THE
UNRAVELLING
OF
MARY REDDISH

David Whitfield

lp

Legend Press Ltd, 51 Gower Street, London, WC1E 6HJ
info@legendtimesgroup.co.uk | www.legendpress.co.uk

Print ISBN 9781917163507
Ebook ISBN 9781917163514
Set in Times.
Cover design by Rose Cooper | www.rosecooper.com

The image on page 294 is printed with permission from Nottinghamshire
Archives

Printed in India

David Whitfield has been a journalist for twenty-five years and is currently working for *The Guardian*. He lives in Nottinghamshire, and used to live less than half a mile away from the site of the asylum featured in this novel, in the Nottingham suburb of Sneinton.

For my parents

This is a work of fiction. However, nearly all of the characters within it were real people, and most of the incidents described in the asylum are based on actual events there. The treatments given to Mary are as recorded in the asylum's case book for 1824-29.

Prologue

The chipped Windsor chair was hanging just above the floor, in the centre of the dimly lit room. Its seat was angled in such a way that anyone fastened within it would find themselves slightly reclined, with their legs only a few inches from the cold stone beneath them.

'Have you ever been fortunate enough to take a ride on a carousel, Mary?' the doctor asked, ushering his patient towards the contraption. 'At a travelling fair, perhaps?'

He pulled hard on one of the four ropes that suspended the chair from the ceiling. Two of the ropes went through the slats at the back of the chair, with the others tied around its front legs. They were all fed through a pulley wheel attached to the ceiling beam, and then down to a smaller wheel which had a wooden handle attached.

'No, sir,' she replied warily.

'For many years it was a favourite of my son,' the doctor continued. 'If ever we came upon one, he would entreat me to take him on it time and time again.' He turned Mary around so that her back was to the chair. 'Why do you think that was?'

'I don't—'

'Because it invariably made him feel much improved in himself,' he said, pushing down on her shoulders until she was sitting in the chair with her legs swinging freely beneath her. He began to secure her limbs to the chair with leather straps, and Mary made a token effort to push herself up, but it was immediately clear that her legs had nothing to brace themselves against. 'Proper circulation of the blood is of the utmost importance, Mary. An irregular distribution of blood throughout the body will invariably lead to mania. However, it can be remedied. A little vertigo can improve both the mind and the body immeasurably.'

Mary glanced at him nervously, then turned her gaze towards the attendant who was standing next to the lower wheel, his foot tapping against the floor and a look of easy indifference upon his face.

'Sir – if I can improve my behaviour in some way, then—'

The doctor leaned over and put his forefinger gently upon her lips. 'This is not a punishment for poor behaviour,' he said. 'It is a treatment, the same as any other. There is nothing to cause you consternation. Have you never seen children rolling down a hill, or running in circles around a stick until they are quite dizzy? They emerge from the experience laughing, Mary. You will find this is remarkably similar.'

Mary began to kick her legs, as the doctor knew that she would; it was a natural and common instinct. Yet just as it did not matter whether a drowning man was an inch or a fathom out of his depth, so it made no difference how far above the ground the patient's feet were; they could struggle for all they were worth, but the chair would not release them.

The doctor pulled once more upon the ropes to check them, took a step back, then turned his head and gave a sharp nod. The attendant began to rotate the handle, and Mary felt her body start to move.

PART ONE

Chapter 1

May 1827 – Mary

Seven miles to walk, in just under two hours. Mary Reddish looked at the mantel clock and reassured herself that, if she left now, she would not be late. It was a journey she had undertaken dozens of times before, and if she went through the fields rather than taking the road, it would save half an hour from her journey, despite the route being more strenuous. A brisk pace across the open countryside would see her arrive on time.

She left the parlour and hung her dirty apron up behind the scullery door. Sundays were supposed to be a half-day, but all too often her tasks seeped into the middle of the afternoon, leaving her little opportunity to do anything with the rest of her day. So this morning, in order to ensure that she finished on time, she had risen at five – an hour earlier than usual – to clean and lay the fires, cook breakfast and prepare a luncheon, make a pie for supper, sweep out the dovecote and heat the water for Mr Barwick's bath, carrying it upstairs one bucket at a time. She had also accompanied him to morning service at St James's, where the sermon had been shorter than she had feared and had not unduly delayed her.

It was now one o'clock. Mary went to her room to change out of her work dress, then let herself out the back door of Manor Farm House, and walked quickly through the cattle pastures at the back of the property. She followed the path at the edge of the field that headed away from Halloughton, and soon the village was lost behind her.

The day was warm, and although it was still only May, the fields and paths were already hardened by a week of late spring sunshine. Within the first quarter of an hour her skirt was stuck to her legs like damp paper, and her hair was clammy against the fabric of her bonnet. She could not afford to be late, however. Her brother Will was about to turn sixteen, and this was the day chosen for the whole family to meet together to mark the occasion. Her parents, Joseph and Elizabeth, her older siblings, Liz, John and Thomas, and, of course, Will himself – the only one of the children still living at home – would all be there.

After an hour, she arrived at the first of three brooks she would have to cross, and stopped to take a drink and splash some water on her face. She had reached halfway; three and a half miles into her walk from Halloughton to Woodborough. Such was the undulating nature of the landscape around her, however, that she could see no more of those two villages than she could the houses and factories of Nottingham in the far distance.

She quickened her pace for the second half of the journey, and arrived in Woodborough with ten minutes to spare, crossing over the Dover Beck before heading towards Towne Street and the comforting sight of the Reddish family house. There had been a time when seven people had lived in this small two-bed cottage, and yet Mary had no recollection of it ever feeling cramped or claustrophobic. When she was very young, she had treated the fields and streams as extensions of the house, and as soon as she grew up she found she could always find a spot in the small backyard to do her work.

She went up the short path and let herself in.

'Here's our Mary!' called out her sister Liz, who was

heavily pregnant with her third child, and who had placed herself where she could be the first to see who came through the door. As she made to get up, Mary gestured at her to stay sitting, but Liz ignored her; and as Mary entered the small room which doubled as kitchen and dining room, she was embraced by not only her sister but also her mother and youngest brother. The older men of the family stood back and watched the warm reunion at arm's length.

'And how's this one?' said Mary, mussing Will's hair as she had done when he was a child, even though he was now taller than her and she had to reach up to do so. 'Sixteen! Who'd have thought it?'

'Not quite, yet,' replied her brother. 'Did you forget what day I was born?'

'None of us has forgot the day you came along,' she replied. 'He was late, wasn't he, Mam?'

'Late?' said her mother. 'Any later and he'd have been born an old man. Nearly finished me for good, he did.'

Will seemed as if he was about to say something about having heard the story of his birth a dozen times before, but Mary shot him a quick look which urged caution; their mother's mood could change at the smallest hint of impropriety or disrespect.

'You look wearied, Mary,' said her father. 'Come and take the weight off.'

Grateful for the offer, she sat down while her mother mashed her a cup of tea. She listened to the conversation between her two older brothers and her parents, grateful to have the opportunity to let the familiar sounds of her family wash over her.

'Five days this week,' her father was saying. 'Three on the fences with Mr Taylor, and two in East Field. Can't complain.'

'And how about you, Mam?' said John. 'Did Harrison see sense at all?'

Mr Harrison was the man who rented out the stocking frame which dominated the small parlour on the other side of the house. The noise of the frame was usually impossible to ignore, with the clank of the pedals and the whirr of the dropping needles echoing through every room for fourteen hours each day. For as long as she could remember, Mary had been used to seeing her mother sitting at the frame, her hands and feet working in unison as she pushed at the pedals and manipulated the handles, hour after hour with barely a break.

Today the frame was silent, but even on a day when it wasn't being used, its presence could still be felt, sucking most of the light away from the large front window where it had been placed in order to prolong Elizabeth's eyesight. All the children had helped out over the years while they were growing up, winding the yarn and seaming the hosiery while their mother knitted, but now Elizabeth was doing it all on her own.

'He says he can't reduce the frame rent,' said her mother resignedly. 'But he can't give out any more work either.'

'He can do both, if he chooses!' exclaimed Thomas. 'I heard he rented out six new frames last week. That's half a dozen new people he's spreading the work around. No wonder there's not enough for someone like you, who's been with him for—'

'Fifteen years,' said Elizabeth, finishing the sentence, 'and with his father before that.' She brought the teapot over to the table and poured Mary a cup. 'But I can't say his father would have done any different. My rent is one and six a week, and it don't matter if I work a hundred hours every week, or an hour, it won't change a thing.'

'I'd like to give him a piece of my mind, then.'

'If you did, I'd probably end up with no hours and no frame,' she replied.

'And Harrison would still find a way to take his one and six every week,' muttered Joseph, and the others nodded at the truth of this. Mary took a sip of the hot tea, noticing that no sugar had been added, and none offered, despite the occasion.

'Now's not the time to vex Harrison, anyway,' said John to his younger brother Thomas.

'And why is that?' asked Mary.

'Because of the job he's found for our Will,' John replied.

Mary stopped herself mid-sip, and put the earthenware cup down on the table. 'What job is this?'

There was silence in the room, and Mary had the uneasy feeling that she was the only one of the family who didn't already know the news.

'As a threader, in town,' said John eventually – the last part being quite unnecessary, as all of those present were well aware that any such job would have to be at one of the large lace-making firms in Nottingham.

Mary knew enough of the trade from her time working in Nottingham to understand the job that Will would be doing: threading the hundreds of needles back on to the machines whenever they came off, a laborious task which would usually take a couple of boys two or three hours to do. He would be on call for probably sixteen hours a day, waiting to head out to whichever factory urgently needed his services. A late evening call would mean him working until past midnight. Mary knew that there were worse jobs, and that the work wasn't that difficult in itself. But the hours were long, and he would be another seven miles further away from her.

'When is this?' asked Mary.

'This time next week.'

'Why is he going into town? I thought the brickyard had work for him?'

John shook his head. 'There's nothing there. And there hasn't been for months.'

'Mr Taylor and his fences, then. Or the orchards – there must be some work there?'

'Picking fruit for a few weeks a year?' said her father. 'There's barely enough work in the fields for me, Mary. How d'you think young Will is going to fare? Harrison is offering a steady job with a steady income. If I was young enough to do it meself, I would.'

'But … a threader?' persisted Mary. 'Could he not learn a trade at Morley's or Hadden's, or one of the other hosiers? I hear Mr Morley is a considerate employer, and pays well.'

It was now John's turn to argue the case. 'There's more money and more work to be had in lace,' he said. 'In ten years, half of those hosiers won't be here.'

Will had been quiet throughout the whole discussion that had taken place concerning him. He now walked over to Mary, put his hand on her shoulder, and told her that everything would be all right.

'But when will I see you?' she said.

'You can see him when the rest of us do,' interjected her mother. 'Now, let's get this table set, you must all be ready to eat.'

Mary knew that she was being overprotective. She also knew that her brother was relatively old to be starting work in such a position; she herself had moved to Nottingham when she was twelve, and had stayed there for seven years until securing the position at Manor Farm House.

But she was seven years older than Will and had always looked out for him. For years, growing up, she had been the one taking care of him while her mother was at the stocking frame, her sister was helping with the hosiery and her brothers were out in the fields. She had known that one day he would have to make his own way, but had always hoped it would be here in their village, not in the dirt and noise of Nottingham.

Her mother was now laying out the meal of herrings, cheese, potatoes and pickled cabbage. The family sat down, said grace and began to eat. Liz started to tell a story about her neighbour who had three children by three different men, and was pregnant with a fourth, but worked only intermittently, and was claiming poor relief for all of them; which Liz thought was a little shameless, because even though it was within the law it meant she received the same as a decent Christian wife with the same number of children. Her mother was inclined to agree, but her father said that nobody quite knew the exact circumstances of anyone, and it was not up to them to decide who received relief and who did not.

Mary was barely listening, however; she was preoccupied with the thought of this being the last time she would see Will while he was living in this house. She found her mind wandering, and must have been distracted for several minutes, because the next thing she knew was that her brother John was saying to her: 'Mary? Are you with us?'

She blinked herself back into her surroundings. 'Sorry, yes, I—'

'You seem a bit distracted by something,' said Liz, before adding, 'or someone?'

Ordinarily this would have been the cue for Mary to give her sister a sharp kick under the table. On most Sundays she met with her intended, Ernest, after she had visited her family; and while her parents knew about the relationship, they didn't wholeheartedly approve of the couple walking about the countryside together, as they would later that afternoon. But Mary was too absorbed in her thoughts even to react to Liz's teasing. She finished her meal, and then helped her mother to clear the table.

As the men began to smoke their tobacco, a rare treat in honour of Will's birthday, Mary took her mother to one side and passed over her weekly wages of four shillings. She knew precisely the precarious state of the family's finances, and wished her offering could have been more. But because board and lodging were included in her job at Manor House Farm, she only received a salary of just over £10 a year, and four shillings was all that she had to give every week.

'You're a good child,' said her mother. 'I wish you had some left to spend on yourself.'

'I'm fine, Mam, there's nothing I need.' She paused, and then said: 'Are you well? You seem a little tired.'

'I'm not tired, love, I'm just getting older. Everything gets a little harder when you get to my age, you'll see. But there's nothing the matter with me.'

'Are you sure? I know it's difficult with just the three of you, and with our Will gone it will be even harder.'

'Don't you worry about us.' She patted Mary on the arm. 'Now, don't you have some place to be?'

'I can linger a while longer,' Mary said, and she stayed talking to her mother until the time when her brothers announced they were going. It was time for the gathering to end. Mary's farewell with Will was quickly over, and as she left the house her eyes were pricked by tears.

She made her way along Towne Street, past the Punch Bowl inn that the family rarely drank at, and up to Lingwood Lane and the school that she had never been able to attend, before reaching Bank Hill and the brickworks where her father and now all three brothers had failed to find regular work. The village seemed to be filled with possibilities that the Reddish family had never been able to exploit.

As she rounded the corner of Bank Hill, close to where she was due to meet Ernest, she saw a familiar face: Arthur, one of Will's friends whom she had always felt fondly towards, largely on account of his having lost his parents at a young age and been brought up by his sisters. She gave her eyes a quick wipe with her shawl, and tried to look normal as he approached.

'Look who it is,' she said.

'And look at you.' He smiled at her, but as he got closer his face became concerned when he saw her blotched cheeks and reddened eyes. 'What's the matter, Mary?'

'Me? Oh, it's nothing,' she said, faltering slightly as she did so. 'Where are you headed?'

'I'm off to meet your Will,' he said. 'Don't tell me nothing's wrong, though. What is it?'

The mention of Will's name set Mary off again, and before

she knew it she was sitting on the hard surface of the road, crying into Arthur's shoulder with his arm around her. In a minute or so, she had recovered enough to be able to tell him what was about to happen to Will.

Arthur said nothing, and Mary looked at him. 'You knew?'

'I did,' the youngster said. 'He told me last week.'

'And you favour him moving to Nottingham?'

Arthur, who was apprenticed to the Baguley family of local shoemakers, and as such was secure with his work in the village, shook his head. 'I'm not in favour or against. But I think he could settle just about anywhere.'

'You don't know what it's like. The smell, the filth … it's a different world.'

'That's as maybe. But what is there for Will here? There's nobody taking people on, far as I can see. And he's only going to Nottingham, not to London or Manchester.'

'Perhaps you're right,' said Mary, dabbing her eyes with the handkerchief Arthur had offered. 'I can see I'm being foolish. But I know how hard it is to come back from town once you've gone there. I could only do it because Mam found out about the job in Halloughton. And I still had to drop my wages to take it.'

'It won't always be the same,' said Arthur. 'There'll be jobs for him here soon enough. My grandad says it's all because of the French wars, and as soon as we get over those we'll be past the worst of it.'

Mary smiled at him. 'You should tell your grandad the French wars finished a good many years ago,' she said. 'But thank you for trying to cheer me up. Ah, here's Ernest coming now.'

He appeared from around the corner, his long stride eating up the ground between them. Mary always admired the way he carried himself, with a confidence that belied his lowly position, and which gave a sense that he knew life held better things in store for him. It was a rare commodity in their village, Mary thought. While she had flitted from job to job

– stitching hose at home in Woodborough, lace finishing in Nottingham, doing domestic work in Halloughton – Ernest had been steadfast throughout his work, and knew exactly where he was heading. He already earned twelve shillings a week as a labourer at the brickyard, and he could expect to almost double that when he became a bricklayer himself in two or three years' time. That would leave them comfortable in their married life, and Mary's four shillings a week from Manor Farm House would not be needed. She would take in jobs at their home to continue to earn a little to give her mother, but she would no longer have to work just to have somewhere to live.

Ernest nodded his greetings at Arthur, and the younger boy departed. The couple made their way down Bank Hill towards the fields, and Mary told him her news: about Will's imminent departure for Nottingham, her concerns for him there, and her worries about her parents now that they would be alone in the house.

'But when we are wed, and living in the village, I'll be able to see them every day,' she added, trying to finish on a hopeful note.

Ernest muttered something non-committal, and they continued walking. He had made a few noises of understanding during her monologue, but nothing to indicate that he was especially sympathetic to her situation.

'What do you think?' she said, after a silence of a minute or so.

'About what?'

'About our Will going to Nottingham, of course.'

Ernest paused, and then said: 'Plenty have done it afore, and plenty'll do it after. He'll be fine, I'd say.'

'And what of me?'

'You'll be fine, too, I'd say. I'll be there to take care of you.'

There was a distance evident in his voice that Mary had never heard before. For a moment she considered holding her tongue; but this was the man she was going to marry. She had rarely been upset when she was in his presence before, and this was not how she thought he would react to her distress.

'Why are you speaking to me in such a way? Does my unhappiness cause you embarrassment?'

He paused and then said: 'Your unhappiness seems to have already been taken care of.'

'What can you mean?'

'It seemed to have already been eased when I first saw you.'

It took Mary a second or two to realise what Ernest was referring to, and then she said: 'With Arthur?'

They were still walking, and Ernest stared down at his feet, watching as each of his long steps ate up almost twice as much ground as hers. But Mary held him by his arm and pulled him back.

'How can have I done wrong?'

Ernest had now physically retreated into himself, his shoulders drawing in as if to protect his inner self from what he now surely realised was a fresh offence that he should not have caused. Nevertheless, he refused to back down, and said: 'His arm was around your shoulders; and your head was upon his arm. In the middle of the street.'

'He was being a comfort to me!' she cried indignantly. She was caught between wanting to laugh off his accusation and giving full vent to the righteous anger that was building inside her. How had they moved so quickly from her requiring solace to her having to defend herself? 'Arthur is Will's oldest friend!' she continued. 'I have known him almost as long as I have known my own brother. What can be the matter with you? I'm sure no one else would remark upon it.'

'No one else is to be your husband,' he said.

'And if they were, would they deny me the pleasure of speaking to an old friend?' She turned her head, and continued walking.

Ernest followed, now half a step behind her.

'That you should doubt me is injury enough,' she continued, almost to herself, yet loud enough that he could hear. 'But to do so on a day such as this, when you see the distress I am in. Do you really love me so poorly? Or do you not love me at all?'

'Of course I do.'

'And I you!' she protested. 'If I am friendly to another, then it is just that and nothing more.'

'Not when we are married,' he persisted.

'What are you saying?'

'Not when we are married,' he repeated, more firmly this time. 'It won't do, Mary. You can't be carrying on with other men.'

'Carrying on? I am twenty-three and he is sixteen, for heaven's sake.'

'It's not the first time. You mayn't think it wrong, but others do. Mam and Dad do.'

Mary almost stumbled, aghast that her own conduct would be something to be discussed among Ernest's family. 'They have spoken of this?'

'Not spoken of it, maybe,' he admitted. 'But they have said in passing they have seen you with him, talking on the street.'

'And what would you have me do? Never speak to Arthur again? Ignore him even when he is standing with Will in the street?'

'Will will not be here,' said Ernest, and his words hit her with such force that she took a step back. It was not their actual meaning, which spoke only the truth, but the casual way in which he had thrown them towards her; an easy point, too easily made.

Mary suddenly wondered whether, rather than Ernest being thoughtless by raising the subject so soon after she had learned of Will's departure, he was actually using that departure to his advantage, to raise a matter that had been bothering him for some time, and to secure more of her for himself once they were married.

She took both of his hands in hers. 'This doesn't stop me loving you,' she said. 'But what you are asking of me serves you ill. We will be married. We will be happy. And I will still see my family, and Will's friends, and Liz's friends, and John's friends, and Thomas's friends.'

'Not Arthur,' he said, quietly but stubbornly.

Mary brought her hands up to his chest, and pushed at him in a mixture of rage and exasperation. 'And if I say no?'

Her push had not shifted him, or even made him lose his balance. 'I won't be made a fool of, and no other man would think different,' he said. 'Will you have a half-day Sunday next?'

'Yes.'

'Then I will be here after service, if you choose to come. If you do not, I'll know what that means.' He set off back towards the village.

Mary's anger barely subsided on the walk home to Halloughton. Indeed, each time she replayed the conversation in her head, she became more furious at the way in which Ernest had manipulated her obvious distress to suit his own needs. Not once had he reassured her. Not once had he told her that all would be well. Instead he was only concerned about some petty, imagined slight.

It was late afternoon now, and the sun seemed even hotter than it had on the walk out earlier. In her rage, Mary had neglected to stop at any of the brooks for a drink, but had stormed through them with the water soaking the bottom of her dress. Now, with still two miles to go, she had an acute thirst that sapped at her energy; and instead of pushing forward, she found herself taking regular stops to compose herself and to regain her breath.

When she eventually arrived back at Manor Farm House, she went straight into the kitchen and drank three cups of water from the jug upon the kitchen table. She calmed herself, brushed away the grass seeds from the front of her skirt, and went into the parlour.

Mr Barwick, a slight man with thick glasses and receding hair, was sitting in his favourite armchair, reading a book. His legs were crossed and he barely looked up at Mary as she entered the room. But he did glance at the mantel clock Mary had checked before leaving, six-and-a-half hours previously, and said: 'You are late, Mary.'

Despite her half-day, over recent weeks it had somehow become common practice for her to return by seven, in order to clear away the supper dishes and see if anything needed attending to. She was minded, now, to let her employer know that this was outside of her normal duties. But she thought better of it, and instead said: 'Is Mrs Barwick returned?'

'She is not. I have received word today that she intends to remain with her sister in Lincoln for a further week.'

Mary's mood immediately took a turn for the worse. The house was a different place when her mistress was absent; quieter, gloomier, more oppressive.

'And, Mary?' continued Mr Barwick.

'Yes, sir?'

'There is no coal in the upstairs scuttles. I would have expected you to have filled them before you left.'

Mary, to her chagrin and his surprise, had to stifle a sob. It was rare for her to cry, yet today it seemed as if she had done little but, and it felt as if there was simply nothing more she could bear. She would have fled the room, but she didn't want Mr Barwick to think that she was rushing out to attend to the coal scuttles, which was the least of her concerns at that particular moment. She laid her palms upon the parlour table, and tried to steady herself. Before she knew it, Mr Barwick was next to her, and his arm was around her. How he had moved there so swiftly she didn't know, but she was now aware of him making a series of low shushing sounds, as if she were a small child rather than a grown woman.

He was the second male to place his arm round her shoulder

that afternoon, but this felt entirely different. His touch was firm, not soft, and his hand was gently rubbing against the top of her arm, reaching down as far as the boundary between the fabric of her chemise and her bare flesh. Mary was suddenly all too conscious that he would only usually see her wearing her full-sleeved working dress.

She pulled her shoulder away slightly, but his grip upon her tightened. The heat of the day, and the clothes she had chosen to wear because of it, were now acting against her; walking across the fields, she had felt no need for her shawl or jacket, but at this moment she would have given anything for the protection they would have offered.

With a determined effort, she twisted sharply to yank her arm away from Mr Barwick. In response, his own arm jerked away from her, traced an arc through the air and then struck a vase placed in the centre of the parlour table. The vase flew off the table, rose over the armchair that Mr Barwick had been sitting in and shattered on the hard floor. It was only now that Mary rushed from the room.

Chapter 2

May 1795 – Ann and Thomas

The Friends' Meeting House was a large, solid building, with a single window facing out on to the street. In the box seat of a nearby cart, Joseph Ashby waited patiently for his wife to conclude the business being attended to inside. His health was failing badly, and the rest of the family had tried to insist that he should not make the journey to accompany her; someone in the village would surely offer to take her there and back instead. But he had insisted, and so now he sat and watched as the sun began to set below the outline of the serene Warwickshire countryside, with a blanket across his knees even though the day was still warm.

Eventually, his wife Margaret emerged from the hall. She walked slowly to the cart, climbed up next to him, and said nothing. He looked at her, and she nodded. 'It is done,' she said. 'It is out of our hands, now.'

Back at the family home in Sezincote, just over the border into Gloucestershire, their daughter Ann was filled with a nervous energy as she busied herself making a late supper and awaited their return. It was not the decision of the meeting that concerned her; she was already resigned to the fact that the women would decide they had done all they could with her, and would pass her case on to the men. Rather, it was the reaction of her parents that gave her a sense of foreboding. There would be no shouting, or recriminations, or any similar display of emotions in a household such as theirs; there was temperance in behaviour at all times. But, still, her father was so poorly, and her mother so worried about him, that she knew her own situation was a distraction they could well do without.

For weeks, Ann's conduct had been the main item for discussion at the women's meetings of the Warwickshire South Society of Friends. There were the other usual matters to be dealt with – the financial accounts from the various branches, requests for removal from one branch to another, the latest epistle coming in from Pennsylvania. But nothing had exercised the members quite as much as the nineteen-year-old who was keeping company with a young man who was not of the faith.

It was past nine o'clock when her parents walked through the door. Ann immediately went to take her father's coat, and to help him to his favourite chair next to the fire. He looked to be utterly exhausted, and a fresh wave of guilt passed through her at the thought that he had felt obliged to travel all the way to the meeting. She served a supper of soup and barley bread, and it was not until all their plates were emptied that she felt able to ask what had taken place at the meeting.

'It was agreed that it was best for the matter to be referred to the men,' answered her mother calmly. 'Michael Pettifer and John Hodgkin will visit you, and Sarah Lamley will accompany them.'

'When will this be?'

'I understand that a date has been set, but I do not know it; I am sure they will be in touch.'

Ann thought she could detect a slight note of archness in her mother's reply, and wondered whether she should end the conversation there, but she pressed on and asked: 'And was anything else said?'

Margaret seemed about to reply; before she could say anything, though, Ann's father began to speak, only for his opening words to immediately be overwhelmed by a violent and prolonged coughing fit, which only subsided when he had been given a small sip of water.

'Ann,' he said eventually, 'please, let your mother be. It is bad enough that she must be present when the behaviour of her daughter is discussed by one and all. I am sure she does not wish to relive it when she is back home.'

'I do not mind,' said Margaret quietly. 'I am only unsure what is left to be said. Ann knows our rules, and she knows that the meeting will certainly follow them. We have discussed it a hundred times. Matters will only change if she desists from keeping the company she does.'

Ann went over to sit next to her mother, and looked at her directly. 'I am sorry,' she said. 'I am truly sorry for ever causing you any distress – both of you. I have always tried to be proper in my behaviour. I have read my scriptures, I have avoided distractions, I have been fair in my dealings with others. I believe that never has my conduct been unbecoming – and it is my sincere, and only, regret that it vexes you as it does. But if you are asking me never to see Thomas again, that is something that I cannot do.'

Ann had met Thomas Morris in Shipston-on-Stour, eight miles away from her own home. Her father was a tenant farmer and grazier, and he would regularly travel to Shipston's sheep market in early summer to sell his unproductive ewes, and a few weeks later to sell the lambs he had raised. Once Ann and her three sisters were old enough, it had become common practice for one of them to accompany him, handing out Society pamphlets and spreading the word to the townspeople and those visiting the market. As first one sister and then another got married and moved to neighbouring villages, the task increasingly fell on Ann and her remaining sister Jane.

It was on one such occasion, when eighteen-year-old Ann was with her father, that an accident befell him. It had been a hot, tiring day at market, with dust and flies everywhere she turned, and Ann felt as if she had walked miles distributing her leaflets. Her father had not sold all of his stock, so had taken the unsold sheep back through the town's narrow alleyways to where he had left his cart, and was fixing the tailboard ready for departure when there was a loud, cracking noise directly next to him. He felt a searing pain in his right leg. The axle of the cart adjacent to him – weakened by journeys along rutted roads, and filled with animals – had given way, and one of the wheels had buckled and trapped Mr Ashby's leg as it collapsed.

For a few minutes, all was chaos. Farmers rushed over to try to raise the wheel off Ann's father's leg, at the same time as the owner of the cart was hurriedly driving the sheep back towards the market pens to lessen the load they had to lift. People going one way collided with sheep going the other, and all the while the face of Mr Ashby was distorted in pain as blood trickled steadily from his wound.

Ann, after offering her a father a few words of comfort as best she could, had the presence of mind to run into the marketplace to ask someone to fetch a doctor. Thomas Morris arrived quickly, made a swift assessment while the cart was being lifted away, quickly fashioned a temporary splint, and then asked four of the strongest-looking men if they could help carry the injured man to a townhouse just off the main square. Ann watched anxiously as her father was carried as if on a throne – two men on each side and the doctor supporting the leg – from the commotion of the marketplace and into the cool, dark sanctuary of the house.

She watched the surgeon go about his work. As gently as he could, he manoeuvred her father's foot first one way and then another, stopping whenever the look of anguish from the patient – who did not utter a single word or sound – became too pronounced. He then placed the ankle in a specific position, took two small wooden splints, put them either side of her father's right ankle, and expertly bound them together with linen bandages.

When he had finished, Ann finally took her gaze away from her father's injury, and looked at the surgeon properly for the first time. He had a firm, broad-set face that looked as if it belonged to a farmhand or blacksmith rather than a man of medicine. It would have been rather an impenetrable face, she thought, had it not been for the liveliness of his eyes, which seemed to her to be seeking something without ever settling upon it.

Mr Morris became aware that she was waiting for him to speak. 'A clean fracture, as far as I can be certain,' he said finally. 'The fibula. The lateral malleolus, to be precise.' Ann looked at him, perplexed, and he quickly added: 'The bone sticking out at the side of the ankle. It's impossible to be sure, but I don't believe there are any bone fragments unaccounted for. Six weeks of rest, with his foot in an elevated position, and then he should be up and about again.'

'Six weeks!' Ann exclaimed.

'I'm afraid so. Time is the only healer with an injury such as this.' Thomas, who had to this point been addressing himself solely to the daughter, and not to the father, suddenly realised that he should be speaking to the patient whose leg he was treating. He turned to Mr Ashby and said: 'You were most fortunate, sir. Multiple fractures are not uncommon from these kinds of accidents.'

'Hmm,' the patient replied, 'I can't say as I feel very fortunate. Six weeks of doing nothing is not going to be easy. But I appreciate your prompt actions, Dr …?'

'Mr,' replied Thomas, 'Mr Morris.'

'As I say, I appreciate what you have done. How much do I owe you?'

Thomas, for his part, was delighted to have the opportunity to set a broken bone. His work to this point in his career had usually involved treating wounds, dealing with common medical complaints and occasionally carrying out minor surgery. Broken bones were one of the more challenging injuries he had to deal with. He looked at the young woman sitting next to Mr Ashby, her handsome features now seemingly unperturbed by the events of the last half-hour, and said, 'Two shillings.'

Ann looked at him with great concern. 'No, Mr Morris,' she said, her voice raised slightly for the very first time. 'I'm quite sure that won't do. Your fees must be a crown, at the very least.'

'I can assure you, two shillings is more than adequate,' Thomas said. 'I wouldn't countenance taking a farthing more.'

'In which case,' said Ann firmly, 'I shall not give you a farthing more; but I shall certainly give you a shilling more, and you will still be undervaluing yourself.' She took three shillings from her purse, and placed them on the table in front of the surgeon. Mr Morris gave her a crutch for her father to use, said that he could return it when he next came back to market, and they parted.

Two weeks later, with Mr Ashby still laid up at home, Ann's sister Jane was delighted to hear that Ann was willing to be the one who went to market in their father's stead. It was an uncomfortable journey, with disagreeable work at the end of it, and she was perfectly happy for Ann to take on the task while their father was incapacitated.

So Ann took the cart and, as she had hoped, on her arrival with the animals in the marketplace, Thomas came out to greet her and to ask her how her father was faring, and whether she needed any assistance with getting the sheep into pens; which she did not, but allowed him to help in any case, and the pair of them managed to spend a short while conversing.

As she was about to head to speak to some of the other graziers, he said to her: 'I must say that your face is very familiar to me. But I cannot fathom where we might have met prior to your father's unfortunate accident; and I am sure I would have remembered had we done so.'

Ann smiled, and replied: 'Have you always been in Shipston? Perhaps you have seen me at market previously?'

He shook his head. 'I am not long arrived here. My home is in Witney, in Oxfordshire; I am only lodging here while I complete my training.'

'You are not fully trained, then?'

'By no means! Indeed, I sometimes believe that a doctor's training is never ended.'

'And had you thought to inform me of this *before* you treated my father?'

He glanced at her to see if she was genuinely displeased, but there was a look on her face that told him she was gently mocking him. 'I assure you,' he said, nevertheless, 'I would never carry out treatment on your father – or any other patient – unless I was entirely satisfied in my ability to do so.'

'I believe you,' Ann said. 'And as for where you might have seen me, I cannot think that you have. However, Witney, you say? My sister Jane is to be married to a man there, and has been often visiting. His name is Thomas Fardon, and he is a baker.'

'The baker!' cried Thomas. 'I believe I may have seen your sister there. Jane, is it? You are the very likeness of her.' He was genuinely delighted to have found a connection with her family, however tenuous.

Throughout the course of the summer, Ann took every opportunity to make further trips to Shipston, whether trying to sell the rest of the ewes for mutton, or taking charitable donations from the Friends to the workhouse just off New Street. With each visit, the amount of time that she was able to spend with Thomas increased; and she continued to see him, despite her early realisation that he was not of her faith. She put the thought to the back of her mind, as if by leaving it there it would somehow resolve itself of its own accord. By the time that the selling season was over and her father had recovered, Ann considered that it would be impossible to contemplate arriving in the town without immediately seeing his familiar figure and broad smile bearing down upon her.

Her younger self would have chastised her for even imagining that she might have fallen in love; who could possibly do so during the course of a few visits over a handful of weeks? Until now, love had been only an abstract notion, something she vaguely ascribed to the relationship between her parents, or her two married sisters and their husbands. It had never taken the form of an actual person who was kind to her, and thoughtful, and treated her as if she was the centre of his world. There was a quality to him that meant she felt entirely safe in his company; and also a hint of something more, that he could take her away from a world of sheep markets and pamphlets and a relative around every corner.

Ann had never lied to her parents before, and she did not want Thomas to be the cause of her doing so for the first time. Up until now she had simply not mentioned him to them, which was an untruth of sorts, but one of omission rather than inclusion. But she wished to see him again, and so one evening she told her parents that she wished to meet – in public, in Shipston-on-Stour – the young surgeon who had treated Mr Ashby there.

There was a long pause, before her mother finally asked her: 'Have you and this man been keeping company?'

'We have been speaking together, in the marketplace.'

'And he is not a Friend?'

'He is not.' She considered embarking upon a description of his fine qualities, but decided against it; her parents would come to their own views regardless. She knew that they would not rail against her, but they would have fully expected her to marry someone who was also a Quaker.

Mr and Mrs Ashby did their best to dissuade her from the course of action she was set upon. They told her that, if she continued, the likely outcome was disownment by the Society; a punishment that fell short of a full banishment from her family, but that meant she would be unable to go to any Quaker meetings, and that to all intents and purposes she would no longer be a Friend.

It did not help matters that Ann's sister Jane was doing everything exactly as it should be ahead of her impending marriage to Thomas Fardon, the baker from the same Oxfordshire village as Thomas Morris. The couple were both Friends, had declared their intention of taking each other in marriage to the Society, had obtained consent from Mr and Mrs Ashby, and had produced a certificate from the Witney branch declaring that the young man was clear of all others and able to marry. The contrast could not have been starker.

A dozen times, Thomas Morris asked to go to speak with Ann's parents, to see if he could win them round. But Ann forbade him; she knew that it was not him personally that her parents objected to, but the idea of him.

In February of 1795, when Ann had been seeing Thomas for several months, Joseph Ashby wrote his will. His middle daughters, Hannah and Jane, would receive £250 upon his death. His eldest, Mary, would get an annual sum of £25. But Ann's inheritance would depend upon her particular circumstances. If she married with the consent of her mother and a group of trustees from the Quaker community, she would receive £500 that had been placed in trust. If, however, she married without their consent, she would only get the interest from this sum, to be paid as and when the trustees considered that it was needed.

Five hundred pounds was an enormous sum; but Ann remained steadfast. By now, it was not simply that she found it hard to imagine a life without Thomas, but that the possibility of ever marrying another man – one who had the approbation of the Society – was unfathomable. Whomever that man might be, he would not be Thomas. She had no quarrel with the Quakers, and still felt her faith strongly herself. But they represented her old life, and Thomas her new, and if it came to choosing between them, she felt it was impossible to go back to her past.

Her situation was discussed over the weeks at successive Quaker meetings; in Brailes, Eatington, Stow-on-the Wold and Shipston. A female Friend was appointed to visit her, followed by another woman and two male Quakers who were also trustees of her father's will. In the middle of it all, her father died, at the age of sixty-one.

None of it made any difference, even her own personal grief at her father's passing. Following his death, Ann moved out of the family home to live in Shipston, where she stayed for more than a year until, in August 1796 – just a week after she had turned twenty-one, and no longer needed her mother's permission to wed under any circumstance – she and Thomas were married in St Edmund's in the town, just a few yards away from the Meeting House where her relationship with him had caused such anxious discussion among her Friends.

Her marriage precipitated an inevitable reaction from the Quakers. A testimony of denial was drawn up and read to her, and on 1 November that same year, at a meeting in Brailes, nine men – family friends, Quaker stalwarts – arrived at the judgement that had seemed all but inescapable since the moment she met Thomas:

Ann Ashby, contrary to the repeated advice of her Friends, hath been married by the priest to one not of our Society. We therefore, for the clearing of truth, believe it our duty to testify against such conduct, and do hereby disown her as a member of our Religious Community. Notwithstanding it is our wish she may be yet encouraged in the attendance of our meetings.

She had not been entirely cut adrift from the community; but what she could do was now limited by the judgement against her. A life that had been set on an identified and comfortable route had been directed significantly off course.

For Thomas, too, the marriage represented a departure from what he had expected, and what was expected of him. His father was a respected blanket maker in Witney, owning a small workshop that employed half a dozen of the hundreds of men and women employed in the village's weaving industry. The presumption was that he would take over the business, join the local guild, marry a local woman and stay in or near Witney, where the work was to be found.

Instead, when he left school he embarked on a seven-year apprenticeship as an apothecary and surgeon, leading to the position in Shipston where he had met Ann. She had immediately struck him as someone who was wholly different to the young women in his home village. There was a serenity and a sureness about her, which he attributed partly to her religion, but not entirely. She made him smile. And her faith intrigued him in itself: Ann believed in God, but had no place for priests; she read the Bible, but did not consider it the word of God; and she ignored all religious festivals completely. His own faith was of a straightforward singing-hymns-and-saying-prayers kind, but hers was much more complex and seemed entirely personal to her. It was only when she was disowned by the Society that he discovered there was no such thing as an entirely personal religion.

Following their marriage, the couple moved to Thomas's home of Witney, and he began working there as a surgeon. They had their first child, also Thomas, but not everything was untroubled in their lives. There were already three surgeons working in Witney, and although Thomas was making a living, every week he found himself travelling further and further afield on his horse in order to treat patients.

Ann, meanwhile, felt somewhat rootless without the Quaker community in her life, despite her efforts not to let the absence affect her. Her sister Jane, who had previously been living in Witney with her baker husband, had moved back to Shipston, where her mother now was, and her other sisters were all in that same area, about twenty miles away from Ann. It was far enough to make visiting something of an undertaking, especially with a baby in tow; but near enough to feel that she *should* be making the journey more often, or that her sisters could be making it in the opposite direction.

As the century drew to a close, the family decided to move away from the area completely. Thomas had found a role as an apothecary in Ingatestone, Essex, and although it was a step down the medical hierarchy – which was firmly established as physician, then surgeon, then apothecary – the work was steady, and he was able to spend a little more time with his family.

Their second son was born in Essex in 1800, and allowed Ann to fulfil a promise that she had wanted to keep for her father, now dead five years.

They had already settled on calling the new child Joseph, after her father. But as Ann sat up nursing the baby in her lying-in bed, with her husband at her side, she turned to him and said: 'I don't believe I ever told you of my father's wishes.'

'His wishes?'

'For his grandchildren's names. With four daughters, he always worried about his family name dying out.'

'Dying out!' replied Thomas, unable to contain his surprise. 'There is an Ashby around every corner of Warwickshire, and Gloucestershire, too.'

'That is *almost* true,' she said. 'But he meant his own small part of the family. He wished that the family name could be preserved, somehow. And he asked all of us – Mary, Hannah, Jane and I – whether we would each give one of our children the middle name of Ashby, in order to achieve this.'

'I see.' Thomas thought for a moment. He knew that Ann's treatment by the Society, and the actions of her parents, were issues that she had never fully resolved in her mind. She had loved her father, and still did so her mother, but they had not stood by her at the time when she had desperately hoped they would; they had chosen their faith over their daughter. Would it be fair on her to have a constant reminder of her family's name? And, equally, would it be fair on baby Joseph as he grew up? 'What would you like?' he asked.

'I think it would make me more contented,' Ann said. 'The others have all done as he wished. I think it would be the respectful course to take.'

'In that case,' replied Thomas, 'we will do it.'

Chapter 3

May 1827 – Mary

Mary was awake long before the band of morning light came through her window and made its familiar way up the chamber wall. It had been a fitful night, filled with half-remembered dreams of Will working in a factory, a stony-faced Ernest looking down on her and Mr Barwick's arm around her shoulder.

She was exhausted from both the lack of sleep and the tribulations of the previous day, but was determined to start early and not provide Mr Barwick with any reason to admonish her. She had not changed out of her clothes from the day before, so she quickly took them off, put on her work dress and a fresh apron, cleaned her teeth with a cloth, rinsed her mouth with water and a little vinegar, picked up her chamber pot and went to the door.

It wouldn't open. Mary tried the handle one way and then the other, but it had been locked from the outside. She peered into the keyhole and could see straight through, so Mr Barwick had clearly taken the key away with him.

She could feel the anxiety begin to rise within her. It was a quarter to six, and Mr Barwick would likely be up and about just before seven. She had to make a swift decision about which would be worse – to try to rouse him by shouting, and risk incurring his anger for being woken; or for him to wake up to find that breakfast had not been prepared, the grates had not been cleaned out and there was no hot water for washing.

Mary looked out of the narrow window overlooking the back of Manor Farm House, which was a jumble of different buildings spliced together over several hundred years to form a whole. The tower house was the only part of the original 14th-century mansion that remained, and Mary's chamber was the only part of that tower that was still occupied – it was too cold in winter, and uncomfortably hot in summer. The windows within it had never been designed for opening. Mary scoured as much of the complex as she could see to check if there was an early glimpse of Mr Barwick to be had. But everything was quiet.

She sat back down on her bed. If Mr Barwick awoke to no breakfast or water then he would certainly be displeased, but there would be mitigating circumstances, and he would surely comprehend that he was the cause of Mary being unable to get out of her room. If, however, she started banging on the door and shouting, Mr Barwick's subsequent mood would be of her own making, and there might be no escaping from it all day. She resolved to do nothing for now.

Her mind was filled with thoughts of Will: of his imminent departure and how he would feel waking up for the first time in a bed that was not his own. Mary did wonder whether she was being too protective of her younger brother. He was almost sixteen, after all, and most boys had already left home and were earning their own way in life by then, whether in a factory, on the land or in a large house.

But there had always been a special link between the pair of them, the youngest two of the five children. Mary was only two years younger than the middle child, Thomas, but because she looked after Will she had continually felt pulled down towards his age, rather than up towards her older siblings. While her sister Elizabeth was sitting next to their mother and stitching gloves, Mary would be changing Will's clout, or preparing his tea, or trying to get him off to sleep so that she could do the housework. It was a different daily life, which served only to exacerbate the six-year gap between Mary and her sister.

Mary was seven when she began looking after Will, and was at an age when she could have helped with the glove-stitching instead. There was a time when she wanted to do so. But if no one in the family was keeping an eye on him, it would have cost a shilling a week to get someone else to take him in every day, and that was more than she would have been able to earn the family by picking up a needle; she was of more use taking care of Will.

And so she was the baby's main carer from six in the morning until eight at night, her mother breaking off her work only to breastfeed him. Sometimes Mrs Reddish would carry on at the stocking frame while feeding, an art she had mastered with the first four children, but if she was also trying to get him to sleep then the clatter of the machine was usually too great for any hope of success.

When Will got too restless, and the others in the household were calling for him to be quietened, Mary would take him outside and try to rock him to sleep, or lie him in a cot and make animal shapes with her hands to distract him. But often she had her own chores to complete, and so – with her mother's permission – she would sometimes give him a drop or two of laudanum to keep him quiet. All the children of the house had been given it while they were babies, although not to the same extent that other mothers in the village appeared to use it; Mrs Reddish was aware of babies who were being given five drops three times a day. More than anything else, she wondered how their mothers could afford it; at a halfpenny for forty drops, it was easy to spend two or three pennies a week if the baby was being given that amount.

She had used it as sparingly as she could with her older children, and Mary was expected to do the same with baby

Will. When he was very young he was given teaspoonfuls of Godfrey's Cordial, but within a matter of weeks the sweet mixture of laudanum and treacle began to be less effective, and he was moved on to straight laudanum instead. If her mother was too busy to feed Will, or if – as seemed to happen increasingly often – her mother's milk was running dry, Mary would add a drop or two of laudanum to some water for him, and within twenty minutes he would be quiet and restful.

It was a Saturday in February 1812, and Will was eight months old. Mr Harrison the frame owner was due to arrive at noon to collect a dozen stockings. Mrs Reddish was desperately trying to finish the last of them, while both Liz and Mary were needed to finish off the stitching on the already produced items. Mary had given Will his drops a half-hour previously, but he was still screaming out from the room above them.

'Did you not give Will anything?' Mrs Reddish asked.

'Yes, Mam.'

'Well, he's making me skittish. Harrison returned two stockings last week because he said they weren't good enough, tho' they were. I can't give him any excuse to do the same this week. Can't you go and shush Will?'

Mary put down her needle and thread, and went up to her brother's cot. Had she given him his dose? She was sure she had, but she was so tired from weeks of him waking every night that she couldn't remember for sure. And even if she had, he had certainly never been like this before; perhaps she had forgotten, after all. She put two more drops into some water, gave them to her younger brother and headed downstairs again.

The three of them focused on their work. Harrison was renowned for refusing to pay for work he considered to be poor quality, and they simply couldn't afford to have items returned to them two weeks in a row. With their heads down, they soon found themselves in a unison of rhythm, the movement of the girls' needles falling into pace with the rattle of the machine.

'Whatever it was you did to Will, it worked, then,' said Liz after about half an hour, and Mary nodded. She continued with her work, but then hesitated. When she thought about this moment later, she was unable to pinpoint what it was that made her decide to go and check on him; it wasn't as if he was being any quieter than usual when he'd been given his dose. But she put down her needle and thread, ignored her mother's inquiring glance as she exited the room, and went upstairs.

The chamber was quiet and still. She went over to Will, and could see that his little chest was barely moving. Grabbing a hand mirror, she placed it over her brother's mouth to see if any breath was coming out; the glass remained defiantly clear. She picked him up, and he was limp; all four limbs hung down from his torso like a raggedy doll.

'Mam!' she shouted as she rushed back down the stairs, still holding the baby. 'Our Will's sickly!'

She bumped into Mrs Reddish at the bottom of the stairs, and thrust the baby into her arms. Her mother quickly put her ear to Will's chest, then said to Mary: 'He's breathing, but barely. Run now, and fetch help.'

Mary rushed out the door and raced to the apothecary's house. She was so out of breath when she arrived that it took her half a precious minute to explain the nature of the emergency, and the apothecary agreed to come with her to the house. He accompanied her back at a far slower pace than she would have wished, stubbornly maintaining a walking speed and never threatening to break into a run.

On arrival, he took a very quick look at Will. He then fixed his eyes upon Mrs Reddish, and said: 'Exactly how much laudanum has this child been given?'

'Two drops,' said Elizabeth, at exactly the same time as Mary said: 'Four drops.' They looked at each other, and Mary tried to mouth an apology to her mother, but the apothecary had started speaking again.

'There's nothing I can do for him,' he said. 'Decreased consciousness. Miosis and bradypnea – shrunken pupils and shallow breathing. A clear case of laudanum poisoning. If his breathing gets any more laboured, you may blow into his mouth if you wish to try to help him recover. But in my experience the child will live, or not, and whichever of those eventualities occurs is now in the hands of God, not of any doctor or mother.' He straightened up from where he had been stooping over to inspect Will. 'If one uses laudanum, then I'm afraid one can expect laudanum poisoning, as sure as night follows day,' he added. 'I shall call for my fee tomorrow.'

'You're not staying?' cried Mrs Reddish.

'Not unless you are willing to pay for me to sit here for hours and do no more than you could do yourself? I thought not – good day to you.'

With that, he was gone. Mother and daughters stared at each other for a moment, then looked down at Will. They smoothed his hair and placed a cold compress upon his forehead, even though it was by no means clear that he had a fever. Mrs Reddish told Liz to go and tell her father, and instructed Mary to sit with Will and keep checking his breathing. Then she lifted herself onto the chair of the knitting machine once more.

'Mam!' said Mary. 'You are surely not going back to work?'

'You heard what he said,' replied Mrs Reddish. 'There's nothing more we can do, but wait and see if his breathing gets worse. You tell me as soon as it does, if it does. But there's plenty more still to be done before Harrison gets here.'

The day dragged on. Harrison arrived, took his stockings and paid in full. Will stayed the same, his face pallid and his small body twitching occasionally as if it knew it was fighting for life. Evening came and went, and still Mary sat by Will's side. Her mother said nothing about the extra drops Will had been given, but Mary could not stop thinking about it. She thought she had been doing right by giving him the drops and quietening him as her mother had asked; but now it felt as if her whole life, not just that of Will's, would be determined by the outcome of the next few hours.

In the early hours of the morning, Mary thought that Will's chest was rising a little higher than it had been. She told her mother, who attempted to feed Will. He took a little milk – only a little, but a little nonetheless.

A few hours later he had another small feed, and by mid-morning it was clear that he was going to live. Mary was giddy with relief, not just for the fact of his survival but because she believed she could not have coped with the heavy weight of guilt that had already settled in her stomach at the thought that she might have caused his death.

It was this episode, more than any other, which gave Mary a close bond with her youngest brother. From that day she looked out for him more than was strictly necessary. Her mother, though, did not mention the incident again, either in terms of Mary's actions or Will's subsequent illness. Her fatalistic approach confused and, for a while, upset Mary. Their family was unusual to have five children who had now nearly all made it to adulthood, and Mary knew that luck had played its part in that. Will's illness was the first time that Mary became aware that her mother would have been just as accepting of the outcome if luck had been on the other side.

It was another two hours before Mary heard the sound of Mr Barwick's footsteps coming up the stairs of the tower house. She suspected that he had delayed coming to release her in order to increase her anxiety – though the suspicion of this did not lessen its effectiveness. By the time the key turned in the lock and the door opened, she was sufficiently agitated to be ready to accept whatever chastisement was coming her way.

Mr Barwick took two steps into the room and closed the

door behind him. For a while he simply looked at her, then finally said: 'That was an expensive vase, Mary.'

'I'm sorry, sir,' she replied, looking down at her feet. 'It was an accident.'

He took a step closer to her. 'Would you have any idea, Mary, how much a vase such as that might cost?'

She shook her head.

'Then humour me, for a moment – how much would you consider the vase would be worth?'

Mary tried to think quickly. There were only one or two glass vases in her family home, and nothing that was even vaguely similar to the china vase that had been broken the previous evening. Stating a price that was too low might be taken as an insult by Mr Barwick; but opting for a price that was too high would be to unnecessarily exacerbate the seriousness of her misdeed.

'A crown?' she offered hesitatingly.

'One crown?'

'Yes, sir.'

He shook his head. 'A guinea, Mary. And would you agree with me that the person responsible for the destruction of the vase should also be responsible for its replacement? Would that be reasonable?'

Her hand flew up to her mouth in shock. 'But, a guinea! That's more than I earn in—'

'In a month,' he agreed, 'however, that is not in dispute. The question is whether it would be reasonable for the person responsible to pay that amount.'

Mary looked down at the floor. She could never agree to pay the amount; neither could she dare refuse. She doubted whether the price he had given her was genuine, but knew there was no way she could prove that it was not.

'One shilling a week, for twenty-one weeks, then?' persisted Mr Barwick, and Mary remained silent. Her wages would be docked whatever her views, and so it seemed better not to express them. But as Mr Barwick left the room, leaving the door unlocked behind him, he murmured: 'Agreed – one shilling a week.'

For the rest of the week, Mary worked long and hard. She cleaned the glass and china, polished the silver, dusted the chambers, swept the dovecote, washed the bedclothes, cooked the meals and kept the coal buckets filled. Partly this was due to Mrs Barwick's imminent return on the Sunday afternoon, but it was also to ensure that she had as little work to do as possible when that day came, and nothing that could feasibly stop her from using her half-day to walk over to Woodborough. She needed to say goodbye to Will before he departed for Nottingham; and she needed to meet Ernest and reassure him that any differences they had in their relationship could be overcome. She was not ready to accede to Ernest's demand that she stop seeing Arthur. But she was willing to meet, and talk, and come to some agreement about how they would live their future life together.

And as the week progressed, her feelings of anger towards Ernest over his behaviour softened slightly. If she put herself in his place, perhaps she could even understand a little of what he had said, even though she did not agree with it. It was certainly true that she had more companions in the village, both men and women, than Ernest had himself. The Reddish home had always been a welcoming house, albeit one where there had often been little or nothing to offer in the way of food or drink to guests who crossed the threshold. Still, in the precious hour or two after work was done, it was rare that there was not another mother from the village to be found at the kitchen table, sometimes there to beg or borrow, but rarely without something of her own to offer, at a later time if not that very day. Their children would often be in tow, and the Reddish youngsters would play hoop-and-stick or skipping with them in the street outside.

Ernest's house, by contrast, had a slightly oppressive air.

He was an only child, and on the two occasions Mary had been to his home she had sat formally, struggling to know what to say, while Ernest's mother served tea and biscuits. It had been a relief to leave the sterility of the house and return to her own chaotic home. But it made her realise just how different his upbringing had been to hers, and what it might be like to have parents who only seemed to seek to constrict their surroundings as much as possible. And perhaps it was also true that her behaviour with those friends that she did have occasionally went beyond what it should – too demonstrative, or too emotional. If Ernest wanted to make that point to her, she would let him.

While her feelings towards Ernest had moderated, however, she was still seething at Mr Barwick's behaviour. A sense of injustice was pricking at the underside of her skin, demanding to be released. Paying off her one-guinea debt would take until October, and during all those months she would only be able to give her mother three shillings a week. That was what pained her: that her mother would suffer for Mr Barwick's severity.

Her mind was filled with thoughts of retribution. But she knew that the only sensible way forward was to keep out of her master's way and make it through the days until his wife's return, which would restore a sense of calm and normality to the house. Mrs Barwick was a practical woman, and not unkind. What had persuaded her to marry Mr Barwick was something Mary could never quite grasp. She was forty-five, while he had just turned sixty – an occasion marked with a dinner at the house that had seen Mary work more than twenty hours extra over the week for no additional pay – and their characters appeared largely incompatible. But it mattered little. All Mary knew was that Mrs Barwick had been instrumental in her getting the job, and it was not one that she could afford to lose.

Mary had spent seven years working in the lace trade before ending up with the Barwicks. Her parents had sent her to Nottingham when she was twelve; Will was old enough by then to be left on his own, and Mary's mother had thought that she would have a better chance of progression in lace than in being a framework knitter at home, where the only progress to be made was in working longer hours and producing more stockings.

She found a job in a small lace workshop, which consisted of two terraced houses knocked together near the centre of the town. Her job was to trim the loose threads off strips of lace, from seven in the morning until eight at night. It was monotonous work, in crowded conditions, and she shared a bed in the same building with three other girls, but she was fed well enough and earned half a crown a week.

The uncomfortable fact was, however, that she was too old for the work. It could be done more quickly – and a shilling a week more cheaply – by a ten-year-old with nimbler fingers. So, after six months, Mary was moved to one of the large warehouse 'dressing rooms' where the lace was stiffened by coating it with a bleach-based mixture and then stretching and drying it on large frames.

From the first day, Mary detested the place and the job. She was used to hard work, but this was nothing less than impossible. The dressing room was heated to ninety degrees, girls frequently fainted and Mary sweated from morning to night. There was no seating provided and she was on her feet all day. As soon as she left the building, the colder air outside would play havoc with her chest, giving her colds, chills and worse. She was exhausted and felt as if her cough would never leave her. The hours were supposed to be eight to eight, but the workers were often obliged to stay until midnight, trudging home through the bitter night air for a few hours of snatched sleep before doing it all again.

Within four years she was on ten shillings a week, but it hardly mattered to her. Most of the money went to her mother, whom she barely felt able to speak to when she saw her, such was her fatigue and state of permanent ill health.

Her mother could see it, too, and when Mary's release finally came about at the age of nineteen, it was largely because of the efforts of Mrs Reddish. She had been told by a friend that a position had become available at Manor Farm House, due to the departure of the previous servant girl in circumstances that were as sudden as they were unexplained.

Seeing an opportunity to have Mary provided with a comfortable job with her own bedchamber, which was also much closer to the family home, Mrs Reddish had undertaken the two-hour walk to the house to present Mary's credentials, fully expecting that the lady of the house would wish to meet her daughter before offering her a position. But Mrs Barwick had hired her on the spot, almost as soon as hearing that the applicant was a young woman of nineteen with an unblemished reputation. In the four years since then, she had never had cause to regret the decision; and neither, at least until the events of the past few days, had Mary.

Mary retired as early as she could on the Saturday night before Mrs Barwick was scheduled to return, but it was still 11.30 before her head touched the pillow. Sleep came to her quickly; however, she had barely been asleep for half an hour when, from the depths of her unconsciousness, she became aware that the door to her chamber was open.

Her eyes sprang open and, still lying on her side as she had been sleeping, she swivelled them round as far as she could without moving her head. Mr Barwick was standing near the end of the bed. He was wearing a long nightshirt and was moving slowly round to the side of the bed that Mary's back was facing.

It was a warm night, and Mary had already kicked off her thin coverlet. She lay motionless in her cotton nightdress. Its fabric extended from her neck down to her ankles, but even if she had been entirely unclothed she would have felt no more exposed than she did at that moment.

The soft pad of Mr Barwick's feet seemed to reverberate around the chamber as he made his way towards her. There was a pause, an indeterminate noise, and then Mary felt the bed sag behind her.

Her mind was incapacitated. Nothing had prepared her for any situation even resembling this. She heard the bed creak once, then again, and sensed that Mr Barwick had shuffled closer towards her. She could feel his breath upon her goosebumped neck.

Then, almost as if it had alighted from nowhere, she felt his hand upon her hip. The palm was resting against the back of her hip bone; his fingers were lightly curled onto the edge of her stomach.

Her body gave a small, involuntary shudder. The hand did not move. Mary let out a breath that she had been holding ever since she had felt the bed sink. And still, the hand did not move.

With great deliberation, she reached up with her right arm, and felt for Mr Barwick's hand. When she found it, it was all she could do not to cry out – it felt warm and damp, and almost slipped out of her grasp as she tried to lift it. But she held it up, moved it backwards away from her body and gently let it drop.

Mr Barwick made no sound. After half a minute or so, she felt him push himself off the bed, and heard his feet scuff their way to the door. From the corner of her eye, she saw him leave her room and close the door. Then there was the sound of the key in the lock.

This time, when morning arrived, there was no question of Mary remaining quiet. She hammered on the door, she banged her chamber pot against the wall, she yelled for all she was worth. Nothing could be allowed to get in the way of her meeting Will and Ernest.

Yet even as she was calling out, she feared that the more noise she made, the more Mr Barwick's resolve would be strengthened. That was the type of man he was: his will was determined entirely by the impact his actions were having upon others, and not by any innate sense of what was right. If he could hear her distress, and feel her panic, he would feed off the knowledge that his behaviour was having the desired effect.

As the minutes and then the hours moved on, Mary was getting ever more desperate. Too quickly, the clock in her room was nearing noon; even if she was released immediately, she would be lucky to make it to Woodborough in time to see Will before he departed, and to meet with Ernest before he gave up waiting for her outside the church.

She looked through the window at the yard below, wondering if she could break the glass and escape that way. But even if she could squeeze through the narrow opening, which was by no means certain, the drop was too great to be accomplished without injury. A twisted ankle would not get her to her destination any quicker.

So instead she kept hollering and thumping against the door, hoping perhaps that someone leaving Halloughton's own church service might hear her and take pity upon her. But if they did hear her, then there was certainly no pity. The door stayed closed until five o'clock when Mary – exhausted, dispirited and slumped against the foot of her bed – heard the door open and saw Mr Barwick come into the room.

All of her anger and energy returned in an instant. She jumped up and tried to break past him, but he caught her by both arms and held her tight.

'You,' he panted, his breath broken up by the effort of holding her, 'are a very stupid girl, Mary.' She tried to wrench herself away from him, but his grip held firm. 'You could have paid off your debt in ten minutes last night.'

Mary broke free from one of his hands, and for a moment

managed to drag him through the door. But he grabbed her hair and yanked her back into the room.

'Let me go!' she screamed. 'You've no right—'

He thrust his head closer to hers, and whispered forcefully in her ear: 'I have every right! You should be grateful I was a gentleman last night. The only reason you're still here is that my wife—'

'Your wife what?' yelled Mary, but already she knew the answer. The sudden departure of the previous servant; Mrs Barwick's insistence on an older replacement; Mr Barwick's attempt upon her on the final night of his wife's absence – this had happened before, and it was only the thought of his wife finding out for a second time that had stopped Mr Barwick in his tracks.

'Just don't think you can corrupt her with your lies,' he continued hoarsely. 'You might think she can help you, but I can make sure no one within twenty miles gives you so much as a second glance if you're dying in the street.'

Coursing with adrenaline, and overwhelmed with the unfairness of it all, Mary made one last attempt to free herself. She jerked both arms upwards, broke free of his grip and gave him a painful blow on the side of the face. He grabbed for her, but instinctively she pushed out at him. Her hands caught him full in the chest and he stumbled backwards, catching his head on the side of the door. As he fell to the floor, Mary glanced upwards just in time to see Mrs Barwick reaching the top of the stairs.

Chapter 4

May 1811 – Ann and Thomas

By 1811, Thomas and Ann Morris were comfortably settled in Hammersmith, a village surrounded by orchards and arable land six miles to the west of London. It was far enough from the city to feel the benefit of open countryside and riverside walks, but close enough to be able to visit without difficulty – more than a dozen coaches a day left the village for busy locations such as Covent Garden, the Strand and Fleet Street, while a fare of just sixpence secured a place on one of the daily boats going down the river to Hungerford market or Queenhithe.

They lived in a house in Grove Place, just off the main thoroughfare of King Street. A third child, Ann, had arrived a year after Joseph, and although the family was now without Thomas Junior – who was about to finish his first year at Repton School – it was a lively household, with the two younger children providing daily distraction for Mr Morris's elderly widowed father who was also living with them. Thomas was working as a surgeon, and Hammersmith itself was thriving: shops and houses were springing up along King Street, and the population had swelled to more than 5,000.

To the outside world – and to the rest of her family – all was well, but Ann Morris had a nagging sense of restlessness that she seemed unable to shake. It was not that she was melancholy, as such; she had too much to keep her occupied to be susceptible to feelings of that nature. But frequently she experienced a persistent uncertainty over whether the path she had chosen was necessarily the right one. She was contented, but nothing more. And she knew that, within a few years, Joseph would also be away at school, Ann would grow up and be married, Thomas's father would not live forever, and she would find herself alone in the house, waiting to see her husband at supper time after he finished his long rounds. Her own mother had passed away a few years previously, as had her eldest sister Mary, and she could easily imagine how her sense of isolation would grow with each subsequent departure from her own small family.

She tried to help out in the community where she could; her personal sense of faith was still strong, despite her disownment by the Quakers, and her natural instinct was to focus on improving the lives of others rather than to spend time considering her own. But she often felt that she was simply picking at the edges of what was really needed. She would fundraise for the orphanage, she would help out at the foundling hospital, but in reality she was only doing what dozens of other ladies of a similar class and temperament had the ability to do. Without the influence and organisation of the Quakers behind her, it felt almost impossible for her to feel that she had accomplished anything of note. She had felt more useful as a teenager, at a time when she was making and distributing soup to local households, mending clothes and handing out Society tracts. Was this, she wondered, the life she had really envisaged when she had given up so much of what she formerly knew?

Thomas was conscious of his wife's feelings, and tried to address them on occasion; but he often considered that the most propitious course of action was to leave his wife in peace. There were times – too many times, perhaps – when he avoided asking about her state of mind, especially at the end of the evening when he was finishing his accounts for that day's work, or making up the medicines he was likely to need for the next. One evening in May, however, when the children and his father had excused themselves from the dining table, Ann's mood appeared so distracted that he felt unable to leave her to her own thoughts.

'Are you well?' he asked her. 'Barely a word passed your lips during dinner.'

'Did it not? I was not aware.'

'And nor does it matter,' said Thomas. 'But has anything occurred to make you so?'

'Not today; no, indeed. But it is the anniversary of the day that my father died. It is sixteen years, now.'

'Of course! Forgive me, I should have known.'

'There is no need for forgiveness. I rather wonder whether I should not let it affect me as it does, after such a time. And yet I find it impossible not to think of him, and to imagine that my conduct – our conduct – contributed in some way to his passing.'

'You cannot think that?'

'I cannot; but I do.'

'Not one of your family has ever suggested as much, though, surely?'

'And I am sure they would not, even if they thought it,' said Ann. 'But who am I to know what is truly on their minds? Jane is in Shipston, Hannah is close by her, and there is little time for either of them to think of visiting their sister eighty miles away.'

'You miss your family, as anyone would,' Thomas answered. As he spoke, the sound of a deep cough came from the parlour at the end of the hallway, and Ann gave him a slightly wistful look.

'You have your own father in the next room,' she replied,

not unkindly. 'Of course, I do not begrudge him; he is always welcome with us, and you must surely know that.'

'And yet?'

'And yet in such circumstances, I would not blame you if you did not understand my – I do not even know what to call it – my unease, perhaps. I barely understand it myself.'

'We could visit Hannah and Jane, though? If that would alleviate your concerns in some way?'

Ann shook her head. 'We should not leave your father for any length of time. And my sisters are but a part of my thoughts. A visit to them would not attend to the greater part. I know that I should be thankful for what I have, and indeed I am. Yet when, at the end of every day, I ask myself of how much use have I been that day, it is a rare occasion where I can be truly gratified with the answer.'

'You are of the utmost use and comfort to me,' he said. His wife said nothing, but started to clear away the supper dishes. 'And to the children, and my father,' he called out, but by now her back was retreating into the kitchen.

Nothing more was said on the matter for the next few days. But one evening shortly afterwards, Thomas arrived home a little earlier than usual, and immediately bustled his wife out of the kitchen and into the parlour, where he bade her sit down in an armchair.

'Whatever is the matter?' she asked, but instead of answering her he produced a copy of that day's *Times* from behind his back, and thrust it in front of her.

'There,' he said, gesturing generally in the direction of the page. 'The one that begins, "General Lunatic Asylum, near Nottingham". Please, do read it.'

Ann cast her eye over the page and found the advertisement in question. '"Wanted",' she read aloud, looking up at her husband briefly, before continuing: '"A director to execute the duties of apothecary, secretary, and principal superintendent;

and also a matron, to regulate the Female Department in this institution. The qualifications of the candidates being equal, a person educated as an apothecary will be preferred; and if the wife of the director can undertake the duties devolving upon the matron, it will prove an additional recommendation."'

'Quite so!' said Thomas excitedly. 'And what do you think?'

'Think of what?' said Ann, bewildered.

'Of us!' he cried. 'As director and matron? Of working together, every day, and of making an actual difference to those who need help? Not of setting a bone here and applying a poultice there, but of *curing* people. Those who are truly afflicted?'

Ann placed the paper on the arm of the chair, and stood up so that she could speak to her husband face to face. 'Can you be serious?' she asked. 'What knowledge have we of insanity? Or of running an establishment such as this?'

'Very little,' he acknowledged. 'But the same will be said of any other applicants, I am quite sure. I am informed that this is to be the first establishment of its kind. There is no one who will have any such experience.'

'There are other asylums – what of those working there?'

'Private asylums, run for profit on the misery of others? Or charitable asylums, depending on handouts for their very survival? This is not like them, Ann. It is an asylum run by the county – not reliant on donations, but paid for through the rates by the people of the county themselves, and with all the attendant support and patronage that such a model entails. We would not be on our own. There would be governors to guide us, a physician, even a surgeon to relive me of those particular duties.'

'You are very well informed, it seems?'

Thomas nodded. 'It was Dr Pennington who first mentioned it to me – his brother, Charles, is to be the physician there.' He paused, and then added: 'I feel sure that, if we were to apply for the positions, he would be willing to make representations on our behalf.'

'That may be so,' said Ann. 'But an asylum? In Nottingham? Where would we live? What about the children, and your father?'

Thomas conceded that he did not have the answers to all his wife's questions; but he asked her to think about the possibility at least, and not to dismiss it out of hand. It was for her, quite as much as for himself, that he had raised the idea in the first place; and he believed her to be entirely capable of coping with whatever challenges the roles might present to them.

He had never envisaged a life where he was responsible for overseeing an asylum, but the more he considered the prospect, the more it appealed. The times during a life when one was able to be involved at the very beginning of a new venture were rare indeed, and to be able to do so with one's wife at one's side, even rarer.

He established that, if successful, the children would live with them in the asylum building, and the only impediment was that there would not be room for his father to be accommodated as well. But he had friends back in Oxfordshire, and when consulted his father made no objection to the plan on his part.

Slowly, over the days and weeks, Ann was persuaded. When she worried about taking the children more than 100 miles away, Thomas reminded her that it was only a dozen or so miles more than when they had moved from Oxfordshire to Essex. When she said she knew nothing of Nottingham, he assured her that it would be no different to any other town of a similar size. And when she expressed reservations about the idea in more general terms, he stressed that he was now forty, and she was thirty-five, and such an opportunity was unlikely to present itself again while they were still young enough to take on such a task.

Thomas did have a genuine interest in how insanity might be treated, or even cured. As with any medical man, he had encountered many disturbed patients during the course of his work, and the traditional remedies that he had prescribed himself were emetics, purges, poultices and the like: physical solutions to attempt to bring about an improvement in the mind. Their success was limited. And while he still believed that medicines such as these had some role to play in the treatment of lunatics, he was beginning to wonder about their efficacy, and was intrigued to know what other methods could be employed.

The position was also undoubtedly his best chance of progressing up the medical ladder. Surgeon and apothecary, his previous jobs, were both subordinate to that of physician, the only one of the three positions to require a university education. But 'director'? That was a previously untested combination of medical, chemical and administrative skills. And while no one had yet established where it came in the medical hierarchy, being in charge of eighty patients undoubtedly meant it was a more elevated position than an apothecary, and probably than most surgeons, too.

They made their applications, and on 4 September they were interviewed and elected to their positions at a meeting of the asylum's visiting governors, held at the General Hospital in Nottingham. Their annual salaries were £100 for Thomas as director, and £30 for Ann as matron. Board and lodging at the asylum were included, but £10 was deducted per year for any of their children living with them. With both boys in school, young Ann would be the only child there, and they would not be wealthy, but they would be secure enough.

Charles Pennington, the asylum's physician and the brother of Robert Rainey Pennington – the well-connected London doctor who had alerted Thomas to the position in the first place – was present at the meeting, and was one of those who voted in favour of their appointment. After the meeting had finished, he walked up to the couple in the company of two men; one was ruddy, with a prominent nasal bridge, and the other was tall and pale with a slightly drawn face, but both had an equally benevolent demeanour.

'My congratulations,' said Dr Pennington. 'Let me introduce you to Mr Dale and Dr Storer. Mr Dale is an apothecary, like yourself' – he looked directly at Thomas – 'and also one of our visiting governors. Dr Storer has been leading the fundraising for the asylum for the past ten years, and has been here in Nottingham for thirty, although you would not believe it to hear him speak.'

Dr Storer smiled and said, with more than a trace of a Scottish accent: 'One can never divest oneself of a Kinross childhood entirely; and neither, of course, would one wish to. Please, call me John. We shall not be standing on ceremony here.'

There were handshakes all round, and curtsies from Ann, before Mr Dale suggested that Mr and Mrs Morris might appreciate the chance to look at the asylum itself. 'The interior is not complete, I'm afraid; some unevenness in the rock below the site was discovered when laying the foundations, which took longer than expected to resolve.'

'And more money than hoped,' added Dr Pennington.

'Indeed,' continued Mr Dale, 'and the schedule was delayed by some months; but the main building is ready, even if it is not yet safe to venture inside all of it. It is a short walk over the other side of town, if you were minded to see it?'

Thomas and Ann agreed that they were very much in favour of such a visit, and the small group set off down St James's Street and towards the asylum. It was cattle market day, and as they walked through the marketplace they passed the sheep pens, cattle stands and tradesmen's stalls that filled the huge space of the square. The sounds and smells took both Ann and Thomas back to the Shipston sheep market where they had met, and though no words passed between them, they knew that the other was thinking the same.

They reached the other side of the square and pushed on

up the hill, skirting the edge of the Lace Market and then out through the eastern side of the town and towards the parish of Sneinton. Just off the Carlton Road, past a gatehouse and at the end of a circular drive, stood the asylum.

It was built as one long block on a gentle upward slope leading away from the narrow streets and tightly-packed houses of Nottingham. The central part of the building housed the apartments for the Morrises and the first-class patients; on either side of this were the two wings, one side for men and one for women. Each wing contained long galleries, or wards, off which were the individual rooms for the second and third-class patients, plus the day rooms and water closets. The galleries looked out over the grounds at the front of the asylum, while the patients' rooms had a view of the airing grounds at the back.

There was little to distinguish it from any other building of a similar size used for a different purpose. The windows were strengthened with cast-iron frames, but had no bars; a wall ran around the airing yards and the building itself, but not around the whole of the grounds. Only when it was completed and the interior was accessible would the casual visitor notice the bolts on the outside of the room doors, the pokers attached by a strong chain to their grates, and the barriers to prevent the male and female patients ever coming into contact with each other.

'Could we look inside at all?' asked Ann, and Dr Storer replied that it would be possible to see a small section, but that the galleries were unsafe for visitors. They walked up the steps, and into a large hallway. Directly in front of them was the matron's parlour, and the committee room; to the left and right were the doors that led straight into the galleries. All around was solidity; the beams of American fir, the stairs of Mansfield stone, the door frames of British oak.

'Excellent,' said Thomas. 'I believe we will be very comfortably situated here.'

The group began to explore further the limited areas that were available to them, and Thomas found himself alone in the committee room with Dr Pennington.

'I wanted to thank you,' Thomas said to the physician, 'for anything you might have done to facilitate our appointment.'

Dr Pennington was silent for a moment, before replying: 'What a remarkably odd thing to say. It's not clear to me why you might believe I had done anything at all?'

'Oh,' Thomas stumbled, 'I don't mean to imply that you had delib— that you had done anything untoward. I simply thought that your brother might have mentioned myself and my wife to you. In passing, perhaps.'

'My brother has his own views, and I have mine,' replied Dr Pennington; and, already, Thomas could discern that Charles was in fact a very different man to his brother. He had imagined that he would simply be an older version of Robert Rainey Pennington, but there were a full nine years between the siblings, and Thomas was beginning to realise that, rather than being a brother by proxy, Dr Pennington would be rather more of an uncle figure, with all the added generational weight that such a position brought with it. 'Any decision I have made has been done on the evidence before me, and the evidence alone,' added the physician, interrupting Thomas's thoughts, and it was clear that the conversation was over.

Despite being successful in their applications, Thomas and Ann were almost wholly unfamiliar with the ways of asylums. So, before they took up their posts, they were told by the governors to make a visit to York, 200 miles from their Hammersmith home, to spend some time in the asylum there, and learn what they could.

The original York Lunatic Asylum, which had opened in 1777, represented the worst aspects of such establishments, with patients chained, isolated, mistreated and largely forgotten about. The lack of care at the asylum had been brought to wider attention when Hannah Mills, a forty-two-year-old widow, died there in 1790, just a few weeks after being admitted due to melancholy.

Hannah Mills was a Quaker, and her Friends in the Society had been denied access to see her during her short stay. When they gained admission following her death, they were shocked by the conditions they found, and resolved to take action to stop the inhumane treatment of the mentally ill. The result was the York Retreat, founded in 1792 less than two miles away from the other asylum; and it was everything that the earlier establishment was not.

It was situated in open countryside, with the building having good views of the grounds with their hedges, trees and small farm with vegetable plots and dairy cows. Inside, patients had their own private rooms, and their care was designed to be as humane as possible. Restraints were used as little as possible. Bleeding and blistering were thought too ineffective to justify their use. Warm baths rather than cold baths would be used to treat cases of melancholia. Medicines in general were to be used sparingly, as they were felt to be an inadequate means of relieving diseases.

Thomas and Ann duly paid their visit, and discovered that there was a gentleness of manner that worked alongside the kindness of treatment. Correct behaviour was reinforced by receiving esteem and respect, rather than by experiencing fear; lucid intervals were encouraged. Patients were motivated to be active, to be outdoors and to make the most of their leisure time.

This was the moral approach that the Morrises would be expected to take at their own asylum. And indeed, from the moment they entered the Retreat, they found it conveyed a sense of calm and well-being that was wholly at odds with the nature of the problems experienced by the patients within it. Mania, dementia, hysteria and imbecility were all in evidence, and yet for the vast majority of each day, the Retreat presented no situation more challenging than would likely be encountered at a large family gathering.

The roles that Thomas and Ann would be taking on in Nottingham were filled at the Retreat by George Jepson and his wife Katharine, both of whom were Quakers; and for Ann, seeing the way in which they managed represented a sudden realisation of how her own strength of faith could finally be brought to bear on those around her. The Jepsons treated their patients with compassion. The couple believed that everyone was equal in the sight of God, and that God – and good – could be found in every person. They placed their trust in social justice, in tolerance and in respect. Ann was determined that she would do the same.

The family moved into the asylum at the end of November. They had nine weeks to get it ready for the first patients, from ordering all the linen, crockery and cutlery to completing the furnishings and recruiting the five members of staff – four attendants, plus a cook – who would help them run the asylum.

A week after arriving, Thomas was invited to dine with Dr Storer at his home of Thurland Hall in the centre of Nottingham. There were more than a dozen other men connected with the asylum – aldermen, justices of the peace, businessmen, a member of parliament – present when he was shown into the drawing room of the grand house, but his host spotted him immediately and came over to greet him.

'Mr Morris,' he said, 'I am delighted you could join us. Are you well settled in?'

'Yes, very agreeably, thank you.'

'You are sufficiently warm? I fear the installation of the heating will be delayed a few weeks yet.'

'Quite so, and the delay will be no inconvenience. The warmth from the fires is felt remarkably well.'

In truth, much of the asylum was freezing, as the small

amount of heat from the open fires was entirely lost to the vast space of the galleries. Whenever the family ventured outside the comfort of their central apartments to visit the rooms on the wings, they wrapped themselves in blankets and endeavoured to make their trips as short as possible. But Thomas felt that now was not the time to raise the issue.

He was introduced to the rest of the gentlemen there, and answered as best he could their various questions about the asylum and his role within it. The assembled party sat down and enjoyed a substantial dinner of veal cutlets, a mutton joint, soups, pies, a whole salmon, pickles and vegetables covered in melting butter. Thomas felt that the evening had largely been a success, right up until the point near the end when Dr Pennington approached him and, after exchanging a few necessary pleasantries, asked him: 'Do we yet have any patients of the first class who are likely to be admitted within the first week?'

The first-class patients were those whose families were able to pay for a superior quality of accommodation; and Mr Morris was forced to admit that there were, as yet, none of these patients registered.

'But you have been advertising the availability of rooms?'

'Of course. In both the *Journal* and the *Review*.'

The physician paused for a moment, and then said: 'It is only first-class patients that will make our house sustainable. Parishes will pay us nine shillings a week for paupers. The families of second-class patients will provide between nine and fourteen shillings. But a first-class patient means no less than fifteen shillings a week. I believe that is a significant difference.'

Thomas was minded to point out that, because there were relatively few spaces available for first-class patients, the number admitted actually made little difference to the overall finances. If seventy of the eighty beds were filled with second- and third-class patients, it would not matter if the first-class apartments stood empty. But he knew that attracting the richest patients was about more than money; it was about prestige. There were those who believed that the asylum would only have a realistic long-term future when it began to successfully divert well-off patients away from established private madhouses.

'Perhaps,' he said to Dr Pennington, 'there might be some other publications that are suitable for advertising. Publications that are for a rather more particular clientele.'

'That, Mr Morris,' said the physician, 'is an excellent idea.'

A light frost had already formed upon the surface of the street outside. Mr Morris looked at his pocket watch and saw that it was only a few minutes shy of ten o'clock. In front of him, a single drinker was stumbling out of the Black Moor's Head, shouting loudly in the direction of those still inside that they should make haste if they did not want to find themselves on the wrong end of a bayonet.

At ten, the curfew began, and after that time the streets would be filled with soldiers of the 15th Hussars and the Royal Horse Guards Blue, brought in by the government to quell the protests by frame breakers that had resurfaced in recent weeks. Thomas pulled the collar of his coat high up around his face, and set off on the short walk back to the asylum.

The oil-fired street lamps barely penetrated the gloom. He walked quickly along Goose Gate and down through Hockley, ill at ease, but unsure whether he was in greater fear of meeting a cavalry detachment or a group of frame breakers as he made his way through the streets.

When he turned a corner and saw the asylum, it was like a beacon guiding him home, and he noticed it in a way he had never done before. Its slight elevation, the gardens which now buffered it on two sides, the row of trees planted at the boundary of the lawns, all combined to give an impression of self-containment: of a building that was serving the town, but was apart from it. It looked like a place of sanctuary, and as he neared the gatehouse he broke into a half-run, such was his eagerness to be home.

As soon as he reached the driveway, he felt a sense of calm begin to descend upon him. He let himself in, locked the main door behind him, and made his way through the hallway to the matron's parlour. The fire was lit, and Mrs Morris was seated at a mahogany table, a sheaf of menu plans spread out in front of her. She rose when she heard him enter, and he went over and kissed her on the cheek.

'I had been starting to worry about you,' said his wife.

'There was no need,' he replied. 'The streets are not busy; I saw only two other souls on my way back.'

'And how did you fare? Were you a success?'

He smiled at her. 'I am the last man to make a striking impression, as you well know. A roomful of the great and good is where I find myself to be the least comfortably situated. But I believe I conducted myself adequately.'

'I'm quite sure you were more than adequate,' replied Ann.

'Is Ann settled?' the director asked, removing his coat and placing it on the back of a chair.

'Yes, for the past hour,' his wife replied. 'She has been racing down the corridors all evening, and was quite exhausted when I put her down.'

'I may just go and look in on her.'

He made his way out of the parlour, and up the stairs to the next floor where most of their rooms were situated. In her small chamber, Ann was fast asleep, with one stockinged leg sticking out over the side of the bedstead. Her father went in, gently tucked her leg back under the blankets and let himself out of the room. For a few minutes more, he and his wife spoke quietly downstairs, as she told him about her work on the asylum menus, and the difficulty she was having finding suppliers for certain fresh goods.

Both were tired, however, and they soon retired to their own bedchamber. Once there, Ann was quickly off, and

Thomas could hear a very gentle snoring coming from her, in time with the rise and fall of her broad frame.

Chapter 5

June 1827 – Mary

Mary had now been locked in the tower house for six days. She was allowed out to empty her chamber pot and to collect her meals, which she ate perfunctorily back in her chamber, but otherwise the rest of the house was off limits.

Mrs Barwick had been distant with her ever since her return. She wasn't quite hostile; perhaps it was the case that, given the circumstances of the departure of the previous house servant, she had her suspicions about what might have been the reason behind the altercation at the top of the stairs. Mary did not know exactly what her mistress had seen, or heard, or indeed what she had subsequently been told by her husband. But her demeanour made clear on which side of the argument she had positioned herself; there would be no female solidarity, and she would be standing firmly beside her husband.

Mary did not blame her. There was little else that a forty-five-year-old woman, from a large family, married to a man fifteen years her senior and with no children of her own, could reasonably be expected to do. For while to all outside appearances she was the lady of the manor, or at least of the Manor Farm House, the reality was somewhat different.

Her husband did not own their home. It had originally been built as a prebendal mansion for Southwell Minster, and was still owned by the church, but was leased to Sir Richard

Sutton of nearby Norwood Park, who subsequently let it out to a series of occupiers of whom Mr Barwick was simply the latest.

Attached to the medieval tower house was a 16th-century hall, and on the other side of that was the main farmhouse that had been added in the 18th century. With the addition of a dovecote and granary, the whole made for a substantial property; but neither Mr Barwick nor his wife had rights over any of it. They were tenants, and nothing more, and while Mr Barwick was able to make a reasonable living from the land, actual ownership of the land itself was two steps removed from him. He acted as if he was a member of the gentry, but in reality was little more than a yeoman farmer. It meant that Mrs Barwick was reliant – more reliant than she wished to be – on the successful running of the farm to ensure that her circumstances, which were tolerable at least, continued as they were. It was not something that she could even consider discarding purely because of a disagreement between her husband and a servant girl.

For her part, Mary was all too aware that another Sunday was approaching; however, she had no expectation of being allowed to visit her parents' house. She had not worked throughout the week, so the thought that Mr Barwick might still give her a half-day off was implausible.

More concerning than even this prospect, though, was Mary's sense that the house appeared to have been functioning adequately ever since she had been confined to her chamber. From what she could see when she went to collect her food, Mr Barwick was being satisfactorily provided with meals by his wife, the house was relatively clean and the crockery and cutlery was washed and dried. There would come a time, of course, when there was too much laundry to be ignored, when Mrs Barwick was disinclined to cook another meal and when the dovecote was impossible to enter because of the smell. But for now, it was disconcerting for Mary to see how smoothly things were running without her. If Mr Barwick got it into his head that she was dispensable, and that her meagre salary could be saved, there was only one outcome that Mary could envisage.

Back in Woodborough, Mrs Reddish was hoping that the following day would bring a visit from her daughter. For Mary to miss one Sunday had been surprising, especially given that it was the day of Will's departure, yet it was not completely unexpected; there had been occasions previously when she had been unable to get away because of illness or because she was needed for extra work, and the day in question may well just have been one of these. But for her to go two weeks in a row without making an appearance would be unusual.

During the week Mrs Reddish had been walking through the village, paying an evening visit to a friend, when she saw Ernest emerging from the Punch Bowl. His head was down and he gave every indication of not having seen his future mother-in-law until he was directly level with her and she called out to him.

'Ah, hullo, Mrs Reddish,' he said, and made as if to carry on, but the older woman stopped him.

'Have you heard from our Mary?' she asked. 'Is she badly?'

'I've not,' he replied, 'and I dare say I don't expect to, neither.'

'Why ever not? Are you not meeting with her tomorrow?'

He shook his head. 'I'm sorry, Mrs Reddish, but we're not courting. You'll no doubt know soon enough, if you don't already.'

'Not courting? Since when?'

'Last week.'

'Last week? But she wasn't here last week, was she?'

'No, that's the point.' He put his hands in his pockets and began to edge away. 'Look, you'll have to ask her, Mrs Reddish. It's not for me to say.'

He walked away, leaving her standing alone – and somewhat bemused – in the middle of the street. It was not even a week since Will had left and gone to the town; now it seemed there might be a reason why her second-youngest child was staying away, too. She missed her whenever she didn't come, of course, and looked forward to each visit, but she also desperately needed the wages she brought every week.

All her married life Elizabeth Reddish had been battling to balance the family books, and at times it felt like an impossible task. When she and Joseph had married, she had felt they were reasonably comfortable, even if they could never be considered well off. The Reddishes were an extended family that had members across a number of villages to the east of Nottingham – Bleasby, Lowdham, Epperstone, East Bridgford – and many of them worked as millers, operating the watermills on the Dover Beck. This was how Joseph had been employed when he met Elizabeth, but like many others he left the trade after years of struggle, and tried instead to earn a living as a framework knitter. He never took to it; he told his wife that his eyesight was not good enough, although she suspected that his mind was too old and his hands too clumsy to adapt to the complicated work.

In the majority of homes in Woodborough where a stocking frame was present, it was the man who was the main operator, while the woman did the seaming and the children did the winding. In the Reddish home, Elizabeth did the knitting, while the children did the winding and the seaming. Joseph, meanwhile, was reduced to working in the fields for a basic rate of one shilling and four pence a day.

And as one century changed to the next, their situation failed to improve; indeed, over the next few years it became worse. Elizabeth found her wages going down from ten to eight shillings a week, at the same time as the price of wheat was going up. With four children to feed following the birth of Mary, Elizabeth never found that she earned enough to buy and hire out her own frames, or take on her own apprentices, which was the way she could have progressed; nor, later, did she have the capital to benefit from the bobbinet boom, when hundreds of workers took advantage of a patent expiration to buy their own bobbinet machines on which they could manufacture brown net lace in their own homes. She stayed throughout as a plain cotton stockinger, never even moving into the more lucrative trade working with silk.

And so she found herself, twenty-one years into her marriage, still living week to week, never being able to save, and always worrying where the money for the next meal was coming from. Meat was a luxury and was limited to some fatty bacon when they could afford it; all the family learned to drink their tea without sugar; new clothes were an impossibility. Every week she knew that the house rent, the cost of food, the rent of the stocking frame and all the sundries such as needles, candles, oil and soap would need to be paid for; while the money coming in varied according to how much work Joseph could obtain. For two-thirds of the year, he would bring in five or six shillings a week; but during the winter when work was scarce, the family would have to rely on poor relief to survive, the parish overseer topping up their income by four shillings a week. To Elizabeth's persistent and sometimes evident annoyance, her husband seemed satisfied with his lot. When he could work, he did; when he could not, he didn't.

Mrs Reddish was worried, however, that the day when he was no longer able to shear a sheep on his own or haul bales of hay across the fields was not too far in the distance. The family had suffered badly during the poor harvests of 1800 and 1816 and the high prices that followed them. Many villagers had moved to Nottingham over the past fifteen years, some driven to the workhouse, and some – on finding the workhouse full – reduced to sweeping the streets for a pittance in the only employment that the city overseers could find them. Joseph had avoided that fate so far, but what would become of the pair of them when he could no longer work at all was a question that vexed Elizabeth every day.

All of this was why Mary's four shillings a week to the family was so important; and Mary knew it as well as her mother did. She was aware of the difference it would make when Mrs Reddish went into the few shops in the village on Monday morning to buy essentials. To her mind, Mr and Mrs Barwick could do with her as they wished, but she couldn't bear the thought that her mother would be suffering both financially and – if she had started to worry about Mary's absence yet – emotionally as well.

The room was oppressively warm. Mary lay on her bed and stared upwards. Her eyes traced the pattern of the cracks in the ceiling, as they had already done dozens of times over the previous few days. Outside she could hear the occasional forlorn bleat of a lamb, but otherwise all was quiet. There were nearly a hundred people living in Halloughton – was there not a single one of them who might notice her absence, she wondered? It was true that she was not on more than nodding terms with any of them, such was the limited opportunity she had been given to interact with them since taking up the job, but still they would usually have seen her collecting milk from the farm at the end of the lane, or putting out eggs for sale at the front of the house.

She already had mild feelings of anxiety about being in enclosed spaces. When she was about four, she had just finished using the privy when she found herself unable to open the door. She pushed up the rudimentary latch as she always did, but for some reason the door failed to open. Later, she would wonder whether one of her older brothers had placed something against the outside of the door as a prank to stop her getting out. At the time, though, she felt she must be doing something wrong, and with increasing urgency had pushed and pulled the door, flicked the latch every way she could and called out for her mam or dad to come and help her. Nothing worked, and the combination of a panicked helplessness and the stench of the privy made her queasy. She was in the act of vomiting noisily into the hole at the very moment Mr Reddish came out to use the privy and discovered his daughter in there.

The chamber wasn't the same as the privy, of course, but it still brought back uncomfortably familiar feelings. She felt disorientated and nauseous knowing that she couldn't escape from her surroundings. The narrow windows, probably too small to pass through even if they had opened, seemed to shrink in size every time she looked at them. The ceiling beams seemed to merge and become interwoven with one another, forming a maze of splintered timber that threatened to crush her. She closed her eyes to make the anxiety go away, but it refused to leave. In exasperation she hit the side of her head with the palm of her hand, to physically try to force it out, and the shock of the blow granted her some brief respite.

Even in the moments when she was able to ignore her suffocating internment, though, and move her mind beyond her chamber walls, it only brought a fresh tranche of disturbing images. Soon after she had arrived, Mrs Barwick had told her the history of the house, although whether the intention was to inform or perturb Mary was never quite clear. The knowledge had not unduly disconcerted Mary at the time, but in her current unsettled frame of mind it assumed a new significance and rooted itself inside her.

Exactly four decades previously, in 1787, the lease on the house had been taken over by a John Prescott, who had soon proceeded with some much-needed renovations. During the course of these, three discoveries were made.

The first was a large key that was found under a stone in the kitchen floor. It appeared not to have any use within the house itself, and was largely forgotten about until the Southwell prebendary, William Jackson, paid a visit to the house seeking for the area under the stone to be excavated.

The new floor that had already been laid was dug out

and, underneath where the key had been, workmen found the opening to a stone-walled passage. They followed the passage as far as they could, but eventually it descended into water and they were unable to follow it any further.

The search had to be abandoned, but the discovery fuelled the rumour already in place that there had once been two secret passages from the house, one to Southwell Minster and the other to Thurgarton Priory. The house, it was claimed, had previously been used as a nunnery; and the purpose of the passages had been to enable the monks from Thurgarton and the clergy from Southwell to surreptitiously visit the nunnery for immoral liaisons with the sisters living there.

The impossibility of following the existing passage meant that it could not be proved that it went to either Southwell or Thurgarton, and the cavity entrance was closed, with the kitchen floor being relaid for a second time.

But then came the third discovery. When a chimney stack was being taken down during further renovation work, a number of human skeletons were found inside a large recess. They were all well preserved, were complete, and had been left there uncovered by earth or by any material. The vast majority of them were skeletons of children.

Mrs Barwick had offered no explanation for the find, but had simply told the story as she knew it. And although Mary had considered the matter for a short while at the time, she had considered it to be ancient history that had little bearing on her own life in the house.

Now, however, it haunted her. She was unable to think of any innocuous reason why the skeletons could be there. Instead, she imagined that the children had been taken to the house from surrounding villages to be abused by the monks, and locked away in a room with the mystery key whenever the monks were absent. Or perhaps they were the outcome of the relationships between the monks and the nuns, born into the dark walls of the nunnery and then killed and hidden when their continued survival threatened the existence of the order.

In lucid moments, she believed this could simply be fanciful thinking on her part. But even then, doubts crept in. What would make the prebendary visit a seemingly unremarkable house three miles away simply because a key had been found under a stone? What could be a reasonable explanation for the indubitable fact that the passage and the skeletons did exist?

And when she let her mind run, the possibilities took on a life of their own. She imagined that there were more skeletons hidden in the walls of her own chamber, and went round the entire room tapping the stonework to see if any section sounded hollow. She pictured the second passage coming up under the floor of her own room - even though the fact there were two storeys beneath her made this an impossibility – and she moved her bed from one position to another, trying to think where in the floor the passage opening could be.

In this state of mind she passed the rest of Saturday, through the night and into Sunday. She felt slightly delirious, and on the occasions she was accompanied downstairs to fetch her food and refill her water jug, she did so in a daze, clutching at the banister and at the sides of tables to stop herself from stumbling. Her nightdress became soaked with sweat and she replaced it with her only other one, but soon that too felt damp against her skin, never seeming likely to dry within the warm confines of her room.

It was in the mid-afternoon of Sunday that Mary, lying motionless on her bed, heard a knock at the front door of the house. There had been no visitors all week, and she jumped off the bed and ran to the window that faced on to the lane.

From that particular window Mary could not see the door, but she could hear the low murmur of two voices, one male and one female. She assumed the first was Mr Barwick, but the second was too muted for her to make it out. She listened for a few minutes, and then heard the door close. It was only when her mother walked past the window on her way back up the road that she realised who the visitor was.

'Mam!' she called out, as she tried to make enough noise

against the narrow strip of window for Mrs Reddish to hear her. But the sound seemed merely to seep away into the centuries-old thickness of the tower walls, and the figure outside kept up its steady walk towards the main road. Mary dashed over to the door to bang it and yell, 'Let me out!', then back over to the window. Her mother was just about to disappear outside the narrow field of vision that the window offered. 'Mam, here!' she shouted one last time, pummelling her fists against the frame, but succeeding only in grazing the sides of her hands against the hard edge of the stone surrounds of the window.

In desperation, she looked around the room and at its sparse contents. She picked up the chamber pot, and hurled it at the window, then rushed over just in time to see her mother look up, take a brief backwards glance and then carry on walking and disappear out of sight.

A swell of pure anger surged over Mary. She was now beyond frustration; an elemental rage was all she had left within her. She grabbed the few portable objects in the room - the water jug and bowl, two candlesticks, her boots – and threw them with all the force she could muster against the door. Then she hauled over her washstand and chest of drawers so that they clattered and broke against the hard floor. Only the bed was left, and Mary struggled to move it, but with a final effort she tipped it onto its side and the mattress and coverlet spilled onto the floor.

The door was hurled open and Mr and Mrs Barwick charged in. They looked at the wrecked room, and the dark yellow liquid dripping down the wall by the window.

'What did you tell my mam?' Mary shouted, and rushed over towards the couple. It was only then that she realised Mr Barwick had a poker in his hand, which he now raised and thrust out towards her, its blackened tip just inches from her face. 'What did you tell her?' she repeated.

'That you had taken badly,' Mr Barwick replied, his eyes not leaving hers and the poker steady in his grasp. 'Which' – he looked again around the room – 'is clearly the case.'

'There's nothing wrong with me!'

'The evidence would suggest otherwise,' said Mr Barwick.

Mary looked towards Mrs Barwick for any indication of support, but there was none to be found there. Instead, there was pity, a look that Mary found much more horrifying than the calm anger being displayed by the master of the house.

'You are not well, Mary,' said Mrs Barwick, in the same tone she might use for a young child. 'We will ask the doctor to come and see you tomorrow. In the meantime, we think it best that you don't come downstairs to collect your meals and water. We will bring them up to you, with anything else you need.'

They backed out of the doorway, protected by the poker as they did so, then closed and locked the door behind them. Mary slumped against the back of the door then collapsed onto the floor.

When she came to, the light upon the wall told her that the sun was setting. She went around the room picking up the items she had thrown, then put the washstand, chest of drawers and bed back onto their feet. There was nothing that could be done about the spillage from the chamber pot; her water was gone, and she would have to wait until more was brought to her before she could attempt to clean it up.

Her mind was humming with thoughts of anything she could have done differently. Could she have somehow broken the window to attract her mother's attention? But the glass was thick and difficult to break. Should she have told Mrs Barwick of her husband's attempt to seduce her, and try to make her see him as he really was? She knew that the answer was that it wouldn't have made a difference; it might even have made matters worse. What could possibly induce Mrs Barwick to choose to believe her, a servant who had lost her mind and destroyed her own room, above her own husband?

She wished she knew what exactly her mother had been

told at the front door. Did Mrs Reddish believe her daughter was unwell in body, in mind, or in both? What arrangements had been made for any return visit? Mary felt she would simply be unable to make it through the doctor's visit, and the days that followed it, if she did not know. Mr Barwick had been leading her every step of the way so far, and she had followed like a fool. It was time for her to take the initiative.

Just after eight o'clock, there was a firm knock upon the door. 'Mary?' called out Mr Barwick. 'Stand away from the door, on the other side of the room.'

The key turned, and he entered carrying a jug of fresh water and a plate of bread and cheese in one hand, and the poker in the other. 'If you move, you don't eat,' he said, and he eyed her warily as he bent down to place the jug and plate by the side of the bed. Mary stood stock-still, and it was only when he began edging back towards the door that she spoke, in a soft voice that was almost a whisper.

'You can do it,' she said, looking down at the floor.

'What did you say?'

She turned her eyes to him, and spoke a little more loudly. 'You can do it. What you wanted to do before. But only if I can see my mam.'

Mr Barwick raised the poker slightly, and looked at her directly. 'Are you quite mad?' he asked.

She shook her head. 'Let me see her, and then you can do it. I won't complain, and it will be between us.'

Instantly, she realised that she had made a mistake. He didn't want her when she was compliant and yielding; he wanted her either when she was struggling beneath him, or was simply too scared to make a move. The power needed to be entirely on his side; if even a trace of it passed over to her, then the chance was lost.

'Wait ...' she called out, but already he was over the threshold.

Chapter 6

February 1812 – Ann and Thomas

Thomas Morris eased himself quietly out of bed, quickly used his toothbrush and tongue scraper, shaved as best he could in cold water with a shaving cake that lathered poorly, got himself dressed and went into the parlour. Two minutes later, he rushed to the water closet and vomited. It was the day of the first patients arriving, 12 February, and he had barely slept all night.

Ann, who had heard his vomiting, joined him in the parlour, and tried to offer him some comfort for the day ahead.

He shook his head at her words of encouragement. 'Never,' he said despondently, 'did I feel more apprehension of my own abilities than at this time.'

'All will be well,' she said. 'I am sure of it.'

'How can you be so certain?'

'Because I know you are capable. And I know that Dr Storer, Dr Pennington and the others will support us. And I know that if we act as Mr and Mrs Jepson do in York, then we shall be doing the right thing.'

Thomas was only faintly reassured. He had spent so many weeks offering encouragement to Ann that they were sufficiently competent for the challenges ahead, that he had given very little time to reassuring himself. He had not allowed his resolution to falter, for fear that it would fade away entirely. But the truth was that he felt underprepared and underqualified for what was ahead of him.

The staff, however, had been endlessly instructed by the Morrises over the course of the previous few weeks. Ann had taken them all round every inch of the asylum, giving them all the information they could possibly need for their work ahead.

'You will start at six in the morning, except for the months of November, December and January, when an extra hour is allowed,' she said. 'Your first task of the day is to wake the patients and remove any foul straw from the chambers. It must be taken to the garden before nine o'clock. Breakfast is at eight, dinner at one, and supper at six. You must count all the items of cutlery out, and count them back in again. No patient is to leave if there is a discrepancy. Patients must retire to bed by nine o'clock, except for the months of November, December and January, when it is an hour earlier. You will be expected to have retired to your chambers by ten thirty every evening. Visiting is every Tuesday between ten and twelve, and any male visitor visiting a female patient must always be accompanied by a female member of staff. Any questions?'

'Can we see a cell?' asked Hannah Greendale.

'You may see a room,' replied Ann. 'Or chamber. Never "cell", please.'

She led them into one of the chambers to take a look. Each patient had their own room, unless they were convalescing, in which case they were placed in a larger room with up to three others. The doors had a spring mortice lock and a bolt on the outside, with a sliding panel for attendants to check on the patients. Inside, there was little furniture: a bedstead, a washstand, a small chest of drawers and a single chair, all bolted to the floor. The small window looked out over the walled airing grounds, and then beyond to two windmills on the top of the hill at the edge of the nearby village of Sneinton.

'There's not much in it,' remarked Hannah.

'The chambers are deliberately as they are,' Ann replied. 'Solitude, stillness, quietness, darkness – these are all things that will help to relieve the symptoms of the afflicted.'

'Not even a mattress, though?' asked Frances Bark, one of the other attendants.

'The patient will need to be assessed first. Most will have mattresses, but those unfortunate enough to be suffering from incontinence will have straw beds and a receptacle beneath. There will be quite enough laundry to do without having to contend with soiled mattresses.'

Another of the attendants, John Clarkson, who had been shuffling uncomfortably from one foot to another, then summoned up the courage to ask: 'These lunatics – how mad are they goin' to be? I don't fancy goin' home black an' blue every day.'

'There are as many types of lunatic as there are birds in the sky,' replied Ann. 'Idiots, imbeciles, melancholics, maniacs. Those suffering from hysteria, dementia, paralysis, epilepsy. One cannot ascribe to them a single type of behaviour; indeed, one cannot ascribe to even a single one of them a typical behaviour. They may be depressed and feeble-minded one day, and violent and incoherent the next. Your role will be to treat them with kindness, patience and forbearance, no matter the provocation. You must forgive all petulance and misbehaviour. Where absolutely necessary, in order to avoid injury to themselves or others, the unhappy sufferers may be restrained – but only when absolutely necessary, and only with the least possible restraint.'

Six patients arrived that first day, all paupers from St Mary's Parish in Nottingham: Deborah Burton, Mary Coates, Alan Bradbury, George Longdeck, James Waplington and Richard Peal. Two days later, another three arrived – Sarah Beattie, Mary Carver and William Joynes. And on the Wednesday of the following week, two more – William Hardy and

George Simpson. The youngest was twenty-seven, the oldest sixty-eight.

The patients would be challenging, they knew; the notes that they had already received about them indicated that at least two were prone to violent fits, three were severely feeble-minded, one had suicidal mania, and another was suffering from a general paralysis which severely affected their speech, walking and general movement. But that was what was expected. All the patients were greeted by Thomas and Ann, checked by the attendants for lice and any signs of infectious diseases, bathed, shown to their rooms and generally welcomed to as great a degree as possible.

Over the first week or two, not everything ran entirely smoothly. The asylum might only have been one-eighth full, but still the timings of the meals were haphazard, with dinner arriving at noon one day and 3 p.m. the next; and while some patients had been provided with clothing by the parish, others had not, meaning there was a scramble to properly clothe those in the latter category.

It also quickly became apparent that the existing notes did not cover all symptoms of lunacy. Thomas was taken aback at the first morning's breakfast when one of the male patients calmly pulled down his breeches, defecated into his porridge, gave the mixture a quick stir and carried on eating. But after a few moments of speechlessness, he called for one of the attendants to remove the bowl and replace it with a fresh one, which the patient proceeded to eat from as if nothing untoward had happened at all.

In practical terms, Ann was in charge of the female wards, as well as all the cooking, cleaning and laundry, while Thomas looked after the male wards and also had overall control. Dr Pennington determined any treatments required by the patients, and the Morrises ensured that they were put into place. There was also a surgeon, Henry Oldknow, who would be brought in specifically for minor operations and setting bones.

And, for the most part, over those first few weeks, it worked. Dr Pennington would visit the asylum every Wednesday to let Thomas know of his proposed course of action for each of the patients, and to his gratification the director found that he was in agreement with the approach taken regarding the majority of them.

Both the director and the physician were agreed that they should avoid the use of bloodletting using leeches. There were a number of reasons why this might be recommended, especially for treating a condition such as lack of feeling in the legs – depleting the blood temporarily could help to reinvigorate the flow of blood around the body, and so alleviate the numbness. But Thomas's view was that the use of leeches was too commonplace and had by no means been proven to be efficacious. Dr Pennington, meanwhile, had seen a number of patients come to him in his private practice whose countenances were very pallid, and he knew from experience that this was a result of copious bloodletting. The two men were in agreement, and Thomas took this as a positive sign that the asylum's treatment regime would be a progressive, modern one.

But when he discovered one of the treatments that was to be used instead, he felt compelled to speak out. Dr Pennington had asked Thomas to obtain a cantharidin powder. This was a toxic substance, commonly known as Spanish fly, which when consumed orally was considered to be an aphrodisiac, but which had wholly different effects when applied to the skin.

'You intend to blister this patient?' he asked, looking up from the prescription book and across the desk at Dr Pennington at their weekly Wednesday meeting.

'Indeed I do.'

'Could I inquire as to the reason?'

'You may indeed.' Dr Pennington opened his medical casebook containing the notes on all the patients. 'He has suffered with a continuous cough since he was brought here. Last week he experienced difficulty swallowing. And I understand that he is often heard expectorating during the night. It is my opinion that blistering of the neck will draw the cause of the affliction away from the affected area. The human body is a remarkable instrument, Mr Morris; it will use its powers of healing where the need is greatest.'

'Quite so,' replied the director. 'And yet he has only been with us for a matter of weeks. Before embarking upon such a course, should we not first exhaust the policies and practices to which we are all committed? He would surely benefit from a long period of rest, of sober living, and of quiet contemplation before such treatments are considered?'

'I fear that quiet contemplation will be an impossibility for any of the patients, while he remains in his current state,' said the physician.

'And yet he presents no immediate danger to the other patients. He has never harmed or threatened to harm any of them. It is only himself to whom he is a danger.'

Dr Pennington shook his head. 'When he is in the paroxysms of mania, anyone who is unfortunate enough to be within one hundred yards of him is in danger.' He looked at the director sympathetically. 'I understand his need for tranquillity and sober reflection. The treatment I am proposing will not be in opposition to those measures, but will walk side by side with them.'

Thomas doubted that having a number of painful blisters upon one's neck was conducive to a sense of tranquillity. But Dr Pennington was in charge of prescriptions and he did not wish to challenge him at such an early stage in their relationship.

The director ordered the cantharidin powder that same

afternoon, and the following day it arrived and he mixed it into a paste with a little water, before calling for the patient to be brought to his consulting room. Using a spatula he applied a healthy amount of the paste to both sides of the neck, and continued with the same treatment every day for the next week.

It had no effect on the patient's health, other than to leave him with a series of painful red welts that stubbornly refused to disappear. Thomas, feeling a little dispirited, spoke to his wife about it when they sat down one evening to eat after a long day; he had told Mrs Clarkson the cook not to stay up to wait upon them, but simply to leave some cold meat, bread and pickles in the kitchen, that they could retrieve themselves.

'What will happen to him?' asked his wife.

The director sighed. 'The visiting governors will wish to see some progress, so I am in no doubt that Dr Pennington will continue with the treatments.'

'And you don't believe that he should?'

Her husband threw up his hands. 'Blistering? There is a good deal of evidence indicating that it could work. And a great deal more indicating that it does not. I should like to see other possibilities explored first – perhaps changing his diet, for example. But Dr Pennington would be the one to determine whether that would happen.'

'What about something that he wouldn't need to determine?'

Thomas looked at his wife. 'Such as?'

'How he fills his time when he is not being treated.' Ann held her husband's gaze. He had ultimate responsibility for all of the patients, but as matron she undoubtedly spent as much time with them, even some of those who were on the male wards, and she was not willing to let anything she had become aware of pass by unnoticed. 'He has ample leisure time,' she continued, 'as do all the patients. But what is he to do with that time?'

'There is the airing yard,' suggested Thomas, but she dismissed him.

'A bare yard with high walls and the same people one sees on the ward every day? I think you or I would have difficulties finding any distraction there. It is the day rooms where diversion is needed. The females have their needlework; at least, those who are allowed it do. What does he have? He cannot read, so the periodicals are of no use to him. All he has is his pipe.'

She was probably right, Thomas thought. He said that he would ask Mr Dale to raise the matter at the next meeting of the house committee, which convened at the asylum every Thursday.

But he considered that the issue went deeper than simply providing additional distractions, helpful though they might be. Even though it had only been a matter of weeks since the asylum opened, he already felt with increasing discomfort that they had been treating symptoms rather than causes. Treatment of the insane was an art, and needed to be based on the moral and physical temperament of the afflicted. To do this, one needed to study their dispositions, characters and feelings.

If one owned a recalcitrant animal, for example, one could happily say that its behaviour and character were one and the same. But the patients were not animals, and their behaviour might be entirely at odds with their actual character. And yet it was only their behaviour that was being assessed, and was then being treated in remarkably similar ways: there were eleven patients, and six had so far been prescribed blistering.

Thomas was already beginning to consider whether such a homogeneous approach was necessarily correct. The philosophy at the York Retreat was that treatment depended on conduct: if patients behaved well, and showed rationality in their actions, then their efforts were recognised; if they did not, then treatments might be used to encourage such behaviour. The widespread use of equivalent treatments across different patients, no matter the presenting conduct, was causing him a deal of consternation.

Thomas continued to work as best he could with Dr Pennington in the months and years that followed. They maintained a cordial relationship, until the occasion when Thomas and Ann returned from a short break – the first they had taken from the asylum – to find the physician at their doorstep at eight o'clock sharp the following morning. Thomas let him inside, and led him to a small meeting room where they could talk without the children or any of the attendants overhearing.

A few cursory pleasantries were exchanged, before Dr Pennington said: 'I regret to inform you that there was a formal complaint while you were absent, from the parents of Mr Strelley.'

Thomas felt his pulse quicken, but resolved to retain his composure. 'Indeed? What was the nature of the complaint?'

'Upon the occasion of their last visit to see their son, they were most perturbed to discover that surgery had been performed upon him since their last visitation. Namely that, unbeknownst to them, his leg had been amputated. I spoke to Mr Oldknow prior to the operation, and gave him my assessment that the infection of Mr Strelley's leg was such that amputation was the only reasonable option. His parents are, thankfully, also minded to think that the operation was necessary. Their complaint,' he continued, 'is that they had not been informed of the seriousness of his situation in the weeks prior to his operation; and that had this been done, they would have been spared the significant distress that awaited them on their most recent visit.'

'I see,' said Thomas, nodding his head. 'And might I inquire as to the relevant stage that this formal complaint has reached?'

'In your absence, it was decided that we should bring in Mr Wakefield and Mr Percy to investigate,' he said, naming two of the more prominent subscribers to the asylum. 'They have completed their investigations, and their findings were presented to the house committee.'

Thomas looked down and saw he had been given the minutes of the committee meeting of 17 August. He began to read, and saw that while it was the case that 'every possible attention was paid by the physician, the surgeon and director during Mr Strelley's illness', according to the report 'it would have been more desirable if the director had given earlier information to the surgeon of the bad state of Mr Strelley's leg, according to the express rule of the institution to that effect, and which the committee expect shall be accurately attended to in future'.

It was also resolved that the director 'be instructed as soon as any of the patients appear to be in a dangerous state, to take the most expeditious means to inform the relations of the same, in a letter to be addressed by the said director to them'.

The director laid the paperwork down on the table as gently as he could; hurling it down in outrage would serve no purpose here. 'I take no responsibility for Mr and Mrs Strelley's lack of knowledge on the matter,' he said.

'You had conveyed to them the urgency of the situation?'

'I had not.'

'Then quite how—'

'I had spoken to the patient's son – Mr and Mrs Strelley's grandson – and explained to him in no uncertain terms the gravity of the diagnosis. He also assured me that he would pass on the information to his grandparents. It is evident that he did not; but am I, then, to be taken to task for the failings of a young man who failed to do as instructed?'

'Perhaps not,' conceded Dr Pennington.

'And yet it appears I have been!' said Thomas, picking up the minutes and waving them in front of his face. 'Could the inquiry not have waited until my return? The surgery had already been carried out – what was the urgency of the investigation? Was it not thought necessary to speak to me to establish the course of events?'

'I can assure you that protocol was simply being followed,' said Dr Pennington. 'The matter was to be investigated and reported to the next meeting of the house committee.'

'And did our dedicated investigators inquire as to why Mr Strelley's leg might be infected in the first place?'

'Perhaps you should be careful what you are suggesting – inadvertently, I am sure,' warned the physician.

'I am not suggesting anything, merely trying to establish a chain of events. The patient had been blistered upon his leg, of that there is no doubt; you prescribed the treatment yourself. His leg became infected, and was then amputated. Should the investigators not have established whether these three elements are linked?'

Dr Pennington fixed his stare upon the director. 'I will inform the members of the committee that you would wish to see your views reflected in any conclusion they come to,' he said. 'And if the existing minutes require amendment, then they shall be.'

He took his leave, and Thomas went straight into the parlour to speak with his wife about what had occurred.

But it wasn't until a full two weeks later that a note appeared in the house committee minutes. It admitted that it did appear that the director had actually informed Mr Strelley's son of his father's situation – nevertheless, the resolution as previously agreed would stand going forward. Even Ann, who was not given to pronouncements that were of a critical nature, felt bound to remark that she had never in all her days seen such a mealy-mouthed apology.

Chapter 7

June 1827 – Mary

The Overseer of the Poor closed the door to his joinery workshop, and set off on the ride from Woodborough to Manor Farm House. The morning's engagement was a distraction he could well do without; he had recently been commissioned to produce six panelled doors for a townhouse in Bingham, and had told the customer they would be finished by the end of the week. This was a promise that was already looking increasingly unlikely even before he was asked by Mr Barwick to attend the farmhouse with the doctor; so being taken away from the work for a significant part of the morning had not placed him in the best frame of mind.

Still, there was little he could do about it. Being a parish overseer would always have to take priority over his paid work, even though it was a role he had not asked for, had never desired and had never received a penny for performing. He had been selected for the role fourteen months previously, and had been given no choice about whether to accept it or not.

At the time, his reaction had been split equally between feeling honoured to be chosen – a vindication of his standing as a respected craftsman in the village – and being indignant at the amount of time that he would have to devote to the job. But over the course of the past year the latter emotion had taken precedence over the former. It was tedious and time-consuming work, collecting the parish rates, distributing poor relief to those who needed it and making sure the books balanced. There was another overseer for the parish, but he often seemed to be away on business in Southwell or Nottingham, and he had been unavailable for this latest undertaking. Meanwhile the parish constable was tied up in dealing with the more serious criminal matters arising in the village.

The overseer had imagined there would be more interesting aspects to his work: a bastardy case, for example, trying to establish who was the father of an illegitimate child so that the man in question could provide support for it, rather than the parish having to do so. However, so far nothing of that nature had arisen, and so his – not inconsiderable – time spent in the role was filled with visiting homes in the village and the rest of the parish. The task was shared with the other overseer, but it was not always a case of simply collecting or handing out money; where possible, the parish preferred villagers to be given items to use rather than money that could be gambled or drunk away, and so he would need to consider the appropriateness, and cost, of giving one family four extra blankets, another a supply of shirts and another a coffin for a grandfather who had been living outside the village in the years before his death and did not have a certificate of settlement.

The extra responsibility had affected his business, of that he had no doubt. He had tried to fit his duties as an overseer around his joinery work, but one had inevitably haemorrhaged into the other, and halfway through the year his income was about one-fifth less than it had been in previous years. The one thing that could be said for the latest task to take him away from his work was that it had indications of being more diverting than the distribution of shirts and blankets.

The eight-mile ride from Woodborough to Halloughton took him just over an hour. He walked up the short path at the front of Manor Farm House and knocked on the door.

Mr Barwick led him into the kitchen, where a man he had never seen before was already sitting at the table. Mr Barwick introduced him as a doctor from outside the parish, who had kindly agreed to attend because the regular physician for the village was indisposed. The gentlemen greeted each other cordially.

'Now,' said the overseer, placing his hat upon the table, 'how may I be of assistance?'

'It is a matter of some delicacy,' replied Mr Barwick, 'and one which I would fervently have wished not to have reached this juncture. But I consider that my own actions are now inevitably being driven by the temperament of the young lady upstairs who, for her own safety, is presently confined to her chamber.'

'Perhaps you could be more specific, sir?'

'I am of the opinion,' said Mr Barwick, 'that she is not in possession of her senses. She has, to put it bluntly, lost her mind, and has been this way for some time. She is violent, and has destroyed property in both the parlour and her chamber. She is uncooperative and rarely speaks. And her moral conduct has … not been correct.'

'In what way?'

'I would prefer not to say. But I believe that a diagnosis may be made without going into the unsavoury details of that element of her behaviour. Indeed, the good doctor here has already made his assessment.'

'He has?' said the overseer doubtfully, and as he spoke the doctor passed him a signed form.

'I am by no means an expert on the matter,' continued Mr Barwick, 'but I understand that for an application to be made to the justices, the legislation requires one signature from a medical person confirming the state and degree of lunacy of the person in question.'

'Indeed,' said the overseer, 'and fortunately, I *do* have some expertise in the matter. And I am clear that it is not for the medical person' – he glanced over at the doctor – 'or for the employer to make the application itself. It is for the family or the parish.'

He was surprised at how easily an authoritative voice came to him; when he had entered the house he had wished his colleague had been accompanying him, but now he was relishing putting into practice what he had learned for his role but had as yet been unable to employ.

He began to read out the signed form the doctor had given him. '"I do hereby certify that Mary Reddish, twenty-three, has been attended by me from the seventh day of May 1827 to the sixteenth day of June 1827, and that, to the best of my knowledge and belief, Mary Reddish is a lunatic, and a proper object to be admitted into the lunatic asylum. Given under my hand this day of etcetera.'" He looked up in surprise. 'You have been attending her for six weeks?'

'I have,' replied the doctor.

'And has she been under any treatment in that time?'

'She has been prescribed as much rest as possible in the past week or so. She has become significantly more distressed in that period.'

He turned away from the doctor and towards Mr Barwick. 'She has been with you for long?'

'For four years.'

'And yet she is chargeable to Woodborough? There is a settlement certificate?'

'There is not,' admitted Mr Barwick, a little reluctantly; the presence of a certificate would have acted as a guarantee from her home parish that, if Mary ever needed support, it would be provided by that parish and not by the place that she had moved to. It would make clear which parish had responsibility for her; and Mr Barwick was keen for there not to be any unseemly wrangling between the respective parish overseers in this particular regard. 'But she has made no application to be settled in Halloughton,' he added quickly. 'Her parents are from Woodborough, and she is Woodborough's responsibility.'

The overseer sighed, and handed the medical form back to the doctor. 'No matter. She is not a pauper and therefore this is not a parish matter. Should her family wish to make an application to the justices themselves, they are free to do so. Good day to you.'

He made as if to pick his hat up and leave, but Mr Barwick placed a firm but gentle hand upon his arm. 'Forgive me,' he said, 'but there may be a misunderstanding. Miss Reddish is no longer in my employ.'

'She is not?'

Mr Barwick shook his head. 'She was dismissed following an incident where she deliberately smashed a vase. Due to her agitation, my wife and I agreed to let her stay in her room until she had recovered sufficiently to leave our house. But I'm afraid that the latest incident has made us fearful for our safety. You are free to speak to my wife if you wish.'

'I intend to do so. But … Miss Reddish's family will not take her?'

'Her mother has visited and is aware of the circumstances. She has some … concerns about her daughter's behaviour. For now, to all intents and purposes, Miss Reddish is a pauper to be looked after by the parish.'

The overseer paused. He did not believe he knew the young woman in question, but he was reasonably sure he had met her relatives; there was a Reddish family in Woodborough, a hard-working mother and a father who was often out of employment, and they did not immediately appear to him to be the sort of people who would abandon their daughter to the asylum.

'I have no cause to believe this to be irregular,' he said cautiously, 'but I wish to see for myself. I intend to make my own judgement. She is upstairs, you say?'

Mr Barwick and the doctor accompanied the overseer up the stairs, and both of them began to follow him into the room, before being informed that their presence was not required.

The overseer went inside, and looked at the young woman sitting on the bed in front of him.

She had a slim figure, and was sitting with one leg crossed over the other, and with her folded hands upon her knee. She wore a long, plain white shift and, despite the heat of the room, a shawl which was wrapped around her shoulders and was passed tightly across her front. Her hair was loose but tucked to one side, where it reached down to her shoulder blade. The room itself had a strong smell of urine and sweat.

'Mary?' he said, and introduced himself. In the absence of a chair, he sat down on the bed as far away from her as possible.

'Are you another doctor?' she said warily.

'I'm not,' he replied, 'but I am here to see if I can help you. Perhaps you could tell me what has been happening?'

Mary, who had already been visited earlier that day by the doctor who was now downstairs, was reluctant to have to speak to anyone else at all. But she vaguely recognised the man in front of her from her visits back to Woodborough; she could not place him, but she thought she had seen his face around the village. He looked sturdier, more trustworthy, than her earlier visitor, and so she told him, as best she could, of what had taken place: of her visit to Woodborough, of her distress at Will's departure and Ernest's treatment of her, of her subsequent incarceration by Mr and Mrs Barwick, and of her mother's visit to the farmhouse. She did not mention Mr Barwick's attempted seduction of her, for fear that it might lead to the exposure of her own offer in return, something she was desperate not to see uncovered. He asked her about her health, her work and her actions over the previous few days. They spoke for twenty minutes, before the overseer took his leave and went downstairs to where the other two men were sitting round the table.

'I don't believe it to be a straightforward case at all,' he said as he sat down. 'I can see no clear evidence of violence.'

'The stains and the dents upon the wall?' prompted Mr Barwick.

'No clear evidence of violence against *others*,' clarified the overseer, who was aware that any justice of the peace was unlikely to commit a patient without considering them to be dangerous. 'I am sure that if every person who threw a pot against a wall was sent to the asylum, it would be filled within a week.'

'And did she tell you she had assaulted me at the top of the stairs? My wife was a witness. In any case, you would not be sending her to the asylum yourself. You would simply be sending her to the magistrate to make that decision.'

'And if the magistrate *did* issue a warrant to convey her to the asylum? The parish would be paying nine shillings a week to keep her there. Dismiss her from your house, if you must; she will only cost the parish two shillings a week in relief, or three shillings in the workhouse. But nine shillings a week? The parish could not afford it even if it was for an incontestable lunatic, which appears to be far from the case here.'

Mr Barwick nodded thoughtfully, and glanced over at the doctor for affirmation. Then he said: 'I understand completely. You are wholly entitled to form your own judgement. And yet, something must be done. There is now a medical certificate which exists stating that Mary Reddish should be admitted to the asylum. I believe, sir, that you, having been made aware of this, are legally obliged to inform the justices of the case within the next week?'

'I am.'

'And there is a penalty for not doing so?'

'Ten pounds.'

'I see,' said Mr Barwick, although he clearly knew that this would be the answer. 'So the magistrate will be made aware of the case, come what may. The issue is whether you consider there is sufficient evidence to support an application for admittance to the asylum.'

The overseer was silent.

'In which case,' continued Mr Barwick, 'perhaps I might present to you two alternative scenarios. In the first, Miss Reddish is a pauper – as indeed she is at the moment – and the parish successfully applies for her to be admitted to the asylum. The parish is liable for nine shillings a week; as you say, a not inconsiderable sum.

'In order to alleviate the burden upon the parish, and because Mary has all but become one of the family during her time here, I would pay four shillings a week for as long as she needs within the facility in order to make a full recovery. This would be, as I'm sure you appreciate, an arrangement between ourselves, not something that would be required to go through the parish records.

'The second scenario is this. The parish makes no application, the magistrate allows her to return to her family, but within weeks they realise that the doctor's diagnosis is correct and that a short period in the asylum would be the most suitable course of action for her. She would then be admitted as a patient of the second class, at a cost of up to fourteen shillings a week, to be shared by the family and the parish. Given the family's situation, I would think it unlikely that the family would contribute more than a shilling or two a week; the parish would therefore be liable for the remainder.' He let the financial implications of this sink in, and then continued: 'You might, perhaps, be under the impression that families are reluctant to see their loved ones committed to the asylum. I feel obliged to inform you that this is very much not the case; I am aware of numerous families where the best course of action has been deemed to be a short period of treatment, especially when the family is attempting to run a business from home and is disrupted from doing so.

'Which of the two scenarios you choose to follow is, of course, entirely your decision. I should make it clear, however, that I would not feel it appropriate for me to make any financial contribution in the second of these circumstances.'

The overseer nodded, and thought for a moment. His parish colleagues would not commend him for making any decision that cost them nine shillings a week; and, even less so, one which cost them twelve or thirteen shillings a week.

'There is, however, a third option,' the overseer said finally, 'and even a fourth. One is that an application is made – whether by the parish or the family – and is subsequently rejected by the magistrate. The other is that Miss Reddish goes to live with her family, behaves well, and no application is ever made.'

'Indeed,' replied Mr Barwick. 'And if the application is rejected, then the proper process will have been navigated, and there will be no further appeal or complaint from these quarters. As to the likelihood of Miss Reddish returning to her family, perhaps getting married, and everything being well, however – perhaps I should relate to you what I said to her mother yesterday.'

He got up from his chair, went over to the overseer and whispered in his ear. The overseer listened intently throughout. When Mr Barwick had finished, he realised that this was not a decision he was going to be able to make on his own. He thanked Mr Barwick and the doctor for their time, and said he would return to Woodborough to consider his views, and discuss the matter with the other parish officials.

It was four days later, on the Friday of the same week, when the overseer made the journey back to Halloughton. On this occasion he was in a horse-drawn cart, sitting on the bench seat next to the driver, with the parish constable in the cart behind, and room still for several more passengers.

It had been a busy week, and not one that was conducive to the completion of the Bingham windows. He had been to see the Reddish family on two occasions. He had met with the other overseer and the assistant overseer to discuss the case. He had then finally, on the Thursday evening, sent a message to Manor Farm House informing them of his intention to arrive at the property at 8 a.m. on the Friday.

Throughout the preceding few days, his view of the matter had been constantly changing. He had his suspicions about the veracity of the doctor's report on Mary Reddish, given that her family had said they had seen no noticeable change in her behaviour over the previous few weeks. And the fact that Mr Barwick was willing to pay four shillings a week for Mary to be in the asylum was certainly irregular.

On the other hand, when he had spoken to her himself, there was no doubt that she appeared agitated and distracted, and not entirely of rational mind. This in itself was not evidence for committal; most of those who required treatment at the asylum had a history of violence to others or attempted suicide, and Mary had displayed neither of these tendencies, save for the alleged assault on Mr Barwick on the stairs. But it was, perhaps, an indication of a mental instability that could potentially spill over into acts of aggression.

The most crucial aspect, in his view, was the family's attitude, and for most of last Sunday's discussion with Mr Barwick and the doctor at the farmhouse, he had been reasonably satisfied that her parents would welcome Mary back into their home. Mary had spoken of them fondly, and there was also a fiancé, he understood, who might perhaps play a role in her rehabilitation.

That had changed, however, when Mr Barwick had whispered to him an additional detail about the matter, and indicated that Mary's mother was also party to the information. It was something that made him less certain that the family – and the fiancé especially, perhaps – would welcome her back unequivocally. It was not a subject that he would have felt comfortable raising with Mr and Mrs Reddish, but he could tell from their demeanour and slightly defensive attitude that it was something they were aware of.

In the end, he and the other overseer, following further discussion with the parish constable, had decided that it was an issue that the magistrate was best placed to decide upon. The parish itself would support the doctor, and put in an application for admission to the asylum, but it would be up to the magistrate – with all his knowledge and experience of these matters – to decide what was best for Mary. If that involved a short period of treatment in a place where she could be helped, then that would be a reasonable and just decision, made with all best intentions and with full understanding of the facts of the case. And if that was the decision, then Mr Barwick's offer of four shillings a week for her care would be one that it was incumbent upon him to accept on behalf of the parish ratepayers.

On arrival at Manor Farm House, the overseer went into the house alone, while the driver turned the cart around in the lane outside, with the parish constable still in the back; the overseer had requested that he should accompany the party on their entire journey.

Inside, Mary and Mr and Mrs Barwick were sitting around the kitchen table, and Mary jumped up as soon as the overseer entered the room. Her face was a picture of excitement, but there was something else there, too: a touch of jumpiness, perhaps, or a sense of a possibility that her emotions might get the better of her. Her few clothes and possessions were contained within a single bag, and the overseer took it as he led her out of the house and towards the cart.

'Why are they coming with us?' Mary said to him quietly as he helped her up the step at the back of the cart. 'We are going to Mam and Dad's, aren't we?'

'You are going to see your parents,' he confirmed, a reply which seemed to leave Mary slightly confused, but there was no time for her to ask further questions, because her former employer was standing directly behind her and making his own way into the cart. The overseer joined them in the back, Mrs Barwick took the seat next to the driver, and they set off. Mary stared for a short while at the parish constable, whose face was unfamiliar, being newly appointed to the role and a relatively recent arrival in the village. She did not have the presence of mind to immediately challenge him on why he was also in the cart, and soon the moment to do so was passed.

It was only a few hundred yards to the main road. They passed the church and went down the small hill at the end of the lane. As they jolted slowly along the rough lane, the overseer kept his eyes on Mary, and saw that not once did she look back at the place that had been her home for the past four years. Her gaze was focused on the road ahead, and he saw that she was holding on to the side of the cart determinedly so as not to lurch into Mr Barwick, who was sitting on the same side as her.

They came to the junction. To the right was Woodborough and, beyond it, Nottingham. For a moment the horse seemed to pull that way – the same way they had approached from a few minutes previously – but instead the driver tugged on the reins and guided the cart and its passengers to the left.

'What are we doing?' shouted Mary, standing up in the unsteady cart and looking back in the other direction towards her parents' home. 'Why are we going this way?'

Mr Barwick grabbed her by the arm and pulled her back down to her seat. Mary tried and failed to pull her arm free, and looked with anguished, pleading eyes at the overseer.

'Where are we going? You said we were going to see Mam and Dad?'

The overseer found himself unable to hold her stare, and turned his head to look down the road which led towards Southwell. 'We are, Mary,' he said quietly. 'We are.'

Chapter 8

December 1816 – Ann and Thomas

Christmas was a special time of the year, even in the asylum. Relatives were allowed to visit on the day before Christmas Eve, and on Christmas Day itself there would be goose and plum pudding for dinner, followed by parlour games in the day rooms, with the tables and chairs pushed back to create space for those who were able to join in. It was the only time of the year that some of the better-behaved men and women were allowed to mix freely, presenting opportunities that the staff were always concerned might be taken advantage of by the patients. In truth, though, this had never happened, and it seemed the patients were so unused to the circumstances that they simply stayed in their usual groups while the games of Buffy Gruffy and Steal the White Loaf took place.

In the Morris family, it was celebrated as a secular occasion. Thomas would have been quite content to attend church, but the beliefs that Ann had been brought up with, and which she still clung to within herself, forbade her from judging any day to be holier than any other. Yet it was still acknowledged as an event by the family, and the countdown to the season began as soon as Goose Fair had come and gone. Every year they took their daughter in hand and walked the short distance into Market Place to see the clowns, the stalls, the dancing bears, and to sample the toffee, brandy snaps, ginger nuts and as much as possible of the rest of the food on offer. Ann was now fifteen, and the Morrises wondered whether this year she might think the attractions too familiar and childish. But they sometimes had to remind themselves that, after seven years, she had now lived in Nottingham almost as long as she had lived outside it, and Goose Fair was – in the same way as the March Fair, May Fair and other annual events – part of the regular rhythm of her new life.

In the run-up to Christmas the three of them would also pay a visit to the theatre on St Mary's Gate, and young Ann would take it upon herself to make some rudimentary decorations to hang up in the patients' day rooms, making sure that there was no material in them that could be used to harm oneself or anyone else. It was the morning of Christmas Eve, 1816, and she and her mother were sitting at the parlour table making wreaths of holly and evergreens that had been brought in for that purpose by the gardener an hour or so previously.

'A fine sight!' said Thomas, as he entered the room and looked at the half-made wreaths. 'This one should have pride of place in the hallway, perhaps?' he added, indicating the one that Ann was working on at that moment. His daughter said nothing but smiled and continued weaving a ribbon and some rosemary between the sprigs already in place.

'Have you been in the day room?' Ann asked her husband, as breakfast was just coming to an end.

'No, there were two admissions to deal with,' he said. 'A new patient, a Mr Housely. And I'm afraid that John Allen has suffered a relapse, and his family are unable to accommodate him over Christmas.'

'Oh, how unfortunate,' said his wife, who remembered Mr Allen as one of the asylum's successes, and was genuinely disappointed to see him return. 'How is he, now?'

'His mind is turbulent,' replied her husband. Ann was about to ask more, but at that point both of the boys entered the room. Joseph was back from school for the holidays, while Thomas had been given a short break from the solicitors' firm to which he was now articled; a position which had come as some relief to his parents, even though it meant they had to financially support him during his long years of training. He had been at his firm just over a year, and at least now seemed to have a degree of focus in his life. He drank rather too well, and was a little too quick to ask his father whether he might have half a crown going spare, but he was on track towards a profession, and that was the most Thomas and Ann had hoped for.

'Well, boys!' said Mr Morris. 'Have you come to help with the decorations?'

'I can see Ann is doing an excellent job,' said his eldest son, 'and I wouldn't wish to intrude. Is there coffee? I seem to have woken with a devilish headache.'

He went over to the table and poured himself a drink, followed by a mildly disapproving look from his father; he had been out late the previous evening, and Thomas had not heard him come home. His son drank half of the coffee in one mouthful, and then went to the kitchen to ask if the cook could prepare him some kippers. Thomas sat down at the table, took up one of the wreaths and began to weave some red ribbon into it.

But at that moment Thomas Greendale, one of the assistants, came running into the parlour with his face ashen. 'Come!' he shouted, and turned to rush out again; but glancing back and seeing they were still emerging from their chairs, he shouted again, 'Quickly! I didn't – I only left them for a minute!'

Thomas ran out of the door, swiftly followed by his wife and eldest son. Joseph hesitated for a moment, not sure whether to go or not, then saw that his sister was about to chase after them. 'I think we should stay here,' he said, trying to take hold of her arm.

'Let me go!' she yelled, shrugging him off and darting after the others. Joseph hesitated for a moment and then rushed after her.

Greendale had left the door unlocked to Gallery A, which was home to the male pauper patients on the ground floor, and he, Thomas, Ann and Thomas Jnr were going through it as the two youngest children came up behind them. The party slowed as they entered the gallery, fearful of what they might find, but Greendale led them at a steady pace past the half-dozen patients who were standing looking at them, and the group carried on beyond all of the chambers, and into the day room at the end of the wing.

There were two figures, in opposite corners of the room. In one corner, partially hidden behind a stool, was George Housely, one of the patients who had been admitted that morning. His knees were drawn up under his chin, his knuckles were bloodied and he did not meet the stares of any of those who had just arrived in the room.

In the other corner was Thomas Clark, a young man in his mid-twenties who had been in the asylum since June of that year. His head was up against the wall at an unnatural angle, and there was no sign of life in his eyes.

Young Ann let out a scream, and her father whirled around. 'In heaven's name, what are you doing here?' he cried. 'Joseph, get her back to the apartment immediately. Thomas, go upstairs and get help.' The children quickly exited the day room, and the director told Greendale to keep a close eye on George Housely in the corner. Then he trod softly over to Thomas Clark, and felt for his pulse.

'Is he alive?' his wife asked, and the director shook his head. Ann cast a look over to the corner to check that Mr Housely had not moved.

'What has he done?' she whispered to her husband; but he had no more information than what he could see before him.

Thomas Jnr came back from the floor above with two more attendants, and between them they took Mr Housely down to the rooms in the basement. If they had expected a struggle, they did not get one; the patient did not move a muscle, not even to straighten his legs out from under his chin.

When he was safely inside the cell, Thomas went back up to the day room, and his father told him to go and fetch Dr Storer from Pelham Street, and Dr Pennington from Castle

Gate. 'And tell them to inform the coroner as well,' he added. 'He will need to see the body.'

The rest of the day passed in something of a fog for Thomas. First the two doctors came, and the director had to tell them all he knew about the victim, and all he knew about the assailant – which was very little – as well as the exact details of the morning's events. Then the coroner for the southern division of Nottingham, Thomas Wright, arrived along with a parish officer, and he had to repeat the information for them. All that he could say was that Thomas Clark was often an aggressive patient, and had been involved in arguments with other patients that had resulted in blows, and it was entirely possible that he had behaved in a confrontational manner with the new arrival George Housely. As for Housely, the admission form said that he was delusional, and entertained a habitual propensity for self-destruction, but had not been excessively violent on previous occasions, and at this stage the director could say no more than that.

With regards to the morning's events, it emerged that the attendant on the floor above where the attack had taken place had rung the bell a few minutes before the incident because he required assistance with a patient who was threatening to throw himself down a stairwell; and Mr Greendale had left his own floor to go upstairs to assist. As soon as the patient upstairs had been restrained, he had returned to the first floor, to be greeted by the terrible scene in the day room.

The coroner thanked those present for their time, and fixed the inquest for the following afternoon, Christmas Day, at the Navigation Inn.

On the wards, the patients were agitated and overwrought; even those on different floors and in different wings knew that something serious had happened. The general noise reached a sustained high level that the attendants had never heard before. Eventually, the shouting, wailing and screaming became so great that Thomas ordered every patient locked in their chamber, leaving the attendants walking nervously up and down the galleries and looking through the door holes to check that no patient was doing harm to themselves.

In the matron's parlour, the children finished off making the wreaths, and then hung them up in the common areas of the ground floor. Later, the family went ahead with a desultory Christmas Eve meal, but it was only the children who ate anything, and as soon as the pudding was completed, the children were allowed to depart to their own chambers.

Ann went over to her husband and stood above him with her arm around his shoulder. 'It is distressing, I know,' she said. 'But we have had a good year; you have had a good year. For the children's sake, shall we try to ensure tomorrow morning is as enjoyable as it can be, under the circumstances? The inquest will be difficult, but it will be over by this time tomorrow.'

'Under the circumstances?' Thomas responded, with a slight edge of bitterness in his voice that he instantly regretted. 'The circumstances are grave, indeed. A man has lost his life, perhaps because of some flaw that I failed to identify in another patient upon admission. Dr Storer and Dr Pennington were considerate enough not to mention it today, but have no doubt that they will be concerned about the impact this will bring with it.'

'Then let them be concerned,' said his wife gently. 'Every day we have dozens of patients with disturbed minds in close proximity with one another. A sensible assessment would surely be that it is unexpected that an incident such as this has not happened before now. The most vigilant attention will never entirely stop those who are determined enough to find the means and opportunity of effecting such violence.'

'And yet to what extent were those means and opportunity enabled by my own actions?' Thomas asked quickly. Then he added, 'I'm sorry, you are right. I'm afraid that sensible assessments appear to be somewhat beyond my grasp at the present moment.'

They spoke for a short while longer, but there was little else that needed saying, and the couple went upstairs soon afterwards. Sleep evaded Thomas for a considerable time, though; and in the long hours of wakefulness he found himself wondering whether his wife's equanimity could be attributed to her character or her former beliefs. She had always been steadfast, patient and kind; but how much of that was innate, and how much of it due to how she had been brought up? He suspected that the truth was that her character and her religion were intertwined, and had been from an early age. But he often wished he had known her when she was younger.

Christmas Day was chilly, in keeping with a year that had been much colder and wetter than usual. The family breakfasted early, as Thomas had the intention of spending a significant part of the morning with patients to assess how the events of the previous day had affected them, before he and his wife attended the afternoon inquest.

He was on the first floor, speaking to one of the pauper patients, when he heard an ungodly scream come from the floor above him. It sounded like the high-pitched scream of a woman, but as he was on the male wing it was impossible for that to be the case.

He ran to the stairs at the end of the gallery, and went up them three at a time to the floor for second-class patients. As he rounded the corner at the top of the stairs, he saw a gruesome sight coming towards him – a patient named Joseph Taylor staggering along the gallery, grasping at the wall as he went and leaving a trail of bloody handprints upon it. There was blood streaming down the side of his face, and his other hand was desperately trying to stem the flow from an unseen wound.

The director rushed towards him, but even as he did so John Allen, who had been readmitted the previous morning, emerged from a room and charged towards the already injured patient.

Thomas paused for a second as his mind strained to make sense of the situation. In that single second, John Allen launched himself at Mr Taylor and struck an earth-shaking blow to the side of his head. There was a weapon of some sort in his hand, a chair leg perhaps, Thomas thought as the patient fell in an instant, cracking his head on the sill of one of the windows overlooking the airing yard as he did so, and crumpling onto the floor.

Thomas thought his own time had surely come; that no sooner had Allen dispatched one victim than he would immediately search out his second. Instead, delivering the fatal blow seemed to have suddenly drained him of all his energy, and he slumped down onto the stone floor just a yard away from the body of his fellow patient. The director did not move, but stayed entirely still in the same position as various attendants rushed past him to tackle and restrain the patient.

To have to endure the coroner being called out on a single occasion to deal with a death at the asylum was distressing enough; to have to do the same thing the very next morning was anguish that was almost beyond what was bearable.

Mr Wright, the coroner, immediately decided that the inquests of both men should be held together that afternoon; the jury was ready, the venue had been booked, and there seemed little point in assembling everyone the day afterwards for the second inquest.

Dr Storer offered to take the Morrises down to the Navigation Inn in his carriage, but the matron kindly declined on her husband's behalf; the walk was only just over a mile, and she felt it would do Thomas some good to be out in the fresh air before the inquest.

So it was that, a matter of hours after the second death, Ann found herself supporting him as they skirted the edge of town and made their way down to the canal and along the towpath towards the Navigation Inn. At times she felt that she was literally, physically supporting him; his legs were unsteady, and at various points they had to stop because he was overcome with dizziness and nausea.

At the points when he felt well enough to speak, the only thing that Thomas could talk about was Joseph Taylor. It was just about feasible to understand how the first victim, Thomas Clark, could have provoked the assault upon him. It was entirely unthinkable to imagine how Mr Taylor could have done the same to John Allen. He had been in the asylum for twenty-one months, and was the most gentlemanly of all the patients: an academic and author who had appeared to have been living a perfectly successful life until the impairment of his mind began. He had run the Dronfield Academy for Boys in Derbyshire, had published a number of respectfully reviewed books on language and on parenting – *A System of English Grammar*, *The Child's True Guide to Knowledge and Virtue*, *A Summary of Parental and Filial Duties* – and he engaged in lively debate in the letters pages of newspapers on matters of grammatical importance. He and his wife Helena had seven children, but when his mental health deteriorated, his house was put up for sale, and a series of fundraising appeals titled 'The Distressing Case of Mr Joseph Taylor of Dronfield' were placed in newspapers across the country by his friends, noting that he had been reduced 'by a severe affliction of his mind, from extensive usefulness, to utter imbecility', and that his family were 'as helpless as they are destitute'. The advertisements warned that he faced the workhouse; but instead, as he entered his sixth decade, he found himself in the asylum.

'Mr Taylor,' Thomas said repeatedly, shaking his head,

and there was nothing his wife could say to comfort him. They made it to the inn just on time, leaving the towpath and crossing over Wilford Street to arrive at the venue just as the coroner was taking his seat. Mr Wright led the witnesses and the jury skilfully through the next hour or two, asking each witness only the questions that related directly to the two deaths or the events leading up to them, and indicating to the jury when a witness had strayed away from the facts and into the realms of speculation and conjecture.

At the end of the evidence, the bare facts had clearly been established by the jury: Thomas Clark, twenty-six, had been killed by a blow to the head delivered by George Housely; and Joseph Taylor, fifty-one, had been killed by a blow to the head delivered by John Allen. But the coroner said he would inform those present of the further findings of himself and the jury the following day.

That evening, the two bodies were removed by the parish from the basement rooms where they had been temporarily stored. Thomas wrote his second letter in two days to the family of a deceased patient, and began to worry about meeting the relatives in person when they turned up at the asylum, inevitably wanting to know how such an incident could possibly happen.

The asylum's house committee had arranged to meet the next day as soon as they had received notification of the coroner's findings, where the director would be further interviewed about the events of Christmas Eve and Christmas Day. The prospect of another interrogation, so soon after the inquests, was more than Thomas could countenance; his wife tried to console him, saying that she was sure the coroner would find no fault with the asylum, but he felt that – however hard she tried to make it otherwise – this was not something that the pair of them were facing together.

Both deaths were on the male wards, and the matron had no responsibility at all for what took place there.

Thomas spent another uneasy night, and eventually he decided to lie down on the parlour sofa so as to avoid disturbing Ann further. When morning came around, it seemed to drag to an even greater degree than the night had done, and when Dr Storer and Dr Pennington arrived just after one o'clock with the coroner's verdict, it was a relief; nothing could be worse than the incessant waiting.

It was Dr Pennington who read out the letter, written that Boxing Day morning from the coroner's home in Chilwell. After reading through the summary of what those assembled already knew from the inquest, Dr Pennington reached the crucial section.

'From every circumstance through the business, no blame appeared to attach to Mr Morris or his servants, as the business for the security of the patients appeared to be conducted in the usual way,' the coroner had written. The director felt his heart rate slow just a fraction.

The letter continued: 'Mr Morris appeared to me in so distressed a situation, I did not think it right to say anything to him on the subject of using precautions to prevent a recurrence of so dreadful a catastrophe, more especially so as Mr Morris acts under the superintendence of so respectable a body of gentlemen.'

And it ended by saying that, while the coroner himself thought that the less publicity given to the events the better, it would be up to Dr Pennington and the committee to decide whether an item on the matter should be prepared for the newspapers.

Dr Pennington folded up the letter, and looked at the committee members. 'There we have it, gentlemen,' he said. 'There are two matters to be addressed this afternoon. To establish whether further precautions are required to avert any such event occurring again. And to determine whether a notice should be sent to the newspapers informing them of the event.'

It was swiftly agreed that an additional assistant was required, in order to ensure that no gallery was left unattended for any period of time, and that the director would keep every patient under proper restraint on admission, until their temper and disposition could be sufficiently ascertained.

'With regards to the issue of publicity,' said Dr Pennington, 'I welcome Mr Wright's indication of his own position on this. However, I believe it would be beneficial for the public to be made aware of the events that have taken place.'

'For what purpose?' asked Thomas.

'For the purpose of openness and transparency,' replied Dr Pennington. 'The public will learn of the events one way or another. It is surely better that they hear about them through official means, making clear that no blame is attached to the asylum or its employees, than for the circumstances to be a whirlwind of gossip, innuendo, or plain mistruths.'

Thomas did not know what to make of this. It was possible that Dr Pennington's views were genuine. It was also possible that he wished the director's inadequacies – for that is how they would be interpreted, no matter the views of the coroner or the committee – to be highlighted, even if it was at the expense of the overall reputation of the asylum. Thomas did not believe the physician would be so short-sighted as to take this position, but he had arrived at a position where he felt he simply did not understand the motivations of many of those around him.

The committee agreed the further measure, and the meeting ended. The notices subsequently appeared in the *Nottingham Review* and *General Advertiser for the Midland Counties* on 3 January 1817, and in the *Nottingham Journal* the day afterwards. For Thomas, when he finally saw the notices in print, it did feel like a further humiliation, and an unnecessary one at that.

But in the wider scheme of things, no amount of public approbation could assail him more than his own feelings of guilt had already done and continued to do. He had spent the first four years at the asylum concerned about how many patients were being cured, how many were being discharged without being substantially helped, and what could be done to improve the ratio between the two. He had never envisaged that two would be carried off in a cart because of blows struck by other patients.

Chapter 9

June 1827 – Mary

It was a perfect summer's morning. In the landscape surrounding the cart that was heading towards Southwell, the haymaking season was just beginning, and men and women were already hard at work in the fields, the early sun catching the blades of their scythes as they arced through the air. Mary saw none of them; or, if she did, she paid them no heed. The landscape was only of interest to her because of any opportunity it afforded her for escape. If they ascended a gentle hill, it gave her a greater opportunity to jump away from the cart. If they passed an orchard of damson trees, it only diverted her because of the potential cover it could offer.

Mary didn't know exactly where they were going, but she knew that Southwell was home to a workhouse, a house of correction, a court and a police station; and her fervent desire was that none of these was her final stop. The overseer might have spoken the truth about going to see her parents, but Mary's aim was to escape from the cart before ever finding out whether or not it was in fact a falsehood.

Throughout the journey, however, Mr Barwick kept a firm grasp upon her arm. For the first few minutes of the journey she attempted to ease herself free, but his grip remained unyielding, and eventually she gave up.

She tried, instead, to engage the overseer in conversation, in order to get more detail from him about their destination, but he either ignored her or gave her non-committal, monosyllabic responses. How much he appeared to have changed, she thought, from the man who had come to visit her in her room just four days previously and had seemed genuinely concerned about her well-being.

The journey into Southwell took just over an hour. They came into the town and turned on to Westgate, where the two western towers of the minster loomed over the shops and houses. The cart then took a right, and continued until the driver stopped outside a vast, derelict building, which had a small structure standing at the end. This was the old Archbishop's Palace, which had been plundered during the Civil War when Cromwell's soldiers stripped the lead from the roof, and the townspeople took anything else that was of value, including the stonework and timber. Now, every fortnight, the building that remained held the magistrates' sessions for the soke of Southwell.

'What is this place?' asked Mary, who could see no obvious signs from her vantage point that they had arrived at a courthouse.

Nobody answered her. Mrs Barwick alighted from the front of the cart, and the overseer made his way to the step at the back. Mr Barwick, however, hung back, not standing up and still keeping hold of Mary. As he eventually pushed himself to his feet, Mary was half a second behind him. He bent down so that his mouth was level with her ear, and said quietly: 'Your mother is inside there, Mary; and I have told her all about the shameless proposition you made to me. If I were you, I wouldn't expect to receive a sympathetic welcome from her.'

Mary, who had not been expecting Mr Barwick to say anything at all to her, let alone the dreadful words he had actually spoken, was taken aback, and for a moment didn't know what to do. But in a split second, without having time to think about either the justification for or consequence of her actions, she rammed the top of her head into the middle of his face; there was a cracking sound, then a yell of pain, and then blood started to pour out of Mr Barwick's nose.

She was horrified; she had never imagined that she could do such a thing, nor even contemplated that her forehead could have been used as a method of attack. But with one of her arms held tight, the other too far from Mr Barwick, and her legs unable to reach around to kick him, she had instinctively assaulted him with the only part of her that could land a heavy blow.

The flash of anger was gone almost as soon as it had arrived, and certainly by the time she saw the result of her action, but by then it was too late. Mr Barwick was slumped on the seat trying to stem the flow of blood, Mrs Barwick was standing at the side of the cart hitting Mary with her fists, and the overseer and constable were trying to drag Mary away from the scene and out of the cart. Another man came out of the courthouse and helped the overseer and constable to get Mary inside the building, where she was thrown onto the floor of a bare room and the door locked behind her.

It was only just over an hour since she had been released from her previous place of confinement; now, once again, she found herself locked up. But twenty minutes later the door opened again, and Mary was led into a large, panelled room and made to sit on a chair in front of a table where a ruddy-faced man was looking down at some paperwork.

She looked to her left and saw Mr and Mrs Barwick, the overseer and a man who looked like an official of some sort. It wasn't until she looked slightly behind her, over her shoulder to the right, that she saw her mother and father, her sister Liz and, sitting next to them, Ernest.

'Mam, Dad ...' she managed to get out, before the official-looking man told her to quieten down, and she stopped herself from saying any more. She couldn't stop looking at them, though, and she smiled at them frantically as she tried to gesture to ask them if they were well. Her parents smiled back, but they were wan smiles, seemingly devoid of genuine affection. Lizzie looked at her in a sympathetic way, but Ernest failed to meet her gaze at all, and instead stared down at the stone floor. Where she had expected to see grief, there was shame; where she had hoped for tenderness, there appeared to be indifference.

For a moment, Mary had forgotten that her family – or mother, at the very least – knew what had transpired between herself and Mr Barwick. But, in a rush, the words that he had said to her in the cart came back to her, and a torrent of embarrassment swept over her. The thought that her mother would know the details of any aspect of her private life was mortifying; to realise that she knew such an intimate particular was almost more than she could bear. And if Ernest knew, too? If he did, it was hard to see that he would be here at all; but if he did not, then there was surely no reason for him not to even be looking at her.

She felt exhausted; the adrenaline that had been pumping through her in the cart had all but disappeared and had left her feeling drained. She thought she heard someone speaking, and looked up to see the ruddy-faced man was talking to her.

'Mary Reddish?' he was saying. 'Do you have a middle name?'

'No, sir.'

'Very good. You are Mary Reddish, then?'

'Yes, sir.'

'Mary Reddish, I am authorised and directed, upon the application of the Overseer of the Poor, to issue warrants for the conveyance of any lunatic, insane person or dangerous idiot to the General Lunatic Asylum for the city and county of Nottingham, with a view to cure, comfort and safe custody. Do you understand?'

For the first time, Mary realised that she was in a court, and that the man in front of her was a magistrate. But, in her shock at the events of the morning so far, she was unable to take in anything else the man had said.

'No, sir,' she said.

'An application has been made for you to be admitted to the asylum,' he said, speaking more slowly than he had been. 'I am to decide whether you are to be taken there.'

'The asylum? But I'm not—'

'That is for me to decide, based on the evidence before me this morning,' the magistrate interrupted, glancing as he did so at the bloodied face of Mr Barwick. 'May I see the certificate?' he asked the court in general, and the overseer presented it to him. The magistrate studied it for a minute or so, then handed it back. 'I believe we should hear first from the gentleman there,' he said, and Mr Barwick rose from his seat and went to stand in front of the justice. His nose had stopped bleeding, but he made a great show of dabbing it frequently with his scarlet-stained handkerchief.

Mary listened as Mr Barwick went through the chronological litany of violent offences that he believed she had committed – the smashing of the vase, the destruction of the room and the assault upon him that very morning. To Mary's ears, the sequence of events sounded harsher than she ever could have believed. At several points she wanted to interrupt and say that the evidence was incorrect, but already her instincts told her that she should bide her time; and so she waited until Mr Barwick had finished, and the magistrate had asked her to speak.

'The vase was an accident,' she said. 'And anyway it was to be taken from my wages. There was no cause to lock me in my room. And then when he wouldn't let me see my mam – I was mad at him, I suppose, but I didn't take it out on him.' She instantly regretted her choice of word that conveyed her anger, given the context of this particular hearing, but it was too late to take it back.

'And the incident outside the court?'

Mary hesitated. Mr Barwick had not mentioned the words that had passed between them; if she was specific about what he had said, it would bring it out into the open. But could she afford not to do so? Without justification for her assault, it would appear to have come from nowhere, and that would make the magistrate's decision an easy one.

'He said something that was very hurtful to me,' she said.

'Which was?'

'That I had – made a proposition to him, and that he had told my mam about it.'

'What sort of proposition?'

Mary could not bring herself to say the words, so the magistrate asked her if she meant a proposition of an obscene nature, and she nodded.

'And did you? Make a proposition of such a nature?'

Mary could feel her body shrivelling beneath her clothing. To speak in such a manner before her parents, her sister, Ernest, the court – it was something she could never have envisaged doing in a hundred years, a thousand. And yet, slowly, another sentiment was also rising within her, and it was one which emboldened her – the knowledge that, if she did reveal everything here, then it would be known to everyone, and she would never have to say it again. Everyone who mattered to her, aside from her brothers, was here in this room; there would be nobody, or barely nobody, whom she would have to tell it to again.

'I did,' she said with as much courage as she could gather, and looking directly at the magistrate as she did so. 'But only because I could see no other way to release myself from my room. A few days previously – it was the night before Mrs Barwick returned – Mr Barwick entered my chamber and attempted to … to join me in my bed.'

'Preposterous!' shouted Mr Barwick, and the magistrate gave him a stern look.

'I did not allow him to,' continued Mary. 'And yet as time went on, I could see no other solution. I am ashamed of what I said to him, but not of why I did it. I feared being locked in that room forever, and I was desperate.'

'The streets of Nottingham,' replied the magistrate, 'are filled with women who became desperate. Desperation is no excuse for such behaviour. Mr Barwick, am I to assume you dispute the account we have just heard?'

'With every fibre of my being!' he said. 'Mary Reddish is a licentious and wanton creature; she is no better than those women on the streets you refer to. The earlier incident was simply the first occasion on which she propositioned me. I had entered her room to check on her well-being—'

'At midnight!' interjected Mary.

'Because I wanted to make sure she was well rested before my wife's return,' he continued, 'and might therefore be able to resume some light household duties. It was then she made an indecent remark not dissimilar to the one we have already heard about.'

'He's lying!' cried Mary. 'He was on my bed – did I drag him there myself?'

'And there have been previous examples of immorality,' Mr Barwick said quickly, keen to press on and divert the magistrate's attention away from that night. 'Forgive me for my necessary explicitness before the court. But I have seen Miss Reddish engaged in acts of intimacy with others, in public. In the field on one occasion, and by the dovecote on another.'

There was a gasp from the family side of the courtroom, and Mary could not immediately tell who it came from. But if she had thought she could have been no more shamed than by the earlier proceedings of the court, then this new allegation put a lie to that; this was the very depths of degradation, no matter that Mr Barwick's false testimony cast him more in the role of voyeur than innocent bystander.

'That's a lie!' shouted Mary, before adding impetuously, and with more than a hint of despair: 'And it's not the first time he has done this! Ask him why the house servant before me left. He did the same to her as he tried to do to me.'

The magistrate looked inquiringly at Mr Barwick, who seemed affronted to be even having to answer the question. 'Nonsense,' he said. 'She received the offer of another position nearer to her family, and decided to accept it, that is all. There was nothing untoward about her departure.'

'Ask Mrs Barwick,' said Mary. 'She knows, I'm sure of it.'

The magistrate turned towards Mrs Barwick. 'Was there, madam?' he asked. 'Was there anything untoward?'

Mrs Barwick had not looked at Mary throughout the morning. She had moved serenely from being aloof in the front seat of the cart to being detached in the courthouse. Mary had tried to catch her eye on one or two occasions; she knew that Mrs Barwick had a number of younger sisters, and perhaps if she faced Mary directly she might picture one of her siblings sitting there in the same spot, and be more sympathetic towards the unwarranted fate that her former employee faced. But there were stronger issues at play than imagined situations in which her own relatives took centre stage.

'There was nothing untoward,' she said firmly. 'The circumstances of her departure were as my husband indicated.'

The magistrate nodded. He continued with his questioning of Mr Barwick, but to the majority of the court it seemed perfunctory now. There was nothing new to emerge, simply the clarification of existing details.

The overseer, for one, was feeling more comfortable about the action he had taken than he had at any point over the past few days. When, in the farmhouse, Mr Barwick had whispered to him about Mary's proposition, he had been somewhat sceptical about whether it was likely that the young woman would do such a thing. When he had been to visit Mary's parents, he had not considered it was a matter he could raise with them, but he felt sure they must have had some level of equivocation about whether it was within Mary's character.

But now all of that was largely irrelevant; Mary's actions outside the court had made it so. She had shown herself to be capable of extreme violence, and in doing so had all but condemned herself to the asylum. It wasn't just the attack itself, but the nature of it – it was uncontrolled, instinctive and almost animalistic. It was hard to square the actions of the young woman outside court with the demeanour of the same person he had met in the upstairs chamber of the farmhouse, but he had seen it with his own eyes, and he didn't doubt the ferocity with which she had launched her assault.

Ernest, meanwhile, felt as if he wanted to flee the courthouse and never set eyes on Mary or her family again. He had been forced to suffer the indignity not only of hearing how a man in his sixties had clambered into the bed of his fiancée, nor simply of how she had made him an obscene offer in return, but of how she had allowed herself to be seen engaging in her own acts of indecency. That was a side of their relationship that he had never pushed Mary on, that he had not imagined broaching until they were married; to see how far she had gone down that road of her own accord was calamitous, and something from which their relationship could never recover even if she avoided the asylum.

And what of Mary herself? To her dismay, she was now seeing the events of the past two weeks with a fresh and awful clarity. After her rejection of Mr Barwick on the night he came to her bed, she had expected to be dismissed, and had been waiting for him to do it; it was entirely within both his power and his character to do so.

But now she saw why he had not taken what would seem like the most straightforward course of action. A servant girl, released from her job and free to tell others about the treatment she had received, was a perilous thing to have living in the next village, especially if there were rumours about the girl who had gone before her. It might not lead to any impact on his livelihood, and would certainly not have any effect on his marriage, but it might possibly just lessen his standing in the community.

A girl who had made wild accusations before being admitted to the asylum, however, that was a different matter entirely. It would leave him entirely blameless; it might even go further and engender some sympathy on his behalf for the slurs and lies he had been obliged to suffer.

And she also saw how meticulously he had planned the sequence of events that had needed to happen for her to arrive at this particular point: ensuring Mrs Barwick would take his side, finding a doctor who would sign the certificate, persuading the overseer to submit the application.

And yet, she had given him his most valuable weapon, with her ill-considered approach to him. It was a weapon he had used to full effect; if he had not told her mother, and then told Mary that he had told her mother, then she would not have unleashed the assault that could well seal her future. Would he have succeeded if she had not propositioned him? Would he have found another way to convince the magistrate that she was violent? No doubt he would have tried, and no doubt the outcome might have been the same; sending her to the asylum was the path of most suffering for her, but it was the path of least contention for the community, after all. Still, she felt as if she had supplied Mr Barwick with the arrows which he was now using to shoot her down.

The magistrate had finished his questioning. He told Mary to stand, and she pushed herself slowly up before facing him with her hands clasped in front of her.

'Mary Reddish,' he said to her, 'the asylum of Nottingham and Nottinghamshire is an institution of some renown, and it is not my intention to populate it with persons whose conduct does not warrant admittance.'

She felt her heart lift a little, but the magistrate continued.

'If you had shown no sign of being a danger to others, then

I would have had no hesitation in returning you to the care of your family.'

'Please, let me expl—'

'Yet the verifiable fact is that you *are* a danger to others. There is a man sitting over there who constitutes all the evidence this court requires.'

'But you don't under—'

'Enough!' said the magistrate severely. 'I have heard quite enough.' He paused before addressing her directly once again. 'Mary Reddish, I find that you have been violent, that your moral conduct has been incorrect, and that you are not of sound mind. You are to be conveyed to the asylum, and safely kept there until you are duly discharged. The outcome of this hearing will be reported to the General Quarter Sessions, and any person aggrieved by the outcome is entitled to appeal to the justices of the peace at that court, giving ten days' notice. Now, vacate the court, all of you; there is plenty to get through this morning.'

Chapter 10

January 1818 – Ann and Thomas

The final years of the decade brought worsening conditions for the people of Nottinghamshire. Poor harvests and a ban on the importation of cheap grains kept the price of wheat consistently high, and with families spending ever-increasing amounts of their meagre income on food, the demand for goods produced by framework knitters dropped away.

The knitters, left at the mercy of frame owners, discovered that there was little mercy to be found. They complained bitterly of working sixteen- to eighteen-hour days for only five or six shillings a week, and the number of workers applying for parochial help soared. Meal, usually used as animal food, replaced bread on the table; and when there came a point where no more economising was possible, the framework knitters took to the streets.

Hundreds of people – men, women and children – marched through the centre of Nottingham, with placards that read 'We ask for bread!' and 'Pity our distress!' Those who found themselves effectively unemployed published an open letter to the lord lieutenant declaring that 'for the last eighteen months we have scarcely known what it is to be free from the pangs of hunger', and describing having to stifle the cries of hunger of their children.

In protest and in desperation, some even dragged their frames into town, pulling them by rope from the back of a cart, and dumped them outside the warehouses so that the hosiers could see how utterly redundant they had become. The hosiers eventually came to an agreement that would see wages increase to a level demanded by the framework knitters; but with no demand for the knitters' work in any case, it made barely any difference.

Sitting in the parlour of his elegant three-storey townhouse in Castle Gate, Dr Charles Pennington was not immune from the realities of everyday life for the working man and woman in Nottingham. Far from it; the years he had spent as a physician at the General Hospital had exposed him to some of the effects that a life of hard labour could have upon the human body, and if there was a disconnect between his own existence and that of those on the streets outside, it was an entirely understandable one that arose from his later years spent treating those who could afford to pay the fees at his own private practice.

He glanced over at his wife Frances, who was reading the local notices in the newspaper. The couple's only son George had moved on from Eton to Cambridge as assuredly as night follows day, and for many years they had lived in companionable partnership in the centre of town, at close quarters to their many friends and former colleagues.

It was the afternoon of Friday 30 January 1818, and in an hour or so they would need to begin their preparations for that evening's dinner engagement. In the meantime, Mrs Pennington was idly looking in the *Nottingham Review* for events that might provide suitable distraction in the future, and had already made note of an insertion from a Mary Noton, respectfully informing the ladies of Nottingham and its vicinity that she was selecting new dresses and millinery in London, which would be ready for inspection at her house in the Poultry on Tuesday next.

'Charles, dear,' she said, and her husband looked up from

the case notes he had been studying. 'There appears to be an item here regarding the asylum.'

'Indeed? What does it say?'

Mrs Pennington adjusted the paper so that she could better read the small print in the top left-hand corner of the page. 'It begins, "To correspondents",' she said. 'And then it says: "LH must send his name and address as soon as possible. In that case, his letter will be printed. The letter, relative to a scene which is said to have been recently exhibited at the Lunatic Asylum, is received, and will be duly considered. We agree with the writer, that if what he states is correct, such conduct loudly calls for a very serious investigation." Whatever can it mean?'

Dr Pennington gestured for his wife to hand over the newspaper, and she did so. He proceeded to read the small item at the top of page three, and then read it again, but he remained no wiser about any event to which the letter writer could be referring.

'I have no idea,' he said. 'Forgive me, but I think it might be necessary for me to pay Dr Storer a visit. I will be back in plenty of time.'

'Really, Charles?' said his wife. 'Dr Storer will be present this evening, will it not wait until then?'

But the physician was already in the hallway putting on his coat. 'I fear not,' he said.

Ann had warned her husband several days previously that they should inform the house committee – or, at the least, either Mr Dale or Dr Pennington – about the small party they intended to hold. And Thomas was aware that, while there was no protocol dictating that he should let the house committee know about the dance, his wife was right that common sense advised in favour of it. But there was a streak of stubbornness and independence within him that some of his past dealings with the committee had brought to the fore, and he was reluctant to go to them cap in hand asking for permission to allow an event in his own home. The governors did have the ultimate jurisdiction over whether he remained in his role as director, but it was also undeniably true that he was ultimately responsible for everything that happened within the asylum's four walls. He had made the decision not to inform them, and the dance had gone ahead as planned.

It was past six o'clock when Dr Pennington and Dr Storer rang the bell to the asylum. They had decided to visit together, so that they could proceed directly to their seven o'clock dinner appointment afterwards. It was a cold evening, and both men stamped their feet against the stone doorstep as they waited for the door to be opened.

It was the matron who greeted them and let them in. 'Gentlemen!' she said. 'Mr Morris did not say he was expecting you?'

'He is not,' replied Dr Storer. 'Forgive our intrusion, but a matter of some urgency has come to light which we would wish to discuss with him as soon as is practicable. Is he available?'

'He is just completing his order for tomorrow,' she said, leading them through to the meeting room where her husband tended to complete his evening's work, spreading out Dr Pennington's prescriptions on the large table and working through them methodically.

The two doctors greeted Thomas cordially, and asked whether he had seen that day's edition of the *Review*. As he had not, Dr Pennington gave him his own copy, and asked him to read the item at the top of page three. He gave the director sufficient time to read through the few lines several times over, and then said, 'You will see why we felt it necessary to bring the matter to your attention this evening.'

'Of course, of course …' Thomas said distractedly, trying to make sense of the words he saw in front of him. 'But – this is absurd!' he added, eventually. 'What editor would see fit to publish such a piece? It is little more than tittle-tattle, and the most vague sort of tittle-tattle at that. It tells the reader nothing, but implies that everything remains a possibility.'

'The editor is known to me,' replied Dr Pennington, 'and he is a respectable man. But it is not the character of the editor that is being brought into question. Rather, the question relates to the nature of the scene that recently took place in this very building. With regards to which, I should say, we are both still very much unenlightened.'

Thomas wondered for a moment how well acquainted Dr Pennington was with the editor, and whether he had been informed about – or even approved, perhaps – the publication of the item. But he dismissed the idea almost as soon as it had been formed; the physician would surely never jeopardise the reputation of the asylum in such a manner. Instead, he explained to both doctors how the event had been a small dance held for the children and some of their friends, that it had not lasted beyond half past ten in the evening, and that the musical accompaniment had been a single pianoforte.

'And yet the noise from such a small dance has clearly reached beyond these walls,' noted Dr Pennington. 'Are we to gather that there was a good deal of commotion generated by the young people present?'

'They are young people who were enjoying themselves,' replied Thomas, unable to keep a note of exasperation out of his voice. 'I daresay there will have been some degree of commotion, if that is how you wish to define the sounds of laughter and good cheer.'

'I have no quarrel with good cheer,' came the reply. 'But the question will inevitably be asked whether the asylum is an appropriate setting for those of a tender age to be indulging in it.'

'Is that quite so? And yet there is no question as to whether it is an appropriate setting to raise a child – my own child?' replied the director. 'You well know that I have raised previously the possibility of a cottage in the grounds being provided as living quarters for my family, and that there has been no further movement regarding the matter. But a simple dance results in an anonymous letter in the newspaper and an immediate visit from yourselves? I appreciate that you are obliged to investigate but, really, gentlemen, I trust that now you are acquainted with the circumstances you will consider the matter closed.'

Dr Pennington shook his head. 'Thank you for providing the additional information,' he said. 'But it is clear that the committee will need to be informed. No doubt some of the members will already have seen the newspaper themselves.'

He apologised to Ann once again for disturbing their evening, and then made his way with Dr Storer away from the asylum and in the direction of their dinner engagement.

'You were a little hard on him,' said Dr Storer, who had been friends with Dr Pennington long enough to feel entitled to make such an observation, and to comfortably foresee that it would not be taken in offence.

'He must assuredly appreciate that the matter is too significant not to be taken further,' the physician replied. 'The asylum is the asylum, and not the Morrises' house.'

'But it is their home, nevertheless?'

'And one which is to be inhabited by the director and his family in a manner commensurate with his position,' said Dr Pennington. 'Perhaps Mr Morris is correct that a cottage within the grounds would be more suitable, but until the day that such a facility is built, there must be an expectation that the building is used appropriately.'

'The governors will decide whether that is the case here, then,' concluded Dr Storer. 'But I am firmly of the belief that Mr Morris is a good man, and an excellent director.'

'I leave the governors to make that decision, based on the evidence before them,' said his companion. 'Now, let us make haste.'

In truth, Dr Pennington had no particular desire to see Thomas removed from his post; and he did not regret that his brother Robert Rainey had recommended him. In his view, Thomas was a competent enough director who simply needed to be guided back to the right path every so often. Dr Pennington was now sixty, while Thomas was forty-seven, and the former understood that every younger generation of medical men needed to be passionate and forthright about new treatments and practices; he had seen it time and again with the freshly qualified doctors who came through the General Hospital.

He did, however, believe that Thomas was simply wrong in some of his beliefs. The director had mentioned on a number of occasions, for example, that he felt too many patients were being blistered; but it was a proven treatment that had been used for many years and would no doubt be used for many more. Change purely in and of itself was not necessarily something to be sought, especially when that change involved only the removal of an existing treatment and not its replacement with anything new.

Dr Pennington was content to let the house committee do its work and investigate what was, in his view, the latest in a series of missteps from the director; not missteps that would justify him losing his job, in all probability, but serious enough for the proper procedures to be followed and propitious action taken.

So it was that, the following Thursday, he was equally content when the investigation was completed and a note published in the house committee minutes to the effect that, while the governors distinctly disapproved of the fact that the dance had taken place, they did not think it called for the severe censure that the paragraph in the *Nottingham Review* conveyed. The committee blamed the director for permitting his children to have their amusement in the asylum; but they also thought it was due to him to add that in his general conduct as director, they felt he was entitled to their commendation. And the next edition of the *Nottingham Review,* in arguing that it had been right to publish the original letter, noted that 'we find that though our Correspondent's charge is not entirely unfounded, yet he has coloured the picture too highly'.

For Charles Pennington, this constituted a fair and reasonable outcome. For Thomas, it was the third time in six years he had received a public judgement in which he was by no means fully exonerated, and in some ways it felt like the most significant yet; more chastening than the investigation he faced after the amputation of Mr Strelley's leg, more public than the deaths of the two patients. It was a direct condemnation of his own actions and, by extension, of how he and Ann raised their children; all played out as a permanent record in the pages of the *Nottingham Review*.

Despite the reassurances that Ann gave him, Thomas felt more doubtful of his abilities than ever before. In addition, the death of his father at the age of eighty, back in the village of Witney where Thomas had grown up, seemed to draw a line under his previous life before the asylum and leave him feeling untethered and rootless. He felt that whatever he now accomplished in his life would be carried out in a void, meaning little to him without his father's awareness and approbation of what he had achieved. He was tired all the time, and either could not get to sleep or struggled to wake.

In his daily life, it was as if he was constantly pulled in three different directions: by the patients, by the physician and by the magistrates. The magistrates felt they needed to retain overall responsibility for running the asylum, the physician was clear that he was best placed to identify the requirements of the patients, the patients had families who demanded constant updates on their progress, and in the middle of all three was the director, aiming to satisfy all parties but frequently unable to do so.

The fifth of August 1826, saw the death of Mary Carver, who was the last of the original eleven patients remaining in the asylum, all of the others having been released or died. She had been a patient for more than fourteen years, and her death prompted a period of soul-searching in Thomas Morris; when he looked back at those first eleven people to be taken under his wing, he wondered with a certain sense of disillusionment how many of them they had genuinely needed to be there. Then there was the patient who had presented with a paralysis that affected their entire body and who, later symptoms showed, actually had a form of syphilis that limited their movement, a rare but clearly physical form of affliction. Another, who had been assessed as delusional and hysterical for thinking her husband was trying to kill her, had only been vindicated when he had murdered their only child, who had been left in his sole care.

Thomas felt that there was no longer any certainty to what the asylum was doing. Were they treating the mind, the body, neither or both? Were their treatments really any better than quack cures? Did a clear system of moral management have any real impact on those with deep-rooted disorders, or were he and the rest of the staff simply scratching ineffectually at the surface of whatever lay beneath? There were times when he felt little more than a gaoler; a well-intentioned gaoler, perhaps, but a gaoler nonetheless.

Chapter 11

June 1827 – Mary

Mary had imagined that, once the magistrate's decision was handed down, she would be taken directly to the asylum. Instead, she was obliged to spend four nights in the court cell awaiting her transfer from Southwell to Nottingham.

The possibility of being taken to the asylum had crossed her mind only fleetingly in the time between her being aware that it could happen, at the start of the court hearing, and the actual ruling being given. Standing alone in the oppressiveness of the courtroom, trying to take in what was happening to her, most of the scenarios playing through her head involved her being taken back to Woodborough to her parents' home, or even returning to employment with Mr and Mrs Barwick in Halloughton.

The worst outcome that she could conceive of was some time in gaol for the assault in the cart on Mr Barwick. And while she was furious with herself for letting him get under her skin in such a manner, there had been a certain satisfaction in seeing him cower beneath her flailing arms – a satisfaction that would surely help to sustain her through whatever period she was forced to spend in prison.

But the asylum? The very thought of it filled Mary with a dread which pervaded her entire body. Compared to what she understood of the gaol and the workhouse – both of which had at one time been home to people she knew from Woodborough

– her knowledge of the asylum was vague, but what she did know was that it was for lunatics: mad men and women who were beyond help, and who were kept locked up for their own safety and that of others. It wasn't for the likes of her.

As far as she was aware – and nothing the magistrate said had indicated otherwise – there was no specified length of sentence for being in the asylum. You were admitted, and you either left, or you didn't. More than anything else, more than the very real fear of being set down in the midst of people who had lost their minds, it was this that struck absolute foreboding into her heart.

For most of the remainder of the Friday of her court appearance, she shook and wept uncontrollably in the cell she had been assigned, though 'cell' barely warranted that description; it was only a locked room with a bucket in the corner for a privy.

Her bowels turned to water, and before long a foul smell was emanating from the bucket, but she was so indifferent to her own needs that she did not call for it to be emptied. It was cleared out after a few hours when some bread and a thin soup were brought to her, but she turned the food away without even attempting to eat it.

By the following morning, she felt spent and empty inside. Her muscles ached from the frequent convulsions of her body, and her throat was sore from the sobs and coughs that had assailed it. The court was a little way outside the main town, but from her room she could still hear the sounds of people going about their usual Saturday morning business: carts upon the cobbled streets, the cries of traders, greetings being shouted from one friend to another.

No one came to visit, and she did not expect them to. Even the briefest recall of her family's faces as she had last seen them in court was enough to convince her of that. Her single consolation was that Will had not been present to see events unfold. He was the one person, she thought, who might have seen things from her own point of view, and at least she had not had to suffer the additional anguish of him turning against her as well.

For four long days, she was held in the room. She could hear occasional comings and goings in the rest of the court building, but there were no further sessions held, and in the evenings when the noise from outside had ebbed away it was largely quiet. An attendant brought her meals and emptied her bucket, but otherwise she was devoid of human contact, and was left alone with her thoughts.

She was not sorry for herself; rather, she felt angry at the absurdity of the actions that had brought her to this point. Approaching Mr Barwick with her foolish proposition – no, it was less than a proposition, she thought, more of a reluctant acquiescence to his desires – and her later assault of him had seemed to be the right course of action at the time, but had only acted to serve his own purposes perfectly. And as she considered her behaviour, she realised that she had not actually made choices at all, but on both occasions had been acting solely on instinct. There had been no point where she had stopped, even for a second, to consider the possible ramifications of her deeds. Her mother had often cautioned her against acting in haste, but Mary feared that her repenting would not be at leisure.

On the morning of the Tuesday, after another interminable night when she had barely slept at all on the thin mattress upon the floor, Mary was taken outside to a waiting cart. There was no Mr or Mrs Barwick present, but the overseer was there, as was the man who had accompanied her to Southwell, who she now knew was the parish constable.

'In you get, Mary,' said the overseer, not unkindly, and she climbed into the back of the cart. The overseer sat opposite her, the constable placed himself next to her and the driver set them on their way.

Passing along the Nottingham road, it seemed unspeakably cruel that the route took them past the turn-offs to, first, Halloughton, and then Woodborough. Salvation lay just a short distance down either of those roads; and yet in reality both destinations were as far away as they could possibly be. Was it really only four days ago that she had travelled in the opposite direction? That journey, when she did not know where she was headed, had seemed to last an age, and she had been able to take in the sights of the surrounding countryside. By contrast, today's flew by in no time at all, and within half an hour they had passed through Burton Joyce and Carlton, and were approaching the outskirts of Nottingham itself.

Before they reached the town, however, the cart turned left through some gateposts next to a small porter's lodge, and there in front of Mary, at the end of a driveway, was the asylum. Its size took her breath away, momentarily; excepting the minster in Southwell, the imposing building was the largest structure she had ever seen, and she couldn't but help stare at it as the cart came to a halt in the circular drive in front of the main steps.

'This is you then, Mary,' said the overseer, as a member of staff in a white uniform came down the steps. The overseer helped her down from the cart, and physically handed her over to the attendant, her slim hand being passed from one man to the other. The asylum towered above her, with seemingly endless rows of windows across its four storeys. It seemed too vast for any purpose, let alone for the housing of the sum total of lunatics in the county.

'Mr Oldknow will need to see the paperwork,' said the attendant to the overseer, and the three of them walked slowly up the steps and through the main door of the asylum. Inside, Mary found herself in a large hallway which led into a corridor, off which were two stairwells and a number of doors. The attendant showed the overseer into one of the rooms, where he remained for fifteen minutes before emerging and saying goodbye to Mary.

'God willing, we'll see you back in Woodborough before too long,' he said, and made his exit through the main door.

Mary felt a greater sense of abandonment at that point than

she had at any time over the previous few days, even going back to when she was locked in her room at Manor Farm House. She had no fondness for the overseer at all – indeed, far from it – but he was the only familiar face that she had seen that day, and now her only link to her former life and home village was gone. She peered through one of the large windows at the front of the building and watched as the cart pulled away.

'Time to get yer sorted, then, missus,' said the attendant, and he took her into a different room where there was a chair and a small table, with a pile of clothes upon it. 'Them there's for you. I don't reckon anyone died in 'em, least not recently. Don't be shy, I won't look.'

He turned away and Mary, unsure of what to do, hesitantly began to undo the top button of her gown, only to be interrupted by a gale of laughter coming from the direction of the attendant.

'Was you really going to do it?' he laughed, shaking his head as he did so. 'You're a right one, eh? Stay there, and I'll get someone from the women's side.' He went out the door, locking it as he did so, and still smiling to himself at the new patient.

A few minutes later, a female attendant arrived, and introduced herself as Mrs Sinclair. She watched as Mary took off her gown, chemise, petticoat and stockings; and the attendant then proceeded to inspect the items for any sign of lice. She patted down the patient to check she had no dangerous items about her, and looked over her body for spots, swelling or any sort of infection. Satisfied, she led Mary over to a small sink in the corner of the room, where she washed her hair thoroughly, combing it through to check for lice as she did so.

Only when she had finished all of this did she present Mary with new clothing. 'Two aprons, three gowns, one shawl, two petticoats, four pairs of stockings, three nightgowns, two nightcaps, two day caps, four chemises, four handkerchiefs, two neckerchiefs, one bonnet, two under-waistcoats, and two pairs of boots,' she said mechanically. 'Take good care of it, mind. The parish pays for it and it don't like having to pay out more than it has to.'

Mary dressed quickly, and Mrs Sinclair placed a wooden comb and a hairbrush with soft bristles on top of the piles of clothes.

She also gave Mary a toothbrush and, when she saw the puzzled look upon the patient's face, said: 'You never used one before? You'll get used to it soon enough; just keep it off your gums. Now, you can pick all these up in a bit when I takes you to your room. First, you need to meet Mr Oldknow.'

The formal assessment and admission were usually carried out by Thomas Morris. However, at the time of Mary's arrival he was away in Wakefield, visiting the asylum there at the request of the house committee. These requests were fairly frequent occurrences, and saw the director travelling all over the country to glean information from various asylums and find out about their best practices. This, at least, was the theory; the director, however, had confessed to Ann that in his view these trips were used rather more as punishments, simply because the committee could effectively order him to go wherever it was they chose. He usually returned from them not significantly wiser, since the Nottingham facility had, after all, been honing its practices for longer than any of the other asylums, but a little more exasperated at the members of the committee.

With Dr Pennington and Dr Storer also otherwise engaged, it had been left to the asylum's surgeon Henry Oldknow to carry out the admission of Mary. She was led into a different room, still on the ground floor, where Mr Oldknow greeted her, sat her down, and explained the absence of the director, before adding: 'You are fortunate to be found a place at all. The asylum is full, and the magistrates have been told not to send any more paup— um, patients of the third class, I should say – here at present. Fortunately, a patient was discharged yesterday and a space became available.'

Mary nodded dumbly, as if she should conceivably be grateful that she was in this unsettling place. Given the male attendant's earlier remarks, she also wondered whether a patient had indeed been discharged, or had actually died in the very clothes she had been allocated.

'Now, I have here your case notes,' the surgeon continued, 'and the overseer has provided me with some details about the events of the past few days. That was a nasty attack outside the courthouse, Mary, on an entirely innocent victim. Perhaps you could tell me why you did it.'

Mary wondered what she could possibly say; after her experience at the court, there was no likelihood that she would wish to relate the whole history of Mr Barwick's unscrupulousness and duplicity towards her.

'I don't know, sir,' she said.

'You don't know?'

She shook her head.

'There was no cause, just or otherwise, for you initiating such an act of violence?'

Mary lifted her head to look directly at Mr Oldknow. 'There was a cause, sir, but not one that I wish to relate.'

'I see.'

He asked her a few more questions that were essentially the same one being asked time and again from a different angle, and then stood up from behind his desk. He went just outside the door to the room, and came back with Mrs Sinclair and the male attendant who had collected her from the cart.

'Do not be alarmed, Mary,' the surgeon said, and it was only the fact of his saying this that caused her to be uneasy. She looked at Mrs Sinclair, and saw that she was carrying a shirt that appeared to have long arms and no buttons down the front. 'Mr Morris will return tomorrow, and will assess you properly then,' continued Mr Oldknow. 'Until that point, it is a standard requirement that you wear this; please stand up.'

Mary had already begun to get up when the two attendants entered the room, but the words of the surgeon made her shrink back into her chair again. The male attendant, however, came up behind her, grabbed her under both arms, and with a strength that belied his moderate frame he hoisted her up and held her firmly in his grip.

'What are you doing?' she cried, but Mrs Sinclair had already taken hold of one of her arms and forced it into the sleeve of the clothing she was holding. Aware that the same thing was about to happen to her other arm, Mary raised it instinctively to keep it out of reach. Mrs Sinclair reached up for it, and without thinking Mary brought her elbow sharply down into the middle of the attendant's face.

'You little b—' began Mrs Sinclair, but before the word was out of her mouth, Mary felt an almighty blow land in the centre of her own face, and she fell to the floor with blood starting to stream from her nose.

All she wanted to do was to bring her hands up to cover her nose and somehow alleviate the pain, but one arm was already secured, and now, with the male attendant who had hit her placing his knee on her chest and pressing her to the ground, she could feel the other one being pushed roughly into a sleeve. When it was in, the attendant forced her to turn over, and she felt a sharp tug as both sleeves were pulled behind her, tightened, and then buckled together so that she was entirely unable to move her arms.

Mr Oldknow had not been entirely straight with Mary; it was by no means a standard requirement for all new patients to wear a strait-waistcoat. But he was inexperienced when it came to admissions, and he would rather a patient be inconvenienced for one night than have the director or physician hold him to account for anything that went amiss with a new patient.

After the two deaths at Christmas 1816, the committee had determined that all new patients should be kept under proper restraint until their disposition could be ascertained, and Mr Oldknow was not prepared to jeopardise his own position by providing a new patient with inappropriate restraint, or no restraint at all.

'Please get up now, Mary,' he said, attempting an authoritative tone in his voice, but being betrayed by a slight tremble which indicated that he had been unsettled by the scenes in front of his desk.

Mary, who was still lying on her front, attempted to get to her knees in order to push herself up, but without the balance that would have been provided by her free arms she toppled over, and fell back onto the floor.

'Help her up, Ellis.'

The male attendant hauled her to her feet, a fresh spill of blood coming from her nose as he did so. He led her out of the room and up the stairs in the hallway, closely followed by Mr Oldknow, and with Mrs Sinclair further behind after going back to collect the pile of Mary's new clothes. On the next floor, the attendant unlocked the door to the female pauper ward, and took Mary through into the gallery.

Ann Morris was standing halfway down the gallery speaking with a patient, but as soon as she saw the quartet enter her ward she walked straight down to speak to them.

'Gracious me!' she said, looking at the two women with bloodied noses. 'What on earth has taken place?'

'A little difficulty during admission,' said Mr Oldknow, 'but nothing that could not be managed.'

'She battered me for no reason, and got what she deserved,' said Mrs Sinclair bitterly.

'But why is she in a camisole?' asked Ann. 'Is it really necessary?'

'I would submit that the state of Mrs Sinclair indicates its necessity,' replied the surgeon. 'In any case, it is only for one night until Mr Morris returns.'

'One night when she will be locked in her own room,' replied the matron, and Mary flinched slightly hearing these words.

'It is for her own safety, as much as that of others,' said Mr Oldknow. 'You are as well aware as I am that this is the procedure to be followed; please do not suggest that it should be circumvented.'

Ann, after a moment's consideration, stepped aside; and the party went forward to the room that had previously been occupied by the recently departed patient. During the exchange in the gallery Mary, whose arms were still being gripped tightly by the attendant she now knew was called Ellis, had attempted to say that it was the use of the camisole that had caused her to react violently, rather than the other way round as Mr Oldknow had indicated; but as soon as she opened her mouth to speak, the attendant tightened his grip to such a painful degree that it took her breath away, and she held back. She continued to do so now, as she was led into her barely furnished room.

'The director will see you tomorrow,' said Mr Oldknow, leading her to the single wooden chair and pushing her down upon it. He and the two attendants backed out of the door, and Mary heard it lock.

The room was long and narrow; ten feet from the door to the window, but only seven feet wide. Under the window was a chest of drawers and a washstand, and against the right-hand wall was the bedstead. It had no mattress, but was topped with straw and a coverlid. Underneath it was a large chamber pot.

Mary pushed herself up from her chair. As she did so, she expected to hear the chair legs scrape against the stone floor, but no sound came, and when she looked down she saw that the chair was bolted to the floor. So were all the other items of furniture in the room.

She went across to the window and looked outside. Directly

below her was a large yard that was divided into six different sections, with the whole yard bordered by a high wall. Beyond the wall she could see a pair of windmills upon a hill, while to the right were gardens and rows of houses.

She suddenly felt claustrophobic, as if there was no air at all in the small room. The window in front of her was closed, and her hands were tightly bound at her back. She turned round, and stood on tiptoes to see if her hands would reach the bottom of the window. She felt the sill between her fingers, reached herself up a bit higher and took hold of the sash. Holding it as firmly as she could while facing backwards, she pushed upwards, and it moved a few inches.

But it would go no further. She turned around, and saw that the pulley was designed so that the window was now at its fullest opening; wide enough to let a little breeze in, but not to give any human any chance of exiting through it. Mary – who by now had been locked up for more than three weeks at the farmhouse and in the court building – bent down so that her mouth was level with the opening, and gulped in mouthfuls of warm air that was undeniably acrid but seemed as fresh to her as she had breathed in a very long time.

The day inched onwards. Within the first few minutes, Mary had examined everything that the room had to offer. She had pulled on the handle of the door and found it to be immovable. She had tried to open the viewing panel but realised it was only possible from the outside. She had inspected her bed and decided that she would need both the blanket and bedspread beneath her to avoid the stiff straw sticking into her body.

The remainder of the time she passed in going over and over – in minute detail – the sequence of events that had led her here, and wondering what she could have done differently at each and every stage. It was difficult for her not to shake the uncomfortable feeling that everything had come together in the only combination of circumstances that would have seen her ending up in the asylum, and that if she had deviated from the course at any stage then she might have saved herself. But she had continued inexorably towards her fate, like an animal trapped in a fast-flowing river, and had somehow not seen or had ignored the overhanging branches that she could have grasped for.

And if ever there was a chance that she might for just a second escape to a daydream that would take her away from her situation, the camisole pulled her back towards it. Not being able to move her arms freely was a torment that she could not have imagined without experiencing it, but as the day progressed it increasingly drove her to a state of distraction. Every slight itch was an unbearable irritation that could not be scratched; every mild ache in her arms became a pain that could not be alleviated.

At some point – Mary didn't know when, exactly, but it was still light outside – Mrs Sinclair came into the room with some bread and water. Mary asked her to scratch a point on the back of her head that had become the focus of all her suffering, and could not be lessened by rubbing it against the wall, but she refused.

Instead, she gave the bread to Mary in chunks that were slightly larger than bite-sized, forcing each one in before Mary had chewed the one before as properly as she would have liked, and then tipped the water into Mary's mouth for too long, so that Mary was obliged to close her mouth and spill the liquid down her gown to stop herself choking.

An hour or so later, the matron came to see her. Her manner was kindly enough, Mary thought, and she asked Mary various questions about how she was feeling and whether she would be expecting any visitors; but she felt unable to speak at all, such was her shock at the situation she was in, and after five minutes the matron said she needed to speak with other patients.

Then she was gone, and Mary saw no one else that day. There were noises from the gallery outside and from the adjacent rooms, but no screaming or crying, just the sounds of people talking and the occasional shout from an attendant to a patient.

It grew dark outside, and Mary realised that she needed to urinate before making any attempt at sleep. She pulled the chamber pot from under the bed, and squatted over it in a way that would keep her gown and petticoat dry. But however she tried to do it, there was no way she could take down her undergarments with her hands tied behind her back. She tried to pull her arms under her backside, but they were tied too closely, so she abandoned the attempt and went back to sit on her bed.

Half an hour later, though, she knew that would have to go ahead. She wondered whether using the chamber pot was a task that Mrs Sinclair had been supposed to help her with, but had chosen not to because of the considerable pain she was no doubt still in from Mary's blow. Or perhaps the chamber pot was not intended to be used as normal, but was placed under the bed in order to catch any liquid filtering through the straw during the night.

Whichever was the case, it didn't matter now. Mary crouched over the chamber pot again and emptied her bladder, the hot liquid turning cold and clammy almost as soon as it hit the fabric of her underclothes. She shuffled back to her bed and lay there waiting for sleep in an embittered combination of humiliation, anxiety and dampness.

Thomas returned in the mid-afternoon of the following day, having caught the early coach from Wakefield. His mood was no better or worse than it had been when he came back from any of his previous similar trips. He was ambivalent about what he had seen while he was away, resentful that he had been sent there in the first place, but pleased to be able to see his wife and daughter again.

As soon as he saw Ann, he could tell that something had

disturbed her good humour, but he let their daughter tell him about her last few days before he sent her away and asked his wife what was wrong.

'The patients will speak to me as they wish, and that I accept,' Ann said. 'They do not know what they are saying. But I do not also expect to be spoken to uncivilly by Mr Oldknow.' She went on to explain the events surrounding Mary Reddish's arrival in the asylum the previous day, staying calm throughout, but clearly upset nevertheless. Thomas was surprised; it wasn't like his wife to be overly concerned about the niceties of language, whoever was speaking to her, and he suspected that the way the surgeon had spoken was not the whole of the matter.

'Was there anything else?' he asked.

Ann hesitated. There was much that she wanted to say: about the inexperience of Mr Oldknow; about her frustration that it had to be either him or Dr Pennington – and not herself, who knew the patients and the procedures better than anybody – who was in charge whenever the director was absent; about having to be answerable to whichever man happened to be arbitrarily placed above her. If she chose to go even further, then she would ask him why it was that she looked after as many patients as he did, but that when their salaries had been increased his had gone up from £100 to £150, and hers had only improved from £30 to £50, meaning the difference between them was even greater than it had been.

None of these issues were her husband's fault, however, so she simply shook her head. 'But please see that poor girl as soon as possible,' she said. 'She has been in that strait-waistcoat in her room ever since she got here. I know when to be scared of a patient, and when not to be, and we should not be frightened of her.'

Thomas spoke to her for a few more minutes, then went outside and called for an attendant to bring down Miss Reddish, before going to his office. A few minutes later, Mrs Sinclair knocked on his door and brought in the patient.

She had a striking face. A handsome face, too, Thomas did not doubt, but there was something about it that put one slightly on edge: the piercing green eyes, the slightly angular profile, the cheekbones that were inching the overall impression towards the margins of hollowness. Perhaps it was just the effect of a sleepless night in the asylum; no one ever slept on their first night.

'Remove the camisole, Mrs Sinclair,' he said.

'Sir?'

'Take it off her immediately.' He said it in such a way that the attendant did not query him again, and began to undo the buckles and pull the sleeves to the front. She made as if to get Mary's arms out from the sleeves, but was shrugged off, and stood uselessly to one side until the garment was removed by Mary herself, and she was dismissed from the room by the director.

By no means could Thomas have been said to have a full assessment of the patient, but freeing the patient from the constraints of the strait-waistcoat was his way of demonstrating that he trusted his wife's instincts. Ten years ago he would not have done it, or even five years ago, but he had reached the stage where he now wondered whether their own instincts were the most potent tools they had available.

'I am Thomas Morris, the director of this asylum,' he said to Mary. 'I will be looking after you.'

PART TWO

Chapter 12

June 1827

Mary stood in the centre of the director's office, rubbing her arms to get her blood circulating properly again following the long hours she had spent constrained in the camisole. As she did so, she took a moment to contemplate the man in front of her, who was looking through the notes on his desk. He was in his fifties, she guessed, with a prominent forehead that gave him a look of solidity, and hair that was swept back in a possible attempt to disguise the fact that it was just beginning to thin. He wore a high-collared waistcoat and a cravat, but no jacket, as if he had been disturbed in the middle of dressing before being called away on more pressing business. He could very easily have been a merchant, or a barrister, or a schoolmaster.

'Mary Reddish,' he said, looking up from his notes.

'Yes, sir,' Mary replied.

'There's no requirement to call me "sir",' said Thomas. '"Mr Morris" will be quite adequate.'

'I would feel more comfortable with "sir", if that wouldn't cause offence, sir.'

Thomas regarded her more closely, and took a moment to consider. He had encountered numerous patients who refused to call him by his name, or who had remained entirely silent when he spoke to them, but never one who had insisted on calling him 'sir'.

'Very well,' he said, 'as you wish. Now, perhaps you could tell me in your own words: why do you think you are here, Mary?'

Her natural instinct was to stay quiet; but already she was beginning to realise that the only way to get out of this place was going to be with the sanction of the man in front of her. 'To get better?' she ventured.

'Ah, but that takes us beyond where we wish to be,' said the director. 'One would hope that getting better is the aim of all the patients here. The question is perhaps better phrased as – why do you think you are here in the first place?'

'I don't know, sir.'

'That is what you told my colleague. But I don't believe it to be the case; your notes indicate that there were very specific events that led to your admission, and I find it difficult to believe that you remained entirely unaware of those events, either then or now. So I ask again – why do you think you are here?'

Mary did not instinctively trust the director any more than she would have trusted the overseer, the parish constable or the magistrate. They were all the same: supposed gentlemen who had taken her life in a direction that she could never have foreseen. She failed to see why a different gentleman in a different suit would be any more honourable than they had been.

'Perhaps that is not for me to say, sir,' she replied. 'It was not my choice to be here.'

Thomas rose from his chair, and went to look out of the window. The grounds were still at their summer best: blooms proliferated from every border, the fruit trees he had planted more than a decade ago had fully matured, and the curve of the driveway as it cut through the green of the lawn was as impressive as it ever was.

'Let me relate to you something that happened almost a year ago,' he said. 'I had a patient named Mary Carver; one of the very first patients to be admitted here. She was, all things considered, very little trouble; she had occasional fits, and was prone to throwing her supper upon the floor, but she was never violent to another soul. In short, she was eminently treatable, and a perfectly good candidate to be entered back into society.

'And yet, in the entire time she was here, she did not speak a word. Not a single one. There were times when I thought she was going to, when she opened her mouth as if she wished to say something, but no word was ever spoken. And it's very difficult to justify sending someone back into society when they cannot or will not communicate.'

He turned round from the window to face Mary.

'She died last year, after fourteen years under my care. And shall I tell you what happened when she died?'

'Yes, sir.'

'Nothing happened. Nothing at all. There were no last-minute words of contrition, no final message that she had been withholding for all those years to be passed on to her loved ones. I spent some time with her in her final days, and I could see in her eyes that she wanted to speak. But after so long without doing so, she was unable to articulate the words. She had simply lost the ability to do so.' He returned to his desk and sat down. 'The opportunity to make ourselves heard does not present itself forever, Mary,' he said. 'There may be a time when one is unable to do so, or is able but is not listened to. This is your opportunity, Mary. It will not be the only one; I don't wish to imply that is so. But I implore you not to be like Mary Carver. She was forty-five when she arrived, you are only twenty-three; you have a good deal of life ahead of you. I would wish you to be cured, and to live the rest of that life away from this institution.'

This was also what Mary most desired. Not a return to her former life; she would never work again at Manor Farm House, and Ernest was lost to her, she felt. But to go back to Woodborough, and her parents and siblings, and to walk by the beck and over the fields; that, to her, was the hope that she had to cling on to.

'I believe that I have a temper, sir,' she said quietly. 'And that I have let it get the better of me.'

'Good.'

'But also that the provocation I suffered was beyond that which I could be expected to endure.'

'I see. What was the nature of the provocation?'

Mary hesitated; she remained reluctant to be specific about Mr Barwick, whom she still feared could influence her well-being in the future. But she knew that she needed to provide the director with something so that he could understand the extent of her mistreatment. And, after all, he was the one who had rid her of the camisole.

'I was confined to my chamber for no good reason, and prevented from seeing my family,' she said. 'And when I rejected the advances of a certain gentleman who wished to … act in a dishonourable manner, he turned against me and misrepresented me to my family.'

Even as she said the words, Mary could see how slight her complaint sounded. She had not been beaten, or starved, or thrown on to the streets. But without going into the detail of how she felt when Mr Barwick had crept into her room, or when she found out he had spoken to her mother at the front door, it was impossible to get across to Mr Morris the deep nature of her distress.

'Nottingham is just beyond these walls, Mary,' he said. 'I could throw a farthing onto its streets, and it could be picked up by a hundred – no, a thousand – unfortunate people who have suffered more greatly than you.'

'I know, sir, but—'

'And yet they have not resorted to the same violence that you inflicted upon your employer,' he continued. 'This is what concerns me, Mary. I am interested in determining the cause for a particular type of behaviour. The cause in your case appears to be … not entirely inconsequential, perhaps, but certainly unsubstantial. What is to say that another similarly unsubstantial cause in the future would not result in a comparable loss of control?'

'It wouldn't, sir,' she said, but Mr Morris shook his head.

'There would need to be evidence of that,' he said. 'In the meantime, get plenty of rest, engage yourself in leisure activities, keep your mind active, and we shall see how you progress. You will find that good behaviour is rewarded with privileges, Mary. We wish you to get better as much as you do.'

Quickly, all too quickly, Mary became accustomed to the routines of the asylum. Up at seven for a breakfast at eight of bread, butter and tea; a long morning spent in the day room; lunch at one of meat, potatoes and suet or rice pudding; a walk around the airing yard; supper of bread, butter and tea or half a pint of beer at six; and locked in her room for bed at nine.

But there were so many things she felt she would never get used to. The ill-fitting clothes which itched and chafed more than her own ever had. The dining bell which determined her movements three times a day. The meat that came with all the bones removed. The early lock-up when there was still some sunlight left in the day. And, most of all, the sound of the key in the lock, and the knowledge that it would be another ten hours before she saw another human face.

Nevertheless, Mary had resolved that the way to freedom was to do as the director had said: to stay calm, to stay reserved, and to prove that her episodes of violence had been the exception rather than the norm. To do this, she decided that she should avoid the other patients as much as possible, on the basis that she did not know what unwanted aggravation they might provide. When one woman, who was rumoured to have killed the man who had attacked her, asked Mary to play a game of bagatelle, she politely declined. When another, whose fits were truly terrifying and could last for twenty minutes or more, tried to engage her in conversation at supper, she moved to a different seat as soon as possible. And when a third, whose mouth was entirely devoid of teeth after she pulled them out for reasons that had never been established, began to sing a bawdy song in the day room for the amusement of the other patients, she turned away and returned to her own chamber. The men she never saw, unless one happened to temporarily hoist himself high enough to peer over the wall of the airing yards, in which case he would swiftly be pulled down again.

Within a few days, Ann rewarded her good behaviour by giving her a job in the kitchen for a few hours every morning. It was heavily supervised, and any sharp items were locked away out of sight; the matron believed she trusted her, but the safety of others still took priority.

It was time away from the tedium of the day room for Mary, however, and as she washed up the crockery she enjoyed the quiet company of the attendant Hannah Greendale, who had been removed from working on the wards after her husband had been found to be supplying alcohol to one of the patients, but who had been allowed to transfer to the kitchen following representations made by Mrs Morris.

On occasion, Hannah would accompany Mary on walks around the grounds. The lack of an exterior wall at the boundary of the site meant that even the most trusted patients were not allowed out alone, but those who were deemed responsible enough were allotted a half-hour every so often to stretch their legs and take in the gardens.

Hannah also helped her when there were things within the ward that she was not sure about: the notice on the gallery wall, for example, which because of her lack of schooling Mary was unable to read, but which Hannah told her were the regulations relating to the conduct of all the members of staff – that they abstain from acts of unnecessary violence against the patients, that they behave with the utmost forbearance, tenderness, patience and humanity, and so on. Mary paled a little at this when she thought of her treatment being forced into the camisole in Mr Oldknow's room, but she said nothing. She was acting as the director had requested, and she did not want anything to jeopardise that.

The director himself, meanwhile, was happy to leave Mary free of treatments for as long as necessary, to assess her temper and disposition for himself. Having missed his weekly Wednesday meeting with Dr Pennington immediately after her admittance when he had been travelling back from Wakefield, however, he knew that the physician would wish to discuss her case in some detail at their meeting the following week.

As the newest patient, she was the first to be discussed. Thomas explained his reasoning to Dr Pennington for avoiding any treatment at this early stage, pointing out that Mary had no long-standing history of violence, had never attempted self-harm or suicide and did not suffer from fits. Therefore it seemed appropriate to ascertain her behaviour once she had been removed from the exciting cause, which appeared to be her relationship with her former master, before embarking upon any potentially unnecessary treatment.

'And yet,' said Dr Pennington, 'she appears to have beaten her former master within an inch of his life?'

'I do not believe that it was quite that serious. A few ineffectual blows, perhaps. There was no weapon of any sort.'

'And also assaulted Mrs Sinclair during her admission, leaving her with a broken nose?'

'That was unfortunate on both sides. Miss Reddish also received a bloodied nose during the altercation.'

'It does seem that serious injury appears to afflict those who cross her path,' noted Dr Pennington. 'And that is before we consider the issue of her moral conduct, which I am led to believe has been improper. What did she have to say about that?'

Thomas was obliged to concede that she had not gone into any detail about it during his conversation with her.

The physician looked at Mary's notes for a while longer,

and then said: 'No, this won't do. I see a pattern of behaviour, and it must be stopped before it begins. A course of antimony tartar will clear out any excess of vigour within her.'

Antimony and potassium tartrate, or antimony tartar, was a powerful emetic, and one that would result in Mary vomiting into a bucket multiple times a day. Thomas had seen its effect on other young women in the house. Elizabeth Rhodes, for example, was just seventeen, and was the youngest patient on the wing. She had been admitted because she had for a long time been flighty, and had complained of persistent headaches, both of which her father was unable to attribute to any hereditary or other cause. She was given the emetic, and was also bled with leeches. Thomas could see little change in her. The director's own view was that emetics were valuable in purging patients who had ingested a poison or who were experiencing intestinal difficulties, but were of limited use in other circumstances. Simply asking Dr Pennington not to go ahead with Mary's prescription would have only one outcome, however.

'I wonder,' he said, at length, 'whether I might be permitted to ask Mr Dale his opinion regarding the most efficacious emetics? My role as apothecary here is greatly limited compared to what it was in my prior employment, and I fear I may not be quite as well informed as Mr Dale. He may also be able to source an alternative that is more … cost-effective?'

Dr Pennington looked doubtful. He was not accustomed to his instructions being queried. But it was hard to deny that Mr Morris's argument of potentially saving money was a persuasive one. He agreed to let the director speak to Mr Dale before proceeding with the prescription.

After four weeks in the asylum, Mary received her first visitor.

Patients were allowed visitors every Tuesday between ten and twelve in the forenoon, and the first three visiting days following her admission went by without anyone travelling to see her. But on the fourth Tuesday, as she was helping to wash up the breakfast crockery under the close supervision of Hannah Greendale, Mrs Sinclair came into the kitchen and told her that she had a visitor, whom she should meet in the airing yard in five minutes.

Mary was elated to learn that someone had come. She had not yet expected that her parents would have forgiven her for her behaviour, both towards Mr Barwick and outside the courtroom, and had thought it might be several more weeks before they relented and came to see her. The fact that they were here after just a month was more than she could have hoped for.

She waited five minutes, which seemed to last an hour, and then made her way to the female paupers' airing yard. Visiting was held there, when the weather permitted, because it was the most visible location in the whole asylum, and could be seen by anyone looking out of the windows at the back of the galleries.

She entered the yard, and looked around for a familiar face. There didn't appear to be any older couples present, and her heart dropped as she realised her parents were not there. Was it one of her siblings, Liz or John, perhaps? But she couldn't see any members of her family. There were half a dozen people whose clothing clearly marked them as visitors, and they were all talking to patients except for one woman in a well-tailored coat and wearing an expensive bonnet, who was standing near one of the corners of the yard, facing away from the asylum.

Mary walked towards her slowly, not daring to call out, or to tap the woman on the shoulder when she reached her. But the woman seemed to sense that someone was behind her, and turned around sharply to look at Mary.

It was Mrs Barwick. In the unfamiliar surroundings, outside of the confines of Manor Farm House, Mary took a second to recognise her former mistress, and when she did so, it was with as great a sense of shock as she could have imagined.

'Good morning, Mary,' said the older woman.

'Have you – come to collect me?' said Mary confusedly, her joy at a potential release being tempered by the thought that she might have to return to Halloughton.

'Of course not,' said Mrs Barwick, before adding as an afterthought: 'Nevertheless – how are you?'

Mary gave a non-committal answer, indicating nothing about her state of mind or the conditions within the asylum. Despite her acute disappointment at discovering her visitor had not come to take her away, she was immediately keen to know the reason for the visit.

'Good,' Mrs Barwick replied, although she appeared distracted and not to have taken in any of the detail of what Mary had said. 'Mary, I wished to ask you something of a rather delicate nature. Is there anywhere else more private we can speak?'

'I think they like you to stay out here.'

'Very well. Come closer and listen properly, I don't intend to repeat myself.'

Mary did as instructed.

'There is a patient in this asylum by the name of Catherine Mills,' said Mrs Barwick. 'Are you familiar with the name?'

'I – I don't think so,' said Mary. There was a Catherine and a Kate that she was vaguely aware of on her wing, but she didn't know either of their full names.

'No matter; you will know her soon enough. There is something I need you to do for me, Mary. Catherine Mills is strongly suspected of committing a serious crime. That is to say, of killing her baby. The how and why are not important. What is important is that the only way in which she is likely to be brought to justice is through a confession. I wish you to acquaint yourself with her, to ingratiate yourself with her, and to induce her to admit to you that she murdered her baby.'

A thousand different questions swirled around Mary's

head. But, to her surprise, the one that actually formed on her lips and she heard herself uttering was: 'Why would anyone believe me if I said she told me she'd done it?'

'That is not your concern,' Mrs Barwick said. 'Your role is to see that she confesses; beyond that, you do not need to concern yourself.'

The truthful answer would have been that, such was the vulnerability of any patient within the asylum, that even the most dubious confession – to whomever it was made, and under what circumstances – would likely be sufficient to condemn them. But Mrs Barwick had no more intention of telling Mary this than she did of admitting why she was interested in the case. Her husband was old friends with a Leicestershire judge who had ambitions to move from the Midland Circuit to the Old Bailey, and who was favourably positioned to make such a move, but who feared that the publicity surrounding an unsolved murder case might possibly jeopardise his chances. The murder itself was not unusual – a baby found cold, lifeless and swaddled in dirty rags in the centre of Loughborough – but the method of killing was: its throat had been cut from one side to the other. While a baby that had been suffocated or starved might not have raised a ripple, this particular death did, and the judge felt that leaving it unsolved tarnished his reputation and threw his aspirations into some peril.

The judge had mentioned the case to Mr Barwick ahead of an upcoming assizes session, pointing out that there was a suspect who had been identified, but that she was now in an asylum; he let it be known that any information obtained about her would be greatly appreciated, not to say well rewarded; and within a few minutes Mr Barwick had seized the opportunity and promised to get what information he could. He would have visited Mary himself, but he felt that his wife was more likely to get a favourable response out of her.

'You will need to know brief details of the circumstances of the case in order to know what exactly you are looking for,' continued Mrs Barwick to Mary. 'Catherine Mills left her home in Knight Thorpe in Leicestershire eight weeks ago. She was found four weeks later in Loughborough, attempting to breastfeed a stranger's baby who had been left for a moment outside a bakery shop. She was taken into custody, and was discovered to have about her person a range of baby clothes that had not yet been worn.

'These events took place a week after the body of a baby had been found in Loughborough marketplace. Now, it is true that there is nothing to link the baby to Catherine Mills. But the possibility that a woman who was found in the same town – attempting to feed another woman's baby, and found with a collection of baby clothes – was innocent of this previous crime is entirely improbable.'

'Could the poor baby not simply have died, and not been murdered?' asked Mary.

'Its throat had been cut,' said Mrs Barwick. 'As even you will understand, it is imperative that the killer is brought to the gallows.'

'This baby was hers, then?'

'A doctor who examined her was unable to establish whether or not she had recently given birth, due to the age of the baby and the time that had passed since her likely confinement. It may well be that she does not confess directly to the murder. That is of no great importance; simply admitting that she has given birth, or that she had been in Loughborough at the time the baby was found, will be sufficient.'

Mary looked behind her to see if anyone had heard this talk of knives, blood and murder. But the yard was as it had been, with the same people walking around in the same small circles. She thought for a moment, but her decision was made swiftly. Scared though she was of the influence of Mr and Mrs Barwick outside the asylum, she owed them nothing, and she did not comprehend how she would benefit from becoming involved in such a scheme.

'Thank you,' she said, 'but I would prefer not to get involved.'

'You are quite sure?'

'I am.'

'I had imagined that you might say that,' said Mrs Barwick. 'Tell me Mary, how is your brother getting on in town – Will, is it?'

Chapter 13

July 1827

Mary looked astounded. 'What do you know about our Will?' she cried, loud enough for two of the other visitors to look up at her. She added in a whispered voice: 'What has this got to do with him?'

'Nothing of a direct nature,' said Mrs Barwick. 'Do not agitate yourself; there is no suggestion that he is the father of the baby in question. But I wondered if you were perhaps aware of his accident?'

'What accident?' Mary replied. She realised that Mrs Barwick must be perfectly aware that she had had no contact with her brother since he left Woodborough at the beginning of June or, if she had not been aware of it previously, then she would be now. But her concern for Will overrode any hesitancy she had regarding being indebted to Mrs Barwick for receiving information about him.

'With his hand,' the older woman replied. 'He was quite badly, I understand. As far as I can gather, he was called out to an urgent job late one evening, but in the middle of rethreading, the machine started up again. I say it was an accident; perhaps it was the owner trying to hurry him along, I don't know. But apparently the needles went right through his hand and came out the other side.'

'No! When was this?'

'A week or so ago, I believe.'

'And how is he?'

'It may surprise you, Mary, to learn that I have not been seeking updates on his condition. I merely thought you would want to know.' She paused to let the information sink in. Then she continued: 'It is a dangerous job, Mary. Something like this was bound to happen sooner or later. It would be much more preferable for him to be placed somewhere like Morley's. I am told they are seeking bag hosiers at the moment; indeed, I am likely to be seeing Richard Morley at a church event this weekend.'

Mary was thinking as quickly as she could. However hard she tried, she could find no connection that existed – besides herself – between Mrs Barwick and Will, and she could not fathom how Mrs Barwick would know about any accident he might have had at work. And yet the circumstances of it seemed entirely plausible.

Furthermore, Mrs Barwick was entirely right in what she said about I & R Morley. They had a reputation as the best hosiery firm to work for in Nottingham, paying the highest wages and even pausing knitting frame rents when there was no work to be had. Mary's mother had applied to work for them in the past but been unsuccessful. If Will could get a job with them as a bag hosier – travelling to all the framework knitters in the villages and taking their produce to the main warehouse in Nottingham – then he would be well paid, secure and safe. He might even have more chance to visit the rest of the family on his travels outside the town.

'And you would be willing to speak to Mr Morley about a position for our Will?' she asked warily, now fully understanding of the deal that Mrs Barwick was offering.

'I would,' came the reply. 'And I would be confident of a positive response. But I would need you to do as I have asked, Mary.'

Mrs Barwick left a short while afterwards, telling Mary that she would be back in a week to determine what progress had been made with Catherine Mills. In the end, Mary considered she had little choice but to accept the task that had been given her; it would potentially be of enormous benefit to her brother, and of detriment only to a woman she had never met and who had likely killed her baby.

Her most immediate problem was that she had never come across Catherine Mills. She might possibly have seen her without knowing it, but Catherine was a second-class patient, and as such was on a different ward and floor entirely. She would never cross Mary's path in the gallery, or the day room, or even in the airing court, because in those places the patients had their own sections according to class; just a few years previously the wall separating the first- and second- class airing yards had been raised in order to cut off communications between the patients.

Mary resolved to ask Hannah Greendale about her on their next walk about the grounds, and she had a chance to do so the following day.

'Catherine Mills?' said Hannah, when Mary had asked what she knew of her. 'She's a piece of work, that one.'

'How do you mean?'

'She has a mouth like a tar,' the attendant replied. 'Miss Mills is no lady, I'm sure.'

'What is her particular affliction?'

'What is not her affliction! She is often overexcited and incoherent. She can be wild, and abusive, and violent. Indeed, she is in the basement currently, for refusing to go to her chamber and for assaulting Mrs Morris.'

Mary's interest was stirred by this information. The rooms in the basement – which were not entirely underground, part of the floor being just above ground level – were used for the refractory patients, those who were temporarily or permanently deemed unmanageable, and who would be too disruptive if left on the higher floors. They were called 'rooms', like the rest of the accommodation in the building, but had more in common with cells than with the chambers on the upper three floors.

'I need to speak with Miss Mills as a matter of some urgency,' she said. 'Are you able to allow me into the basement to see her?'

'Heavens, no!' replied Hannah. 'It would be more than my job is worth. Why would you possibly need to see her?'

'And how long is it likely to be before she returns to her ward?' asked Mary, ignoring the question.

Hannah shrugged her shoulders. 'She could be out tomorrow, or it could be another week. She's been in and out of here for years. A spell in the basement will be of no consequence to her.'

A thought began to occur to Mary. The basement cells would be the place where she had the best – perhaps the only – chance of making contact with Catherine Mills; but how to gain access there? If Hannah would not take her, then no one else would. The only other option was to get sent there herself, by committing some sort of infraction that she knew would see her punished.

She was silent for a few minutes, and then said to the assistant: 'If I told you I was going to do something that I knew was wrong, but for a good reason, would you speak up for me later, and let people know my reasons? And that I had committed the act in sound mind, not through insanity?'

Hannah Greendale stopped walking, forcing Mary to stop with her. Hannah, who had been at the asylum since the start, was now forty-seven, and had seen every type of patient come and go through its doors, from those who sat silently and never spoke, to those who hurled themselves against windows and door frames in order to fatally hurt themselves.

Mary appeared to her to be one of the most level-headed patients she had come across, and there was also undoubtedly a small element of the maternal in the way in which she had taken her under her wing, guiding her work in the kitchen and choosing to be the person who escorted her on walks outside.

Hannah also had no special fondness for the Morrises, having been – she felt – unfairly demoted to the kitchen after her husband had been dismissed for supplying alcohol. She understood that her husband deserved to be let go, but she did not consider that his actions should reflect upon her, and leave her in a position where after fifteen years' service at the asylum she was working as a kitchen maid with little chance of a return to the galleries and the job that she had enjoyed doing previously.

Despite all of this, though, she could not possibly sanction what she understood Mary to be asking. No patient was worth risking her job for, and if she had learned one thing over the past decade and the half, it was that it was better never to get involved, no matter what the particular issue at hand.

'That's not something I can do,' she said to Mary, before adding: 'And I think you should be careful. Pretending to be something you're not, and then trying to get someone to stick up for you later? This must be the worst place in the world to do something like that.'

Mary thanked her for her honesty, and they continued their walk without remarking upon the matter further.

Later that evening, Thomas was busy making his second rounds of the day. With the asylum filled with eighty patients, there was less than a minute or so to be spent in each patient's chamber – time enough to ask how they were, check that any treatment had been received and then move on. It was rare that he had any chance to speak to a patient at length, unless they were in his own consulting room for a specific occasion.

On this occasion, however, after arriving in Mary's room and asking about her state of mind that day, she responded by asking him how much longer she would need to remain in the asylum.

'You can't be asking Mr Morris that!' shouted Mrs Sinclair, who was accompanying the director on his rounds. 'He has dozens of patients to see; do you expect him to have all their notes in his head? It's not all about you, Mary Reddish.'

'Please,' said Thomas to the attendant, 'it's perfectly acceptable for the patients to ask questions.' Then, turning to Mary, he added: 'But I'm afraid I can't give you a specific answer. It depends entirely upon your progress.'

'But I have been here more than two weeks, sir, and you cannot say I have not behaved well. You said that that good behaviour would be rewarded.'

'As indeed it has,' replied the director, 'with additional privileges. Not every patient has the opportunity to work, or to walk in the grounds.'

'But what about me getting out?'

'Getting out? Two weeks of good behaviour is inconsequential, Mary, especially to someone with your own history. We would need to assess you over several months to be sure that you were able to live safely back in the community.'

Mary gasped audibly. 'Several months?' she said, falling back towards her bed and steadying herself with her hand. 'But – I thought I would only be here a few weeks, at the most!'

'There is no predetermined period of admission,' said Thomas, a little sternly. 'It is your behaviour that has brought you here, and your behaviour that will determine when you leave. But a few days of good behaviour following an assault on an attendant – that is undoubtedly not sufficient, Mary.'

Mrs Sinclair, who had been the recipient of that earlier assault, let a smirk form on her face, which Mary immediately noticed. 'Sir!' she said. 'I cannot stay that long! My brother, he—'

'Every patient will have loved ones on the outside,' said the director, turning and walking towards the door. 'Would you have us send them back into their family homes before they are recovered?'

'I am no danger to my family, sir—' began Mary, placing her hand on his elbow to try and halt his progress out of the room.

Mrs Sinclair took hold of Mary's arm and twisted it behind

her back, causing her to stoop down low to try and relieve the pressure.

'You're hurting me!' cried Mary, but the attendant pushed her arm even further, until it was bent back as far as it would go. 'Get off!' she yelled, but the force remained constant and Mary could feel the pain streaking up her arm to her neck, a pure pain that allowed her no respite. With all her might she pushed her shoulder hard into Mrs Sinclair's side, shoving the attendant into the wall and driving all of the wind from her. Half a second later there was a crack as her head struck the frame of the door, and she slumped unconscious to the floor.

Slowly coming round, Mary heard the sounds – the running, the shouting – and she realised that it was her own body that was being hauled out of her room and dragged down two flights of stairs, but she felt detached from everything that was going on. She saw the white flashes of the attendants' uniforms, she was vaguely aware of fists hitting her stomach, but it was as if it was happening to someone else. Not just her mind but her body had switched off, and she was taken down to the basement without a single coherent thought going through her mind.

It must have been in the early hours of the morning when she came round. She was lying on the floor of the cell, her abdomen aching from the blows she had received, and a terrible dryness in her mouth. There was a single mattress on the cell floor, a bucket in the corner and nothing else within the space. There was an arched window, but only the very top of it let in a small amount of moonlight, the rest of it looking directly onto the exterior wall that was pressed close against the windowpanes.

She tried to sit up and remember what she had done, but the act of pushing herself up proved too painful, and it was all she could do to haul herself over to rest on the dirty mattress. Memory came more easily to her, however. How had she let herself lose her temper once again? She could recall that she had been in pain, too much pain, and had experienced the single, overpowering feeling that all she wanted was for it to stop.

But what connected that thought, of wanting her arm to stop hurting, with the action of pushing Mrs Sinclair into the wall? There was no process that had been gone through, it was surely pure instinct. Or was it, she wondered? There was a certain recklessness and excess of force about the action she had taken; perhaps, deep down, she knew that it would result in her being taken where she wanted, which was down to the basement. Because of Will she was now desperate to remove herself from the asylum, and desperation called for extreme measures.

The truth was, she didn't know. But if there was indeed any method to her madness, then she believed she was applying it without fully being aware that she was doing so; in which case, could it really be characterised as method at all?

Mary suddenly felt nauseous, and went to kneel over the bucket. She retched half a dozen times, but nothing came out except a small amount of phlegm. The only effect was to make her stomach ache even more than it had already, and she crawled back to lie on her mattress.

'You'll be awake, then?' called a voice from through the wall next to her. It was a woman's voice, not unfriendly, and seemingly well educated.

Mary was startled, and sat up as best she could, but remained silent.

'I heard you come arsy-varsey down the stairs last night,' the voice said loudly. 'Who brought you down – was it Ellis? He's a crafty one, he is. Two bob says he got an eyeful of your notch on the way down.'

At this, the woman who had been speaking broke out into raucous laughter, which continued for a good half-minute before subsiding. Mary was entirely baffled by the content of the speech, by the hilarity that followed it, and above all by the coarseness of the language, which fitted with the information Hannah Greendale had given her previously, but which seemed wholly at odds with the apparently cultivated voice underpinning it.

'Are you – are you Catherine Mills?' Mary called back. She tried to make her voice loud enough to be heard by the other patient, but not so loud that it would wake any sleeping attendant nearby – not that she was sure there *were* any attendants in this part of the asylum. The act of speaking hurt her mouth, and she reached up to discover that she had a split lip in addition to her other injuries.

'Who wants to know?' said the voice.

'My name is Mary.'

'Just Mary, is it?'

'Mary Reddish.'

'And how do you know *my* name?'

Mary, whose mind still felt fogged from her recent period of insensibility, needed to quickly consider why she might plausibly be aware of her neighbour's identity. 'I – I think I must have heard someone say you were already here when they brought me down,' she said hurriedly. 'At least, they said a name, but I wasn't sure if I had it right.'

It sounded unconvincing to her own ears, but there was no response from the other cell, so it seemed she had been believed.

After a few more moments had passed, she called out: 'How long have you been here?'

'In this shithole generally? It's my second home, young Mary. About a month this time, and it's certainly not my first. In this particular *bit* of the shithole? Who knows? A day, maybe.'

Mary wondered how it was that her own voice gave away her age so obviously. She couldn't quite place the age of the other woman; older than she was, certainly, but by how many years she would struggle to hazard a guess.

'And could I ask – why are you here? In the – the whole place, not down here.'

From the next cell, there was the unmistakeable sound of Catherine Mills letting out a long, loud fart. 'Christ!' Mary heard her say. 'A proper cheeser – you had better be glad this wall's here, Mary! Though even a wall might not save you from that.'

There followed the same guffaw that had been heard a few minutes previously, and once again Mary bided her time until the laughter subsided, while wondering again at the incongruity of the language when set against the gentility of the tone.

'What was it you said?' the voice next door said finally.

'I asked why you were in this place.'

There was a pause. 'You'd need to ask Mr Morris that. Have you met him?'

'Of course.'

'He's a gentleman, and no mistake. And he's tried his best with me; but every so often I just feel as queer as Dick's hatband, you know?'

'Not really.'

'I'm out of sorts; I can't put my finger on it. Ow, shit, you little bugger!'

'What have I said?'

'Not you! A buggering louse … there, I've got the fucker. But you know what I think me biggest problem is, Mary? You know why I think I'm sometimes a bit queer?'

'I'm quite sure I don't.'

'Men, Mary; it's men. It's either honey or turds, am I wrong? I was stepping out with a gentleman, Mary, by the name of Henry, and a few weeks ago I paid him a visit to find him there, right there in the parlour, with some whore – fair enough, not a whore, perhaps, but common as a barber's chair – so I said to him, get her out this house, and he pointed out that it was his house, which it was, and so I had no option but to leave, and so now I'm on my own again, and my John without anyone to look up to as a father. Does that seem right to you?'

Mary sensed the slight possibility of an opening. 'Your John,' she asked, 'how old is he?'

'Nine, nine and a half, I should say.'

'And who is looking after him if his father is not there?'

'His father? Oh, Henry is not his father, though I was hoping he might be one day. His useless shit-sack of a father is long gone. My mother and sister look after John when I am in this place.'

'And is he your only child?'

'One is enough, Mary. I'm not getting belly-full again.'

Throughout the conversation, Mary had allowed her voice to get louder, as she grew increasingly confident that no attendant slept or kept watch overnight near to the refractory cells. Now, however, she thought she heard a noise from the top of the stairs that led down to the basement. Through the gap in the window she could see that it was starting to get light outside, and she wondered if the sound was an attendant making their early rounds of the building.

There were no further noises, though, and Mary breathed a sigh of relief. Although the room was hard and bare, it was warm enough thanks to its position below ground, and at this moment she felt safer there than if she was having to deal with a visit from an attendant or doctor. But she suddenly felt an overwhelming tiredness, as if the events of the evening before had suddenly caught up with her, and she told Catherine that she was going back to sleep.

'Off you go, then!' came the reply.

Mary heard a movement in the next-door cell, and then the sound of Catherine reciting a poem in a sing-song voice:

'All you that in your beds do lie,
Turn to your wives, and occupy
And when that you have done your best
Turn arse to arse, and take your rest …'

The familiar laughter travelled through the wall to Mary once again. She found it strangely comforting.

Later that morning, the physician and the director were in the ground-floor meeting room, ostensibly having a discussion that would result in a decision about Mary, but both knowing that there was only one way in which the discussion would end.

'And what did Mr Dale say about the emetic?' asked Dr Pennington.

'I must confess that I have not yet had the opportunity to ask him.'

'How unfortunate,' replied the physician. 'Still, there can be no doubt that the latest assault by Miss Reddish reinforces the urgency of treatment. She must be given two grains of antimony tartar, three times a day, beginning immediately.'

Thomas nodded. There was little he could say in opposition to the physician now that Mary had assaulted Mrs Sinclair for the second time in the space of a month. But he had a vague sense of being let down by her, something that he had rarely experienced with other patients; he felt that, by seeking permission to speak with Mr Dale, he had bought Mary some time to prove herself, yet all she had done was to prove herself unworthy of his efforts.

The prescription was made up by the director, who then went down to the basement to administer the emetic himself. Mr Ellis, the assistant, was outside the cell on his arrival, and he called out to Mary that Mr Morris was entering the room.

'Ah, Mr Morris, is it?' shouted Catherine from the other call. 'Good morning, sir!'

'Good morning, Catherine.'

'How is your dear wife this morning, sir? Did she wear you out last night?'

'Conjugal relations of others are not your concern, Catherine,' he replied, and went into the cell in front of him.

Mary already looked as if she had been in the basement for

a week, not a matter of hours. Her hair hung limply about her face, and her eyes had the look of someone who could not get enough rest inside them even if they slept for days.

'I have some medicine for you,' he said. His tone was cool, which was something she would have picked up on had she felt more like her normal self, but all she wanted him to do was to hand over the medicine and leave. She took the small tablet from him, swallowed it down with some of the cup of water that Ellis had left earlier in the morning, and sank back down on the mattress again.

For a few minutes, she felt perfectly normal. Then she could feel sweat starting to form on her forehead, under her armpits, down the ridge of her back. She fanned herself as best she could with the fabric of her gown, but the sweating increased, and she found herself feeling desperate for fresh air. Her body burning, she drank the rest of the water, wishing she had more to splash on to her face, and called out to the attendant to see if he could refill her cup.

But even before she had time to see if he would reply, a wave of nausea swept through her entire body; it was as if she could feel her innards being forced up as far as they could towards her throat. And when they could go no further, when the pressure within her was at breaking point, she stumbled over to the corner of the room and vomited copiously into the bucket.

Chapter 14

July - September 1827

Mary stayed in the basement for two days, and was taken back upstairs at the same time as Catherine Mills. This was her first chance to see, albeit briefly, the woman upon whom so much of her future apparently rested.

She was in her late thirties, Mary thought, although her guess could easily be wrong by half a dozen years either way. Physically, she was similar to herself: slim, even thin, but taller by perhaps an inch, and with her hair done up in a tight bun. It was not the figure of a new mother, Mary thought, but perhaps she was one of those women whose shape returned swiftly after giving birth, as it had with Mary's sister. Mary half expected an off-colour comment to be thrown her way as Catherine was taken away, but the other woman was silent as she was carried up the stairs.

The course of emetics continued in accordance with Dr Pennington's instructions – two grains of antimony tartar, three times a day – and Mary felt drained. She had been physically sick before, of course; there were several bouts of illness that had been passed around the Reddish children in her younger years, and more recently she had eaten something in the fields around Manor Farm House that had caused her to vomit twice on the way home and twice more when she reached her chamber.

But this was different. Those previous occasions had

followed a familiar and almost reassuring pattern: a rising sense of nausea, followed by half a minute or so of actual vomiting, and then a feeling of blessed relief which lasted for a good twenty minutes before the nausea began again. Now, there was no feeling of relief, just different levels of nausea. Even after she had *been* sick, she still *felt* sick. The way her entire body felt was dictated by those small pills, and she didn't feel clean or purged or expunged, just weak and sore and dispirited.

When she returned to her room, she tried to resist the first occasion on which Mrs Sinclair and Mr Ellis came to give her the medicine. She turned her head when the former approached her with the pill, and clamped her mouth shut when the latter held her in a headlock and tried to prise her jaw open with his dirty, stubby fingers. She fought back, briefly biting at one of his fingers to get it out of her mouth, but received a sharp blow to the head for her troubles.

While Mr Ellis held her, Mrs Sinclair went away and returned with something small and metallic in her hand. This was the implement used to force-feed patients when the need arose. It was nothing more than the key to a door lock, which would be inserted between the patient's teeth and then turned through ninety degrees until the mouth was sufficiently open for liquid food to be poured down it.

It was crude, and its crudity was demonstrated by the occasional patient who could be seen walking along the galleries with at least one front tooth missing. However, the year previously, a patient from Derby, Thomas Pattinson, had died at the asylum after persistently refusing all forms of nourishment, and it had been determined that this fate would not be allowed to befall any patient again; and so the key came out whenever a patient was refusing to eat or take medication.

Aware of the dental disfigurement of some of her fellow patients – most of whom had not had many teeth to start with – Mary swallowed the pill.

The next time the attendants came round, she attempted to

pretend to swallow the pill, hiding it under her tongue to avoid detection, but it was easily spotted, and she was rewarded with another clout to the head. She found a small stone in the gallery, no doubt brought in from the airing yard on the bottom of someone's shoe, and practised hiding that in her mouth, attempting to get it as far back under her tongue without ingesting it, but only succeeded in swallowing it straight down and almost choking.

There were no more walks around the grounds at the front of the house for her. She lost her job in the kitchen; she was no longer trusted to be around any sort of kitchen implement. The single candle that was in her room was removed, and the evenings dragged by in endless darkness as soon as the sun had dropped down below the level of her windowsill.

While her walks in the grounds with Hannah had ended, the attendant was still to be found in the gallery, and when she next saw her, Mary took the opportunity to ask her more details about Catherine Mills.

'When you told me that Miss Mills was no lady,' she said, 'why did you say that? Had you expected her to be so?'

'Why, yes!' replied Hannah. 'She has been here so often that everyone knows her story. She is quite well-to-do, I believe. Her home is an old manor house called Knight Thorpe Hall, where she lives with her mother and sister.'

'And yet, as you say, her manner is far from ladylike?'

'She is foul, and coarse,' replied Hannah. 'I do not know whether I'd like to wash out that mouth of hers, or punch it.'

Mary was interested to hear that Catherine's home was in Knight Thorpe, as Mrs Barwick had also said; it added a little weight to what she had been told. She pondered for a moment, and then continued: 'So Miss Mills is well off, or at least her family is. But why, then, is she a patient of the second class, and not the first? Surely her family could afford a few extra shillings a week?'

'I wouldn't like to say,' replied Hannah. 'Her mother does come to visit her, so I don't believe they are entirely estranged. But—'

'But what?'

'All I know is that the child she had was not with a husband. She had to go to one of them bastardy hearings to prove that he was the father. Now, there are some families who probably wouldn't let that affect how they felt about the mother of that child. And there are some who probably would.'

Without her kitchen work, it would have been easy for Mary to lie in her chamber, staring at the wall and thinking only of the next pill to be forced down her throat, but from her own experience – getting up early with a head full of cold to go to the warehouse dressing room, forcing her aching body out of bed to light the fires at Manor Farm House – she knew that she would feel better if she was actively involved in doing something.

She asked Mrs Morris if she could be employed anywhere else, and was offered the laundry room, which she immediately accepted. This was the most unpopular place to work in the entire asylum, dealing on a daily basis with soiled sheets and urine-soaked clothing, and was viewed largely as a punishment rather than an opportunity to get out of the galleries and day rooms.

But Mary – even in her weakened, dispirited state – was glad to be given it. And within a day or so it became clear that her new job could, just possibly, be a godsend. Taking in the laundry and washing it was only half of the job; the other half was redistributing it back to the wards. Ideally this would have been done by someone who was actually from the ward in question, but as none of the first-class – and very few of the second-class – patients actually worked, it was left to the pauper patients such as Mary to take the fresh laundry back to those wards.

On the first occasion when she went up to ward F on the second floor, where Catherine was accommodated, she didn't see her, and assumed the older woman must be in her room or out in the airing yard. On the second, she did manage to glimpse her in the day room, but she was holding court to a group of around half a dozen women, telling a story that was being met with a mixture of laughter and embarrassment. There was no opportunity to go and speak with her.

But on the third occasion, Mary was emerging from the day room where she had left her pile of laundry, when she noticed Catherine entering the washroom and water closets. A single door led to both rooms, where the modern water closets provided a level of comfort that most of the patients had never experienced before – although the smell that emanated from them had initially proved little better than that in the most basic of privies, necessitating the installation of extra ventilation a few years previously.

Mary looked around quickly, and saw that the attendant who would be unlocking the main door to let her out of the ward was talking to a patient at the other end of the gallery. In an instant she had slipped inside the washroom door, just in time to see Catherine entering one of the stalls.

'Catherine!' she called, and the older woman looked around. 'It's Mary?' she added, and she could see Catherine look at her with no recognition at all, until something clicked into place from the brief glimpse they had had of each other outside the basement cells.

'Ah, Mary,' she said. 'What are you doing here?'

Mary was taken aback; she recognised none of the buoyant quality to Catherine's voice that had been so evident in their basement conversations. It was flat and monotone, as if it was an effort for her to talk at all. Mary had also not fully considered what to say to her. After their initial talk in the basement, where Catherine said she only had one child, Mary had been unable to get any additional information out of her, as she had become increasingly unintelligible. She appeared to be more lucid now, but it was difficult for Mary to know how to begin.

'I – I just wanted to see how you were?'

'Why would you concern yourself with me?'

'I thought that – perhaps, after our time in the basement – our welfare would be of interest to the other?'

Catherine gave a derisory snort. 'In that case, I'd be of interest to half the asylum,' she said. 'Do you know how many women I've shared time with, Mary? This is my sixth time inside. Don't bother wasting your time on me, Mary, there are better things for you to worry about.'

Mary was finding it difficult to adjust to this new version of Catherine: her coherence, her relative calmness, the lack of swearing. 'I'm sorry if I have offended you,' she said.

Catherine looked at Mary's downcast face and doleful eyes, and softened a little. It wasn't quite the case that, in Mary, she saw herself as she had been at Mary's age, which was also around the time of her first admission; there were too many differences between the two women. But what she did see in Mary, a little, was a glimpse of how her own child might be in a decade or so. Would he appear quite so vulnerable, quite so eager not to displease? Would there be a time when he would need helping in the same way that Mary clearly did now?'

'You've not offended me,' said Catherine. 'But I am about to piss myself. So any conversation about how I am is going to have to wait.'

Mary smiled to herself at this brief glimpse of the old Catherine. She could not hang around while Catherine used the water closet, however; the attendant waiting to accompany her back down to the laundry would be wondering what had become of her.

'And I have to go,' she said. 'But perhaps I could see you another time? I am on this ward most days.'

'You do as you see fit,' came the reply, amid the sound of a petticoat being gathered up. 'I'll still be here.'

Over the next few weeks, Mary made sure to give herself as much time with Catherine as she could legitimately manage. It was not always possible; sometimes Catherine was nowhere to be found, and sometimes the attendant – depending on who it was – stuck closely by Mary's side as she made her rounds. But on other occasions she was able to attract Catherine's attention in the day and have a quiet word with her in the corner, or return to the scene of their previous meeting in the washroom.

Slowly, and with many backward steps, Mary found out more. Catherine told her how she had been apprehended in Loughborough, supposedly for trying to feed a baby that was not hers, although she could remember little of the incident herself. She wasn't sure why she had been in Loughborough, and not her home village of Knight Thorpe nearby, and she did not know how long she had been in Loughborough, but she did recall that her son was being looked after by her mother, which was fine, because he had been cared for in such a manner many times before, and for long periods.

Mary couldn't quite establish all the exact details, but it seemed that Catherine had first been admitted nearly a decade previously, and again at regular intervals over the years. But however many times – and in different ways – Mary asked her about having had a second child recently, Catherine was adamant that she had not.

Mary never felt in any danger around her. If the past weeks had taught her anything, it was that she was quickly aware if someone was a threat to her, and she had none of those feelings with Catherine. But she was less sure about what Catherine might have done in the past, and in particular she wanted to ask why she had been found with baby clothes, when she had no baby of her own. To do so, however, would be to admit to prior knowledge of the details of her case, and that was something she knew she could not do.

She continued speaking to Catherine when she could. But sometimes she felt too ill to even leave her room, as the ordeal of the antimony tartar regime persisted. Three times a day she would take the cursed pill, and three times a day she would heave her guts into the bucket in the corner of her room.

On occasion, she would not make it to the bucket. Such was the raw power of the emetic that, if she had fallen asleep through exhaustion, or had vomited twice in quick succession and mistakenly thought that there was nothing left to expel, she would sometimes be taken by surprise and not even have time to cross the room. She would purge herself onto her own clothes, trying to catch as much of the vile liquid as she could in her apron, but usually spilling it on the rest of her garments and the bedclothes.

Anxious to escape the stench that was right under her nose, she would strip off her outer layer of clothing. If there were spare items to put on, she would do so; if there were not, she would wait until she had access to the washroom to clean the soiled gown and apron as best she could, clean off the worst of her sickness and then put the clothes into the laundry at the first opportunity.

But if Mr Ellis or Mrs Sinclair ever saw her in her chamber partially dressed, they would not allow her to remain that way, claiming that she was indecent and was offending the sensibilities of the other patients, even though they would not see her when she was confined to her room. They made her put her fetid clothing back on, denied her access to the washroom when she should have been granted it and carried out spot checks to make sure that she had not taken it off again.

It became a remorseless circle. The antimony tartar made her constantly nauseous, and apprehensive about eating; the threat of being force-fed made her take food; the combination of the food and the smell of her gown made her sick again; and that made her even more nauseous and reluctant to eat.

Eventually, she decided that she would not wear any soiled gown, no matter what threats the attendants employed. If they put it on her, she would remove it as soon as they had left her chamber.

And so, inevitably, before long she was in the strait-waistcoat once again. She was made to wear it over her stinking gown, so that she had the double punishment of the foul smell and being unable to move freely. This was her situation when, on 15 September, she was placed in the rotatory chair for the first time.

The chair had only been introduced to the asylum that year, but it had been used as a tool for treating mental disorders since 1804, initially by Joseph Mason Cox, whose *Practical Observations on Insanity* of the same year sang its praises. Dr Cox, the physician at the private Fishponds Lunatic Asylum in Bristol, had conducted experiments on patients from which he concluded that the circulatory motion of the chair – around a hundred revolutions per minute – was beneficial in a number of ways that helped cure patients of their maladies. It unblocked the stomach, it improved circulation and it induced vomiting in those for whom even emetics did not work. Its main effect, aside from nausea, was fatigue, and patients had been known to sleep for hours following a session in the chair, awakening feeling calm and refreshed.

Other asylums including Glasgow and Wakefield had previously employed the chair, but the latter had not done so since 1821, and its introduction in Nottingham was towards the end of its period of popularity, with doubts already emerging about its efficaciousness as a treatment. Dr Pennington was enthusiastic, however, and it was he who determined that Mary Reddish should be submitted to its effects.

When Mary was taken down to the basement on that Saturday morning, she was not sure where she was going, but presumed that she was due another spell in the refractory cell because of her refusal to wear her gown. Once Mr Ellis had pulled her past the cell entrances, however, and further on down the corridor to a single door that stood right at the end of the passage, she knew that the previous cell was not her destination.

Mr Morris and Dr Pennington were stood by the door, and while the former avoided her gaze, the latter took her arm, guided her into the chair, and strapped her in, with her feet dangling just high enough so that they could not reach the ground. He told her of the chair's soothing effects, and likened the experience to that of a baby being lulled to sleep by its mother. Then he nodded at Ellis to turn the handle that rotated the chair.

For a few seconds, Mary experienced a pleasant sensation that was not unlike being gently rocked. But then the handle was turned more quickly and the chair began to build momentum, spinning fast enough that Mary was unable to focus on any particular point in the room as it passed by with each rotation. She closed her eyes, but that instantly made things worse; the nausea rose in her immediately and she swallowed in order to try and keep it down.

Opening her eyes again, she could see various blurry shapes as they flashed past: the dark suit of Dr Pennington, the white coat of Ellis, the glimpse of daylight at the top of the basement window. They were beginning to merge into one, forming a dizzying montage of shapes and colours that were forcing their way in on her.

'Let me out!' she called, trying to attract the attention of Mr Morris. Again, she closed her eyes, and this time she kept them shut. It was no comfort, however; the awful, sickening vertigo was threatening to overwhelm her. 'Make it stop!' she now screamed, but the chair continued to rotate, faster and faster, and Mary knew she had to somehow get out, even if it meant flying out of the chair and into one of the walls. She pulled hard against the straps, and twisted her body to try and squirm out from the seat; yet she was held fast.

She vomited, copiously, and she was revolving so fast that the contents of her stomach hit her in the face as she completed her next rotation, covering her with the foul liquids that were the only remaining contents of her insides. A second or two later, Mary could feel the motion of the chair start to reduce slightly, and when she realised that it was really coming to a halt, she burst into tears at the sheer, unadulterated relief of having survived. She was on the verge of fainting, and her head felt as if it had been cleaved with an axe, but she had made it through.

Then, almost imperceptibly, the chair began to move in the opposite direction. Mary looked upwards and saw, to her horror, that all that the previous rotation of the chair had done was to twist the two supporting ropes around each other; and that now, to get back to the point from which she had started, she would have to endure the same experience all over again, in the opposite direction.

'No!' she wailed desperately, but even before the sound had left her mouth, the chair had gathered pace and was spinning once again on its dreaded, unbearable journey. Within a minute, she had involuntarily emptied her bladder; soon afterwards, her bowels had voided. But by then, it barely mattered. She lost consciousness halfway through the return trip, and when the chair finally came to a halt, Ellis had to lift the dead weight of her insensible body high on his shoulder in order to carry her away.

Throughout it all, Thomas stood in the doorway, watching as the treatment took place before his eyes.

Chapter 15

October 1827

'Surely,' said Thomas angrily, 'it must be evident to you that the chair is entirely punitive, not curative?'

'On the contrary,' replied Dr Pennington, 'I believe there is significant and substantial evidence regarding its positive effect on the brain and the nervous system.'

'You have read Dr Cox's writings upon the matter, presumably?'

'Naturally.'

'And is it not apparent from his case studies that *fear* of the chair is the sole motivating factor in the behavioural changes of the patients he describes? One might as well threaten a patient with drowning, or with placing a tiger in their parlour – it would have the same effect.'

Exasperated, he got up from the table where he was sitting opposite the physician, and began to pace distractedly around the room.

'I do not doubt that fear of the chair works effectively in combination with its improving physical qualities,' replied the physician. 'But work it most certainly does.'

'You consider that it has worked upon Mary Reddish?'

'Not entirely; she is not yet cured of being a violent lunatic. But she is now restful, and when I checked her after her most recent treatment, her pulse was fifty-nine and her inhalations were sixteen; that is a considerable improvement.'

'Had you considered that any one of us might conceivably be turned *into* a violent lunatic as a result of dread of the revolving chair?'

'The rotatory chair.'

'Rotatory chair, revolving chair, swinging chair, whirling chair, whirligig, it matters not what you call it!' exclaimed Thomas. 'Whatever name it is given, it remains an instrument of simple torture and nothing more.'

'The chair will cure her.'

'By inducing her to vomit? She has done nothing but vomit for the past two months. It is my understanding that where the chair is used – if, by God's grace, it should be used at all – it is where the use of usual emetics has failed. That is not the case here.'

Now it was Dr Pennington's turn to get up from his seat. 'You are familiar, presumably, with Samuel Tuke's view that there are very few cases of insanity where the disorder is caused by an inherently mischievous or malevolent disposition?'

'Of course.'

'And that the great majority of cases are caused by these dispositions being excited by unnatural or improper circumstances?'

'Indeed, and I concur with those views greatly.'

'I do not,' said Dr Pennington. 'I do not believe, for example, that one might be *turned* into a violent lunatic by a ride upon the chair. One's disposition must already be inclined in that direction. And to overturn that – to reverse it – is not simply a matter of hoping that it will go away; it must be driven out. If tartar does not work, then the chair must be tried. If the chair does not work, she must be purged. If purges do not work, then the shower-bath must be employed. Do you see? There is something within her that must be expelled, and it is my responsibility to determine what it is that will successfully achieve that.'

'Our responsibility,' corrected Thomas.

'Excuse me?'

'The welfare of patients is our joint responsibility.'

Dr Pennington fixed the director with a firm stare. 'I am in charge of all matters medical,' he said rigidly.

'And I am in charge of running the asylum.'

This was a moment that Thomas had known would come; his only surprise was that it had not come earlier. He was well aware that Dr Pennington, by virtue of his status as physician as well as his long-standing position of eminence in the Nottingham community, had an assumption that he was effectively in control of the asylum. In addition to the particular responsibilities of his role, he was elected rather than appointed, and had been on the panel that had appointed the director.

And yet nowhere was it explicitly stated that he was in charge. It was not written in the by-laws, rules, orders, regulations or the articles of union that the physician held sway over the director. The ultimate power lay with the governors, and both men were subject to their decision-making processes.

'Do you intend to contradict me?' asked Dr Pennington. 'In which case, perhaps I could ask you a question. Who do you think would support you? The governors? The committee? The subscribers?'

'None of them, I concede,' answered Thomas. 'But the patients themselves might benefit from an approach that was not established upon an assumption that their disposition was innately malign; and, indeed, their families would welcome that as well.'

'And Miss Reddish, for example; how concerned about her welfare are her relatives? Has there been any visitation at all? I believe there has not. It is my management of her case that will determine her recovery.'

Thomas was deflated. He felt as if he was battling against not just Dr Pennington, but the whole asylum establishment. But, for the first time, he also had a sense of something else; a small glimpse of how, just possibly, he could make a real difference. He did not yet know the details, and he certainly did not know whether his was a plan that could be carried out to a successful conclusion. But he had an undeniable perception that the way forward did not involve dragging unconscious, doubly incontinent patients out of whirling chairs.

'Furnish me with the details of Miss Reddish's further treatment,' he said. 'I will ensure it is carried out.'

Later that day, he articulated his frustrations to Ann. She, too, was disheartened by the way in which the treatment used was different to that which they had expected, and that they had seen first-hand at the York Retreat; but she did not have the regular direct contact with Dr Pennington that drove her husband to such great degrees of distraction.

'And it is not just the chair,' Thomas was saying. 'Everywhere one looks, there are patients suffering from his foolish perceptions. What was the name of that girl from Weston who left a few months ago?'

'Elizabeth Rhodes?'

'That's her. Seventeen years old, and he bled her dry. He used to rail against the dangers of excessive leeching, but he is quick enough to prescribe it. And what of that young man from Mansfield and his antimonial ointment? Is Dr Pennington quite so devoted to antimony that he not only prescribes it orally, but also orders it to be applied to the most sensitive parts of a gentleman's body? It had no favourable effect, and succeeded only in producing a full crop of pustules.'

Ann waited patiently while Thomas reeled off a list of other patients who could by no account have been said to have benefited from the physician's prescriptions.

'I could not agree with you more,' she said, when he had run out of steam.

'But then what are we to do about it?' replied Thomas. 'I cannot deny that he is in charge of treatment.'

'Of treatment, yes,' replied his wife. 'But of care? Can we not say that we are both equally in charge of that?' Thomas looked at her inquiringly, and she continued: 'Do you ever ask yourself whether we have abided by the principles that we witnessed at York, and agreed to follow? If you do, then you must see that we have not.'

'How so?'

Ann held her arms out as if to convey the whole of the asylum. 'We had pledged that kindness and compassion would be just as important as pills and purges. Are they? It is not simply about Dr Pennington's leeches and ointments, Thomas. What would you say to all those patients on whom we have used straps, or wrist locks, or camisoles? Did we not say that as little restraint as possible should be used?'

'It is impossible for *no* such equipment to be used,' he argued. 'Even at York they use a little.'

'But we should only use it as a last resort for preventative reasons, to stop them harming themselves or others,' replied the matron. 'Can we truly say that we have always explored every other option before resorting to restraint? Or that it has never been used as a punishment?'

Thomas knew that she had a point. He also knew, however, that as the asylum numbers had grown, it had become too difficult to cope without the use of restraint, and more than occasionally. Sometimes patients simply had to be stopped from doing what it was their instinct to do, not just if that was harming themselves or attacking other patients, but at the lesser end of the scale as well. When a patient hurled the contents of their chamber pot at you for two mornings in a row, who would begrudge the director who restrained them so that they could not do it again on the third morning?

Thomas explained this to his wife, but she shook her head. 'If there is a moral as well as a medical approach, then they must work together, not against each other,' she said. 'There cannot be empathy in the galleries and day rooms, and cruelty in the treatment rooms.'

'You are right. But again – what are we to do about it?'

There was now a distinct chill in the air as autumn edged nearer to winter. It was the time of year when, in the outside world, Mary would grab for a shawl whenever she went out, and would leave her boots by the fire before retiring to bed in the hope that they would not stiffen with frost overnight. In the asylum, though, it was generally warm. The heated pipe and flue system kept all areas of the building at a steady temperature, and although that temperature was a few degrees lower than most of the patients would have liked, the prospect of getting through the coldest weather was less daunting than it would have been outside.

Mary had hoped – indeed, expected – to be out of the asylum and back in Woodborough before the year was out. But now she found herself unable to look beyond the next day, or sometimes even the next hour. Her life was a constant round of vomiting and recovery, but the periods of recovery seemed harder to negotiate than they had, and she found herself growing steadily weaker.

Her sessions in the chair continued, and each lasted longer than the one before. The first had only taken five minutes, but soon that figure was up to ten, and then fifteen. She would not have to endure only a single 'journey' of the chair – the initial clockwise rotation, and then the spinning back anticlockwise as the ropes unwound themselves – but one, or sometimes even two, repeats. At some point, she would pass out, and would come around later on her chamber bed, the room slowly coming into focus as she grasped at her surroundings, trying to make sense of where she was and what had happened to her.

Following her second session in the chair, she had an upset stomach for days, and discovered that Mrs Morris appeared to have taken a special interest in her recovery: she brought her cups of tea infused with rhubarb, ginger and peppermint, and often stayed with her while she made sure that Mary consumed all of the drink.

The matron did not say a great deal, Mary came to realise, but what she did was said in a kind way, and was helpful to her. She made Mary appreciate that, distressing as what she was undergoing might be, there was a definite pattern to it, and that having this was far preferable to not knowing what was around the corner. Mary knew that each session in the chair would leave her feeling sick for a while, then empty and fatigued for a while longer, then hungry, then relatively normal, and then fearful of the next treatment that was coming. If she could fortify herself for these different stages, and know that each was both distinct and finite, then she would be better prepared to negotiate them.

The other aspect of her life in the asylum that was of comfort to her was her meetings with Catherine. To begin with, the meetings in themselves provided little solace; they were only important because of what information she could obtain that would be useful to Mrs Barwick. But as the days and weeks progressed, Mary looked forward more and more to finding time to talk with Catherine, and was disappointed when she was unable to do so.

She found, though, that when she did speak with Catherine, her mood was impossible to predict. Sometimes she would be coherent but gloomy, other times confused but exuberant, and very often a mixture of all these behaviours and more. It was when she was at her most high-spirited that Mary was able to find out more about her.

On one occasion, when Mary was behind with her work, Catherine offered to help her take the fresh sheets to all the rooms on her ward, and as they were about to exit the penultimate room, Mary stopped her and asked: 'Tell me, do you ever wonder why you were found trying to feed another woman's baby?'

'Fucked if I know,' said Catherine. 'If I did, I wouldn't be here, would I?'

'No, but – is there any reason why you might want to do that?'

'Couldn't tell you. These' – she placed her hands over her small chest – 'were never any good to me. Didn't help me with my own child, so I'm buggered if I know why I'd try to feed anyone else's.'

Mary hesitated, before saying: 'Would you like to have another child?'

Catherine made as if to walk away and out of the room, but then turned round. 'Do you want them, Mary?'

'I don't know – one day, perhaps?'

Catherine shook her head. 'Be careful what you wish for, Mary.'

'I'm sure that's not—'

'Let me finish. Be careful, not for your sake – but for theirs. You'll be fine with them, I can see that. But will they be fine with you? How will they feel about a mother who's been in here? You can't take it for granted that they'll turn out okay. My John has, but he's spent half his life with his grandmother and aunt, bless them. People are in here for a reason, Mary.'

'I'm not. Not for a good one, anyway.'

'Of course you're not.' There was more she could have added, but she left it there.

Several weeks after her first visit, Mrs Barwick came to see Mary again. She was forced to wait longer on this occasion, because Mary was on her rounds until nearly eleven o'clock, by which time the visiting period was almost halfway through. There was a light drizzle in the air when she finally made her way out into the airing yard where Mrs Barwick was.

'What progress have you made, Mary?' she said immediately, clearly irritated by the length of time she had been left waiting.

'Did you speak with Mr Morley about our Will?' asked Mary.

'I did.'

'And what did he say?'

'He said there are always positions available for young men with the right temperament who are willing to work hard.

Now, don't prevaricate, Mary – what have you discovered about Catherine Mills?'

Mary was caught between saying something that could potentially help Will, and saying what she believed to be the truth. She was more than prepared to do the former, if she genuinely believed that it would be of benefit to her brother. But she had a legitimate fear that any deception on her part might rebound twice as hard upon Will, and so she told the truth.

'I don't believe she killed her baby,' said Mary simply. 'I don't believe that she *had* a baby at all.'

'Where is the evidence for this?'

Mary admitted that there was no evidence to speak of. 'Perhaps that is why I don't think she did it,' she added.

'The baby clothes in her bag, Mary! The stealing of another woman's child! Are you blind to these? Has she explained them?'

'No.'

'Then it is up to you, Mary, to ensure that she cannot do so.' She put her arm around Mary's shoulder, but in a way that was largely intimidating rather than comforting. 'It is not just your brother who might benefit from this information,' she said. 'It could be that Mr Barwick and myself could help you get out of this place.'

Mary looked at her sceptically. 'You can't make that happen.'

'True – to a degree. I cannot sign your discharge papers. But remember that it is your behaviour towards the two of us that has landed you in here, Mary. A word from either of us in your favour would certainly not do your cause any harm.'

'I don't care for myself,' said Mary, although her words were rooted more in a disbelief that Mrs Barwick could have any impact on her length of incarceration than in any genuine disinterest in her own prospects. 'It is Will I want you to help. And I … I won't speak to Catherine again until you give me your word that you will secure him a position at Morley's.'

'Is that so? And what makes you think that you are in any position to negotiate?'

'You returned here, didn't you?' asked Mary defiantly. 'You would not be here again if you did not need my help. Perhaps you have even visited Catherine in this very yard, and she would not speak to you?'

'You have always been a disrespectful little thing, Mary,' said Mrs Barwick. 'If we were outside of this place you would not be speaking to me in such a manner. But I believe we understand each other. I will speak to Mr Morley about a position—'

'Not just any position, the job as bag hosier.'

'About *that* position, then; and if I do that, you will speak to Catherine Mills again. If she will not admit to having a baby, then get her to admit to being in Loughborough when the body was found.'

'When will Will be moving?' Mary pressed. 'I need to know.'

'By the end of the week. But get me something.' Mrs Barwick turned on her heels and walked quickly away from the yard.

Mary stayed for a few minutes, wondering whether she had any reason to trust that Mrs Barwick would take the action she had promised. Then she realised that there was little point in considering it further; Mrs Barwick would act as she saw fit, and all Mary could do was to keep her end of the bargain and hope that Mrs Barwick kept hers.

She went back into the main building, where an attendant was waiting to take her back up to ward E on the first floor. But before she reached the stairs, Mr Morris came out of a doorway and asked her to join him in his office. She took the seat in front of his desk, with the director behind it, and he asked her how she was faring.

'I am as I was when you saw me yesterday evening, sir,' she replied.

'Of course,' he said. 'But you will appreciate, Mary, that

it is not always possible for me to get a sense of your well-being during my rounds. Often Mr Ellis or Mrs Sinclair will be present in order to give you your medicine, and there are so many other patients to see as well. So I ask you again, how are you feeling, in very general terms?'

It seemed like a question to which there was one right and one wrong answer, and Mary's only concern was to choose the one which did not lead to further sessions in the chair. If she said she was improved, it might indicate to the director that the chair was working. If she said she was no better, he might consider that more sessions were needed.

'I am the same, sir,' she said, 'as I was before I entered this place. That is to say, I am of sound mind, with no cause to be here.'

'And yet even since you have been here, you have carried out two unprovoked assaults?'

'Assaults? Perhaps, if you choose to use that word. But unprovoked? That is something I would never accept. Is forcing my arms behind my back in a camisole, or shoving a vile pill down my throat, not a provocation?'

'Everything that has been done is for your own benefit.'

'It has only served to injure me or keep me in a state of sickness!' she replied. 'Nothing has been done to benefit me from the moment I came here – indeed, even before I arrived. I am only here because of the unjustified treatment I received. To be locked in one's room and unable to see one's family? To be forced to fend off the attentions of a man some forty years older? Are these to be considered matters of routine, which one should let slide past with barely a glance?'

A terrible thought struck Mary for the first time. Was it possible that Mr and Mrs Barwick had engineered the whole process of events that led to her being admitted to the asylum, purely for the purposes of meeting with Catherine Mills? For a second she wondered whether it could actually be feasible that they had done so, but common sense soon took over. They could not possibly have known for sure that the overseer would support them, or that Mary would assault Mr Barwick in the cart, or that Catherine Mills would be admitted to the asylum just before Mary, or that Mary would be in a position to meet with Catherine. It was pure chance – the couple had set the chain of events in motion, but where it had gone since then was due to happenstance and her own actions.

'Many people go through experiences such as you have described,' said Mr Morris. 'But they do not resort to violence as you have done.'

'Then they are better people than I,' Mary replied bitterly. 'And for that I only have myself to blame. But could I ask – who is it that has decided that it is the object of the provocation who should be punished, and not the provoker himself? If a badger kills a bee that has stung it, is it the fault of the badger, or the bee?'

'You are the badger, then?' asked Mr Morris.

'Would that I was,' said Mary abjectly. 'I don't truly know what I am, sir. But I do not feel that I am the bee.'

Mr Morris sat back in his chair, with the hint of a smile upon his face.

Chapter 16

October 1827

Thomas awoke the next morning at exactly half past six, the same time he did every day. There was a lantern clock in the parlour that struck every half-hour, which the director and matron could hear quite clearly from their bedchamber, but it was only the sound at six thirty that roused him; his body had conditioned itself to sleep through all of the others.

The attendant who started at six had already lit the fire in the parlour, taking the sharpness off the early morning cold, and by the time Ann joined him a quarter of an hour later there was a comfortable warmth spreading throughout the space around them. At a quarter to seven they ate a quick breakfast of coffee and toast, with Thomas also taking a lightly boiled egg on his plate, before going their separate ways.

The director went straight outside to carry out a check of the building and make sure that all windows and doors were secure. Then he went up to the top floor galleries, where the attendants were in the process of unlocking the patients' chambers, to make his first rounds of the day.

Already, the familiar sounds of the asylum waking up were drifting towards him as he climbed the three flights of stairs. It had been a relatively quiet night; there were always some instances of patients banging on doors, but there had not been the persistent shouting and crying that was often prevalent.

Perhaps the darkness and solitude of the locked rooms did sometimes have a calming effect.

By this time of the morning, however, there was a constant commotion: the first daily shouts of greeting and insult, the sound of boots walking upon hard gallery floors, of keys being turned in locks, of patients calling to be released because their chamber pot was full.

As Thomas passed the central apartments, he paused to check on the welfare of the first-class patients. He duly noted Mr Walker's complaint that he was quite sure he had been provided with a tallow candle overnight rather than his usual beeswax, and said he would investigate. He went up past the pauper patients on the first floor, and was briefly notified by one of the attendants that Mr Hannington, who had been admitted with cerebral affliction, had severely bitten himself overnight and was bleeding from a number of wounds. He told the member of staff that the patient should be moved immediately to the basement, where he would attend to him shortly. He made it to the top floor, and managed to carry out his rounds on two wards before eight o'clock arrived, and all the patients were taken to breakfast.

Ann, meanwhile, had left the parlour to go straight to the kitchen and speak to the two assistants working there, before checking that the laundry maid had arrived and knew what her immediate duties were; there had been an outbreak of diarrhoea on one of the wards and, while there were no indications that it had a more serious cause, she wished all the laundry from that ward to be washed twice. She tested the water supply, established that once again it was poor, and told the maid that she would need to visit the corporation pump during the course of the day.

Like her husband, she paused at eight to oversee breakfast – milk pottage, tea and dry toast – on her own side of the asylum, and then sat down to complete her orders for the day: more starch and soap, a delivery of pork and mutton and extra supplies of rice, oatmeal and sugar.

After breakfast, the more trusted patients went off to their various jobs, while those who were not permitted to be in employment retired to the day rooms and waited for the airing yards to open. Ann went to each of the female wards to supervise the patients who needed assistance with bathing; a difficult task, made more so by the absence of warm water for those being bathed. While his wife was upstairs, Thomas was down in the basement to patch up Mr Hannington. He took a diversion on his way back to the wards to check on the progress of a privy that was being built in one of the female yards, and then returned to finish off his rounds. He ordered poultices for a patient suffering from continual fever, tested the mobility of another afflicted with temporary paralysis, checked on the frequency of fits of another who had been experiencing paroxysms for the past week, and agreed to the use of the mouth clamp for another who was refusing to eat and whose appearance was becoming emaciated.

Finally, at eleven o'clock, his rounds were completed, and he made his way downstairs to meet with Ann in the parlour of their apartment. Five minutes later, as she had been invited to do, Hannah Greendale joined them.

'Please sit down, Hannah,' said Ann. The attendant did so, with the air of someone who didn't know why she was there but who had every expectation that it was not for positive reasons.

'And don't be alarmed,' added Thomas. 'We just wish to ask you something. You have been with us a long time, have you not, Hannah?'

'Since the beginning, sir.'

'And are you happy in your work?'

The attendant, who had decidedly not been happy ever since she had been transferred to the kitchen, hesitated.

'You may speak frankly, Hannah,' added Ann.

'I liked it better with the patients on the wards than in the kitchen, then.'

'I see. And presumably you would wish to return to your previous position?'

Hannah nodded.

'Very well,' said the matron. 'You are a good worker, Hannah, and I can't recall a day where you have ever been sick. It was ill-considered of us to move you to the kitchen after Mr Greendale was dismissed; one shouldn't punish the wife for the transgressions of the husband.'

'Thank you,' replied Hannah, who was slightly perplexed by this belated acknowledgement.

'But before you move,' said Thomas, 'we would like to ask for your help with a matter that needs the assistance of someone who works in the kitchen, such as yourself. Are you willing to do that?'

'Yes, sir.'

'Excellent. You are well acquainted with the patient Mary Reddish, I believe?'

'She worked with me in the kitchen, and I have also accompanied her on walks around the grounds.'

The director gave her a sheet of paper. 'How is your reading, Hannah?'

'I get by, sir.'

'Very good. Mrs Morris will help you understand these instructions, and they will soon become as familiar to you as the general rules. They represent the revised diet for Mary Reddish, which must be followed to the letter; and also her new exercise regime. She will take her meals in her room, so as not to distinguish her meals from those of others in the day rooms. And you will personally be in charge of ensuring that she undertakes twice-daily walks in the grounds, as laid out in the plans.'

'In addition,' said the matron, 'Mary is to be moved to the quietest chamber, the one furthest from the day room. It is a double chamber and she will have plenty of space. She will be the last to be woken in the morning, and I will ensure that any noisy patients in neighbouring rooms are moved accordingly. Is that all clear?'

'I think so.'

'You must know so, Hannah; not think so,' said Thomas. 'And I cannot emphasise too strongly that details of this must not be revealed to anyone. Not to the other attendants, not to any other patient, not even to Mr Greendale. Do you agree?'

'Yes.'

'Good. The instructions begin with immediate effect, and when they are completed you will be transferred back to ward duties.'

Hannah thanked them both, and left the room. She was glad to be resuming her walks with Mary, whose company she had missed over the previous weeks. But that was nothing compared to the fact of getting her former job back.

The next person to be called in was Mr Ellis. He was less well known to the Morrises, having been there a matter of months rather than years, and his cooperation was by no means guaranteed.

After the couple had explained to them what it was they wanted him to do, he looked at them dubiously.

'That doesn't sound right to me,' he said.

'It is in accordance with the course of action that has been prescribed for Miss Reddish,' said Ann.

'So Dr Pennington knows about it, does he?'

The director and matron exchanged quick glances. They had half expected the conversation to go this particular way; now they had to bring it back round again.

'What is your annual salary, Ellis?' asked Thomas.

'Twenty pounds.'

'Indeed. And the reason I know that it is twenty pounds, is because I pay your wages. Not Dr Pennington, or the governors, or the house committee.'

'And?'

'And the same principles that are applied to patients also apply to staff. Good behaviour is rewarded, and poor behaviour results in sanctions. If you agree to the measure we have proposed, your salary will increase to twenty-three pounds.'

'Twenty-five.'

'This is not a negotiation, Mr Ellis. If you wish to accept the offer, please do so. If you choose not to, then I am sure there are others who would be happy to benefit from a similar offer.'

'And if I decide Dr Pennington should know about it?'

'It would be a temporary and minor irritation to myself and Mrs Morris, but undoubtedly the end of your association with the asylum.'

Ellis turned away, as if he wanted to give the firm impression that he needed some time to think about the offer that had been made. Mr and Mrs Morris already knew that they had won him over.

The final call required was to speak to the apothecary and governor James Dale. Although Thomas and Mr Dale were still close, it was an inescapable fact that they had seen less of each other since the Morrises' son Thomas Jnr had married Mr Dale's daughter Jemima the previous year. For months prior to the wedding, the two families had been almost permanently intertwined, planning the event and also keeping a discreet eye upon the courting couple. Since the day had passed, however, there had been an understandable lessening of contact, as if the unnaturally high level of association previously enjoyed had somehow needed to be compensated for in the weeks and months that followed.

They still greeted each other warmly, though, when they met at the Flying Horse Inn on the south-eastern side of the marketplace. The huge space of the square always looked to Thomas as if it was abandoned outside of market days, and this afternoon was no exception, with a few carriages and a handful of people lost to the expanse and the tall buildings that surrounded it.

He arrived slightly late, and spent several minutes searching through the maze of oak-lined rooms to check that he had not missed Mr Dale sitting in some dim corner, before the two men found each other, took a glass of porter each and sat down.

They spent the first fifteen minutes or so giving each other their thoughts on the agreeableness or otherwise of Thomas Jnr and Jemima's living accommodation – with a little concern expressed on both sides that it was perhaps beyond the couple's means, given Thomas's still-modest solicitor's salary – and generally updating the other on the well-being of all family members.

'And how is the asylum?' asked Mr Dale when the conversation about the family had come to a natural pause. 'The opportunity to become reacquainted is always most welcome, of course; but I wondered perhaps if there were some other matters that you wished to discuss?'

Thomas was impressed, not for the first time, at the perspicacity of his friend. 'You anticipate my purpose,' he said, 'although I hasten to add that I too would always appreciate any opportunity of meeting, for whatever reason.'

'You are free to ask of me whatever you choose, whenever you choose to do,' said Mr Dale. 'Please, tell me what is on your mind.'

Thomas proceeded to provide the details of the Mary Reddish case, his concerns over her treatment and the outline of his plan for remedying the situation. He did not say so, but her welfare had become the touchstone by which he felt his role at the asylum could be judged: help her, and he could help others; fail her, and he would have failed them all. The reason he did not explicitly say this was to avoid the possibility of Mr Dale inferring any sort of inappropriateness in his relationship with the young patient, which was by no means the situation, but which Mr Morris was keen should avoid entering even the outermost thoughts of his friend.

Despite this, Mr Dale himself realised that the predicament of this Mary Reddish was clearly of very high significance to the director, and he asked a series of further questions, probing her background, temperament, symptoms and behaviour. He questioned the exact frequency and amount of emetic she had been given, and the full details of her treatment in the rotatory chair.

When he felt he had all the necessary information, he sat back in his chair and asked: 'Tell me, Thomas, something that I consider I have never properly asked you before. Why did you come to the asylum? You had a steady job as an apothecary, your children were settled and your father was with you – why abandon all of that?'

'For Ann,' Thomas replied immediately. 'There was no role for her to play in Hammersmith. And yet, here, she is in charge of half the asylum – and the better half, no doubt, thanks to her work.'

'I wholeheartedly understand and agree,' said Mr Dale. 'But what of you? There must surely have been ample opportunities elsewhere to work in a location where she was given a role of responsibility, without alighting upon a lunatic asylum. Why did you come here so very specifically?'

Thomas took a sip of his porter, and thought for a moment.

'And please,' added Mr Dale, while his friend was still pondering, 'bear no thought to my own circumstances and career. If the apothecary trade bored you to distraction then you are entirely free to admit so.'

'Not at all!' laughed Thomas. 'But one does feel – or I did, assuredly – that in any such role, one is simply a small part of something more sizeable. One can do one's utmost to treat a patient to the best of one's ability, but it will have little impact if they are living in unsanitary conditions, working in a dangerous environment, or sharing their life with someone who makes every waking hour a misery.'

'The impact will also be limited if a fellow doctor is prescribing treatments that you consider to be unnecessary,' added Mr Dale.

'Well, quite,' agreed Thomas. 'But to have responsibility for someone's entire welfare – to be able to determine how they eat, sleep, work – that, surely, is a privilege beyond comparison, and one which Mrs Morris and I are most indebted to be able to undertake.'

'And yet one in which, in this particular case and perhaps others, you feel you are hamstrung by the particular circumstances?'

'Exactly so. Which is why I am about to ask you whether you would consider an undertaking which, in all due probability, I do not expect you to have to perform; but which if you did – if the appropriate time ever arose – I would consider myself to be eternally grateful.'

He went on to lay out the particular sequence of events that could result in him asking Mr Dale for his assistance; and exactly what form that assistance might take when it came.

Mr Dale fully comprehended that he was being asked to take sides. He was not completely averse to doing so in individual cases, but in truth he respected the judgement of both Mr Morris and Dr Pennington equally. He was better acquainted with the former, but he had known the latter for longer. To do as Mr Morris was asking was not something that he would enter into lightly.

'I do not seek a decision now,' added Thomas. 'I appreciate the potential consequences of what I am asking. And if you think it inappropriate that I have asked at all, then I most mournfully regret doing so.'

'I understand your reasons,' said Mr Dale, not disagreeably. 'But you will also recognise the delicacy of the situation in which it places me. Before I make my decision, I would ask for one condition to be met.' And he told him what it was.

Back at the asylum, Mary was on her laundry rounds and was standing in the doorway to the day room on gallery F, on the second floor. She had been hoping to speak to Catherine, who was by herself in the corner of the room at the small bagatelle table, but something about the way Catherine was conducting herself held Mary back. Catherine was taking the cue and potting one ball at a time in the same hole in the middle of the table, before retrieving it and potting the same ball back into the same hole, over and over. There was something relentless and monotonous about her actions that Mary had not seen before, and it made her hesitate.

'Mind yourself, Mary,' said Hannah Greendale as she appeared in the same doorway from the gallery, and turned her body to squeeze past her. 'Ah, there you are Catherine,' she said, looking over to the bagatelle table. 'Time for you to take this, if we're going to get rid of that cough of yours.'

Hannah walked towards the corner of the room, carrying a spoon in one hand and a small vial of liquid in the other: it was spermaceti wax dissolved in an egg yolk, one of a number of remedies including castor oil and ethyl nitrate that Catherine had been receiving for a persistent, hacking cough.

It happened so quickly that, later that afternoon, Mary – still shaken as she sat on her bed – could only see the memory of it, and did not believe that she had experienced it in the actual moment. Catherine, in one single moment, swirled around with the bagatelle cue in her hand, and with the speed of a bullwhip brought it down forcefully on Hannah's arm. Perhaps she had been aiming for the vial; perhaps it was just an uncontrolled, maniacal swing. Hannah cried out in pain, dropped the liquid and fell to her knees. As she did so, Catherine took two wild steps towards her, and then stood above the attendant and jabbed towards her with her finger.

'Keep that vile, disgusting stuff away from me!' she shouted, and Hannah cowered into a ball on the floor.

Ann, who had heard the commotion from down the gallery,

ran into the room and Catherine immediately turned her attention to her.

'Fuck you!' she screamed, and then, even louder, to Mary: 'Fuck you, too!' She grabbed between her legs, thrust her crotch towards Ann and Mary, and shrieked: 'And you can both fuck this as well! Fucking whores!' With barely a pause, she reached underneath the bagatelle table, lifted it up and hurled it towards the doorway. The wooden balls flew in all directions, and the matron and her patient instinctively ducked and began to edge away from the day room. They had almost made it to the safety of the gallery outside, when the cue that Catherine had been using came hurtling towards them as well. It sped through the space of the day room, split the very air between the two women and landed harmlessly on the gallery floor.

Chapter 17

December 1827

When Mary was about eight years old, her parents had spoken to her gently after supper one evening, and warned her to stay away from one of their Woodborough neighbours. The woman in question, Mrs Allen, had previously been a friendly presence on the street, walking round to the Reddishes' home unannounced, and usually stopping to chat to Mary if they came across each other in the street outside.

Initially, there had been no indication to Mary of why she had been told to stay clear of Mrs Allen. Her parents would not tell her and, unusually, neither would any of her older siblings. But inevitably word began to reach her from other children that Mrs Allen was touched in the head, and had been so ever since a few weeks after giving birth to her second child. She swore incessantly, kicked out viciously at those going past her front yard, and shouted so loudly that she could be heard down the end of the street.

As Mary thought about the scene she had witnessed in the day room, it seemed to her that there were obvious parallels between her former neighbour's behaviour and that of Catherine – the shouting, the swearing, the violence. But nothing about the similarities made sense. Catherine, she was sure, had not recently had a baby. And while Mrs Allen's behaviour appeared to be permanently offensive for several weeks, Catherine's went in fits and starts; she could be entirely normal one week and then a screaming devil the next.

Mrs Barwick had not yet paid a return visit to the asylum, and Mary did not know what she would say to her when she did. She wanted to give her some information that would help Will, and perhaps even herself, but in all conscience she could still not provide Mrs Barwick with any evidence that Catherine had even had a baby, let alone killed it. (She wondered, also, how it was that the magistrate who Mrs Barwick was trying to help had ever made the connection between Catherine and the poor dead child; was there in fact any link at all, or was she simply a convenient woman who had been found in a state of distress in the wrong place at the wrong time?)

But Catherine's wild outburst in the day room had shown Mary an entirely different side to her; and it scared Mary. The asylum was filled with patients who could turn violent at any time, but Mary felt that she knew who they were, and she avoided them. The sudden attack from Catherine – and the personal nature of it – had left her on edge, and extremely doubtful about the woman she had even started to think of as a friend. If Catherine could turn like that, in an instant, against Hannah, against Mrs Morris, and against herself, was she also someone who was capable of killing a baby, in a fit of rage?

Mary was trusting that Mrs Barwick would already have moved Will to a new place of employment, but she knew that any new position could be swept from under him – in a matter of hours, not days – if Mrs Barwick felt that Mary had not fulfilled her end of the bargain.

There was one simple solution to this: Mary could just tell Mrs Barwick what she wished to hear. Mary did not believe that the murdered baby was Catherine's, but she could simply tell Mrs Barwick that Catherine had admitted being in Loughborough at the time the baby was killed. Mary would have played her part, Will's salvation would be assured, and justice could take its course; Catherine would just have to take her chances at the assizes.

Already, though – and despite the attack in the day room – Mary wondered if this was something she could do. It was true that Catherine had not yet explained away the baby clothes in her bag when she was taken into custody, and Mary could persuade herself that this presented sufficient doubt to justify sending Catherine to court. On the other hand, Catherine's welfare had – somehow – become important to her. The truth was that she had grown to like her, and still liked her in spite of her violence. Catherine was honest and irreverent, and while her vulgarity sometimes threatened to overwhelm the rest of her character, Mary had a feeling that she might be playing a part: not one that Catherine was aware she was playing, perhaps, but a role nevertheless. She did not seem a natural fit within the asylum, and that drew Mary to her more than anything else ever could.

Catherine was banished to the basement following her loss of control, which meant that Mary would be unable to speak to her for the foreseeable future. But she nevertheless had the opportunity to talk about her, when Mrs Morris unexpectedly approached her in the laundry room one afternoon.

It had been in the same room, a few months previously, that the matron had seen one of the first indications that Mary was a patient who was deserving of all the help she could give. Ann had been about to walk into the room where Mary and another patient were using box irons to tackle two large piles of creased bedsheets, when she saw an interaction that made her stop and pause.

The other patient, who was smaller even than Mary, looked frail and was struggling slightly with the box iron, which was weighed down with heavy coals to keep it warm. Her pile of ironing was significantly larger than Mary's and it was clear that she was not keeping pace.

As Ann stood and watched, Mary took an armful of clothes from the other pile, placed it upon her own and carried on without saying a word. The matron went into the room, collected what she needed to and departed. But later, she found herself passing the laundry room again just as the ironing was being completed, at the same time that Mrs Sinclair was in the room. The attendant was chastising Mary for taking so long over her pile. Ann peeked her head around the door, expecting Mary to explain that she had ironed half of the other patient's pile, as well as her own. But instead she stayed silent, her head down, and accepted the admonishment the attendant was giving her.

On that occasion, Ann had wondered whether she should say anything to Mary later, pointing out that her selflessness had not gone unnoticed. She had decided against it, but wondered whether that had been the right decision.

She entered the room now, and the heat hit her with the same force that it always did. All along the back wall were the large tubs of water placed on the iron bar grate above the wide fireplace, at various stages of preparation as they were heated to be used for cleaning the patients' clothes. Steam rose from the tubs and filled the room, causing streams of condensation on the windows which, like those in the chambers, could only be opened a matter of inches.

'Mary Reddish!' she called, and Mary emerged from the steam as if from a coastal fog.

'Yes, miss?'

'Please accompany me outside for a moment.' Ann unlocked the side door, and the two women went out into the damp and drizzly December air. 'How have you been feeling in yourself, Mary?' asked the matron.

'Very well, thank you.'

'You are happy with your new chamber?'

'Yes, thank you.' Mary had, of course, noticed all the changes that had recently taken place in her care: the move to a quieter room, the meals she was given, the resumption of her walks in the grounds, the changes in her treatment. But she had not particularly questioned the changes; she was used to different aspects of her life in the asylum being constantly adjusted at the whims of those in charge. These recent changes were undoubtedly more pleasant than some she had experienced previously; there was no benefit in her drawing attention to them.

'I am glad to hear it,' said Ann. 'And Mary – I believe it is the case that you have formed a friendship with Catherine Mills? Is that correct?'

'I'm not …' Mary hesitated.

'You do not need to be alarmed, Mary. You are not in trouble.'

'But how do you—'

'It is my job to be aware of what is taking place on the wards. And clearly you were present at the unfortunate incident the other day. Now, let us say that you have been seeing Miss Mills regularly over the past few weeks. Tell me, what have you observed?'

'How do you mean?'

'What is her behaviour like?'

'She can be loud, and crude; but other times she's as normal as you like.'

'And when does she appear loud and crude? Do not fret, I am not expecting you to make a diagnosis.'

'I don't know; every few weeks, maybe? It's hard for me to say, Mrs Morris. I just know she seems normal for a few weeks at a time, and then changes.'

'And has she told you anything about her family circumstances?'

'Only that she has a mam and sister who look after her child; John, he is called.'

'I see. And is there anything else you wish to tell me, Mary?'

More than anything, Mary wanted to let Mrs Morris know about Mrs Barwick's visit, and what she had been asked to do for her; but in the back of her mind she felt that anything she said could rebound on Will.

'No, miss.'

'Thank you, Mary,' said the matron. 'That will be all.'

The pair went back inside, and Mrs Morris locked the door behind them.

'The chair?' exclaimed Ann, walking briskly into the small room that Mr Morris used for his apothecary preparations. 'What reason is there for Miss Mills to be given the chair?'

Thomas looked up from the powder that he was mixing, five grains of mercury submuriate to one grain of antimony tartar. 'I am sorry,' he said, 'I should have told you, but – I have been so busy with these preparations.'

'But now that I am here – please tell me why another of my patients is to be placed in the chair.'

Thomas sighed. 'Dr Pennington believes that there is a particular justification with Miss Mills.'

'Which is?'

'I understand she has difficulty with her ...' He paused before adding, with some discomfort: 'With her monthly curses.'

'The word is menstruation, Thomas. And a doctor should be quite able to say it.'

'She is adversely affected by her menstruation, then. Her catamenial discharge has been the cause of significant discomfort to her, on previous admissions as well as this one.'

'I am aware of the issue. And the chair will help her how?'

'Dr Cox wrote that the chair is useful in the treatment of uterine disorders, and Dr Pennington appears to be in agreement with him.'

'Of course he does,' said the matron resignedly. 'But why now? Miss Mills has been admitted on numerous occasions previously without having such treatment. Surely this is simply punishment for her behaviour the other day?'

'Dr Pennington would undoubtedly argue that is not the case. Indeed, I believe it might be, in part, because Dr

Pennington ascribes a little of the recent improvement in Mary Reddish to the good effects of the chair.'

Ann looked at him archly. 'He does?'

'He does.'

'I see. And yet our arrangement with Mr Ellis? That is proceeding well?'

'Perfectly well.'

'So Dr Pennington is not attending Mary's sessions in the chair?'

'He is not. It is perhaps the case that he would not trust me to carry out the sessions to the letter of his instructions, knowing my own views. But he trusts Ellis implicitly.'

'Quite.' Mrs Morris thought for a moment. 'And would it not be possible to come to a similar arrangement with regards to Miss Mills, in order to save her suffering, as has been arrived at with Miss Reddish?'

Her husband threw his hands up in exasperation. 'What would you have me do?' he asked. 'I am endeavouring to help one patient in the way I see fit, and as you well know it is proving quite difficult enough. Would you have me do the same for every patient who suffers from Dr Pennington's purges, and blistering, and sessions in the chair? Do you not consider that such a course of action might be brought to his attention? We are trying to help one patient in a particular way, but we cannot do it for all. Not yet, at least.'

During this small speech his voice had become increasingly loud, and he ended it with what could only be described as a shout.

'Why must you become so intemperate?' said his wife quietly.

'And how can you remain so tranquil?' he retorted. 'It can only be because you do not have to deal with Dr Pennington day after day and week after week. We both agree that we should not stand by and see "your" patients suffer unnecessarily, but I am afraid the burden for attempting to rectify this falls largely on my own shoulders. And I may be attempting to change the outcome for one patient only, but I am trying, nevertheless.'

Ann did not shout back in return. Instead she said, in a slow, steady voice: 'Who is it who comforts these women who are sobbing because they do not know when they will see their children again? Who is it who tells them not to forget the faces of the babies who have been taken from them just minutes after birth? Who is it who has to persuade them to keep living for at least another day, when they are distraught because the stocking they have tried to hang themselves with has not held their weight? That is me, Thomas; so please do not suggest that the burden does not fall equally upon me. It is precisely because I want the best for my patients that I am asking you whether Miss Mills could benefit from the same regime as Miss Reddish. While you and Dr Pennington discuss the next treatments, it is my staff and I who must hold these women's hands and provide a comforting voice. Neither of which I have ever seen on one of Dr Pennington's precious prescriptions, but which I would suggest are equally valuable nevertheless.'

Thomas's face fell, and he went over to his wife. 'Forgive me,' he said, 'for my ill-thought words. My temper is my weakness; I should not have raised my voice.'

She reached forward and gave him a small peck on the cheek. 'Your passion is also a strength,' she said. 'But it may occasionally be misdirected.'

Catherine had already had her session in the chair by the time Mary finally managed to speak to her, on Christmas Eve. She was sitting alone in the day room, a deck of cards spread out on the small table in front of her, but not in any pattern that suggested a game had either been played or was imminent. Mary went over and touched the other woman lightly on the arm.

'Catherine,' she said quietly, 'are you well?'

At other occasions, Catherine would have responded with

a smile or, if she was in one of her exuberant periods, some sort of crude remark. But now she said nothing at all, and barely raised her eyes to look at Mary. Her countenance was pale, and her eyes seemed to have had the life taken from them. Of all the patients in the asylum, Mary recognised best the effects of Catherine's treatment in that small, gloomy basement room.

'You have been suffering, I know,' said Mary. 'I know the chair only too well. I wish there was something I could do to help.' Instinctively, she put her arms around Catherine and held her for a moment; there was no embrace in return, but neither was she pushed away.

She stayed in the room for a few more minutes, which was as long as she dared, until she knew she had to leave in order to continue with her rounds. And as she made her way out of the ward and down to the next floor, she had an overpowering feeling which she had rarely experienced before, but which now manifested itself in a physical form: her shift felt itchy against her body, her neck was hot and she had the beginnings of a headache.

The feeling was guilt. She felt guilty for saying that she knew how Catherine felt, when the truth was that her own circumstances had recently changed so markedly for the better. She felt guilty for not being able to tell her that things would improve, because she had no certainty that they actually would for Catherine.

And most of all, she felt guilty for wanting to be acquainted with Catherine in order to ascertain what information she could get from her. She thought that her initial reasons for doing so were justifiable. But sitting in the day room just now, next to the pale imitation of the woman she had first met down in the basement – now so weakened and reduced – she had paused to wonder at whether she was able to put the needs of others in front of her own. She believed she had always done so in the past, but what she concluded with regards to her dealings with Catherine did not sit well with her.

In this state of distraction, with her mind largely on her past, current and future conduct, she went out of the gallery, and down the central stairway that led to the main entrance hall. As she turned the corner, one of the first-class patients coming in the opposite direction collided with her. She had time to take in his everyday clothes, his breeches and his waistcoat – and then he was slamming into her, the force of him knocking her off balance and forcing her to put her hand against the wall to steady herself.

She regained her composure and glanced up, expecting to see an apologetic face looking at her, but instead she felt a sharp, stinging blow to her cheek, and then a warm shot of saliva landing on the centre of her face. As she raised her own hands to ward off any further blows, the man shoved her once more and then walked – not in any hurry – in the direction of the central apartments.

Mary sat down on one of the stairs, and wiped her face with her sleeve. There was a cut on her cheek where the man had struck her. She was shocked; but it was the fact that she was shocked that shocked her even further. Despite the attack from Catherine, she had been walking through the wards and day rooms, the corridors and the stairs, with barely a thought for where she was, she realised. Perhaps the extra care and attention that she was being given had provided her with a false sense of her own safety. But this was not a townhouse, or a theatre, or an inn. It was a place for people who would grab you, spit at you and hit you without a moment's thought. She had been too complacent.

Through Christmas and into the new year, Mary tried to see Catherine when she could, but often she was out of the ward, or confined to her chamber within it. Mary's mood grew darker, despite the wound on her face healing, and the continued improvement in her own living conditions and treatment. There seemed to be no way that she would ever be able to find the information that Mrs Barwick sought, even if she had wanted to do so. That meant she had no means of securing Will's long-term future, in addition to no way of determining whether Mrs Barwick had made good on her promise to move him in the short term. And as for her own future, it was something that she no longer wished to dwell upon.

Chapter 18

January 1828

'I am concerned about Miss Reddish,' said Ann, putting down the shift that she was mending, and looking over towards her husband. 'Her development is not what I had hoped.'

'Indeed?' he replied. 'Her physical well-being has surely made advances. She is less lethargic, she appears stronger, even her skin has improved. And she seems lively enough when I speak to her.'

The matron shook her head. 'That is not what I mean. On the outside she gives every indication of improving in mind and bodily health, but there is something within her that has been lost.'

'Such as?'

'Something that may be indefinable.'

'Try for me, my dear.'

'In that case – she seems to be accepting of her situation. Resigned to it, perhaps. I can see no indication that she truly believes she will return to her former life.'

'Whether that happens is for us to determine, not her.'

'The "us" being yourself and Dr Pennington, not you and I,' Ann replied. 'He will have to agree to her discharge; and there must be no indication from her that she is not ready. If we were to take her to him now, would he agree to her release?'

Thomas thought for a moment, and then said that it was

likely that Dr Pennington would not. 'But what more can we do?' he asked. 'We are doing what we can. If it is her belief in herself that needs to change, what could we possibly do that would accomplish that?'

'I don't know,' said his wife. 'Perhaps we should ask her.'

They brought her in to speak to them that afternoon and, now that he was looking for it, Thomas could see what his wife meant. Mary looked healthy, and she spoke in the same quiet but firm manner that she always had. But there was something different about those green eyes: they did not have the same intensity they once had, and did not follow one's small movements and gestures.

'How are you feeling, Mary?' asked Thomas.

'Very well, thank you, sir.'

'You are comfortable in your new chamber?'

'Very much so, I'm sure.'

'And tell me – do you have any thoughts of what you would do if you were to be discharged?'

Her eyes flickered for the first time. 'Am I to be released, then?'

'No, no – I apologise, I should not have raised your hopes. It is simply that I wondered about your familial situation. I believe it's the case that your former mistress has visited you here, but no members of your family. I have also written to your mother and father to inform them of your progress, but received no response. Are you estranged from them?'

'They are estranged from me, perhaps,' said Mary softly.

'I see,' said the director, although he did not, quite. 'Is there no relative to whom you remain close?'

'My brother?' she replied brightly. 'Will, my youngest brother.'

'And he has also not been to visit?'

'I believe he either does not know where I am, or has not

had the opportunity, sir,' she said. 'If he was able to, I feel sure that he would.'

Thomas nodded. It was the general policy of the asylum not to encourage visits. If family members wanted to come, then they could, and two hours were set aside every Tuesday morning for such a purpose. But in broad terms it was considered that visits by relations could act to the disadvantage of both patients and visitor. The patient would be overwhelmed and often quiet during the visit, but afterwards would become overstimulated by the memories and thoughts of home the visit had engendered, especially if the exciting cause of their malady arose from a domestic scenario. And the relative would be surprised at how quiet the patient was throughout the visit, and they would wonder, sometimes aloud, why they were spending fifteen shillings a week to incarcerate someone quite so placid. So there was rarely any encouragement for visits to go ahead; and there was certainly no precedent for patients being taken to see relatives outside of the asylum.

'Where is he, this brother of yours?' asked Thomas.

'I am hopeful that he now works at Morley's, sir.'

'I know it. If he is there, then he is much better placed than he could otherwise have been.'

'Yes, sir.'

The director glanced at his wife, and then said to Mary: 'Do you feel that it would be of benefit to your recovery to see how he is faring?'

Mary's face lit up immediately. 'Really, sir? It would be everything I have been thinking about these past weeks!'

'Caution yourself, Mary – you would not be taken to meet with him. You would just be taken to see him from a distance, to reassure yourself that he is well and is situated where you believe him to be.'

'That does not matter, sir, thank you – seeing him will be enough.'

If Thomas had needed any strengthening of his opinion that this unusual course of action was justified, then the change in Mary's demeanour provided it instantly. She was almost a different person: gay, lively and bright-eyed. She thanked the couple several more times, both before and after a date was set for the outing, and then went back to her work.

I & R Morley occupied a factory-warehouse site that took up the whole eastern side of Fletcher Gate in the town centre, a relatively short walk from the asylum. As Thomas, Ann and Mary made their way up Goose Gate one early Thursday evening, the director was taken back to the time he had made the same walk just over sixteen years previously, on his way to meet Dr Storer, Mr Dale, Dr Pennington and the others at Thurland Hall, shortly after his arrival in Nottingham.

The town had changed since then, he thought, and not for the better. The ineffective whale-oil street lamps had been replaced by modern gaslights at least, but there was little else that he could see that was an improvement. Nottingham was noisier, smellier and – from the evidence in front of him – poorer, too; where before he had encountered one or two beggars on his walk, now there was one on every corner, and they appeared to be significantly younger and thinner. He stopped when he could to hand out a few pennies here and there, but his change was soon exhausted and he quickened his pace past the remaining vagrants, ashamed that he could offer no more charity.

Mary, meanwhile, was happy to walk as quickly as possible; not simply because she was keen to see Will, but because the acrid black smoke that lingered above every street was badly stinging her eyes. In the grounds of the asylum, she could smell the town, and sometimes see a haze of smog above it when she was in the grounds for her exercise, but she could not feel it and taste it like she could now.

They passed the boisterous Druids' Tavern in Warser Gate, turned into Fletcher Gate and arrived at the vast premises of Morley's. 'I shall go in and ask after your brother,' said

Thomas to Mary. 'It may well be that his work for the day is not yet completed, but we will at the least know that he is due back to the factory from his travels this evening.'

He crossed over to the other side of the road and went to the main door of the factory. A group of women workers was leaving as he arrived there, and he stood to let them pass, their shawls billowing in the cold wind as they stepped out into the street. Ann and Mary stood silently and waited, with the former casting the occasional nervous glance back towards the tavern and anyone who might be emerging from it.

For ten long minutes they waited, until the figure of Thomas appeared in the doorway silhouetted against the faint light from inside the factory. Mary could not help herself; she ran across the street and called out to the director before he was fully out of the door.

'Is he there?' she shouted. 'Did they say he was there?'

She ran up against him, and he held her arms loosely. 'Come this way a little, Mary,' he said agitatedly, manoeuvring her away from the door.

But she wrenched herself free, and said, 'Tell me!'

'He is not there,' said Thomas, in some consternation. 'I asked them to go through all their files – that was why I took so long. But they have never had a record of a Will or William Reddish. I am sorry, Mary.'

Ann had by now joined the pair, and she was there just in time to grab hold of Mary's legs as they collapsed beneath her. Between them, the couple half walked, half carried Mary fifty yards away from the factory entrance and the unwanted attention the scene had already caused.

'Mary,' said Ann, sitting her down on a freezing cold step, 'speak to me.' She took hold of her hands and squeezed them tightly, as if that alone would bring her back to full consciousness. Mary said nothing, but even as the matron looked at her, she could see her begin to come to life, looking around confusedly. 'You have had a shock, Mary, but Mr Morris and I are here, and we will look after you.'

Mary nodded briefly, and then it seemed that the memory of the last few minutes came surging back over her. She began to talk, garrulously and mostly incoherently, and while the couple could not make out many of the words she was saying, it appeared that she was asking them to take her to the place where her brother had originally been employed, to see if she could find him.

Thomas and Ann exchanged a quick look above Mary's seated form, and the matron shook her head. Nothing good could come of any further action this evening. All they could do was get her back to the asylum and hope that she had exhausted herself into sleep.

The Morrises talked long into the night. Ann would never articulate the sentiment, but there was an unspoken sense between them that the director himself had failed: he had suggested and encouraged the visit to Morley's, he had been convinced that it would do Mary some good, and ultimately he was responsible for the care of all patients, both male and female.

'I feel that she is ready to be saved,' he said dispiritedly, 'but we cannot see the route ahead. It is there, but we are blind to it.'

'We should not be too hard on ourselves,' replied his wife. 'It was circumstances that worked against our favour, not the idea itself. If Mary's brother had been at Morley's then we would not be having this discussion.'

'But do we have the right to let Mary's future stand or fall upon the whims of circumstance?' he asked, shaking his head as he did so. 'I should have visited the factory before taking her there; it was not fair to submit her to that.'

Ann was silent for a short while, as she considered what to say. Her faith was not something that the couple often discussed, partly because they accepted each for what they were, but also because her Quakerism had been such a barrier to their relationship; to discuss it would bring back memories that might be better left untouched. She still maintained her faith, however, and she felt that now was one of the occasions when she had to say what she believed to be the truth.

'There is God in Mary,' she said, 'just as there is in everyone. But she does not know it. Her life has been spent looking outwardly at the needs and feelings of others – her parents, her brothers and sisters, even her employer – as if that will bring her peace.'

'As have you, surely?' Thomas suggested, but his wife dismissed his intervention.

'She has to look within herself first,' she responded. 'Only then will she find the strength she needs to enable her to help others in the way she wants.'

'I understand,' said the director. 'But how can we make her look within herself? Can she not only accomplish that through her own actions?'

'We can guide her,' said Ann. 'At the moment she has lost all hope, because she feels that she can fall no further; she feels that she gone down as far as she can. She is removed from her home, her parents have disowned her, and she is fervently worried about her brother. But the reason there is still hope is because she *can* fall further.'

'I'm afraid you have rather lost me.'

'Make her see that neither she, nor her brother, is at the bottom,' said Ann. 'Give her the strength firstly to stay as she is, and then to pull herself upwards, taking her brother with her if necessary. She must be made to appreciate the precariousness of the position she is in; only then will she have the encouragement to improve her lot.'

They waited another two days to see whether Mary improved. But her condition deteriorated; she was listless, and tired, and had to be persuaded into going for her daily walk. On the third day, when Thomas was still completing his morning rounds,

Ann went to get Mary from the laundry, told her to collect her shawl and then led her out of the asylum and back on the road into town.

'Are we going to see Will now, then?' asked Mary, and the matron shook her head. She marched Mary past the vastness of Arkwright's lace mill and towards the marketplace, then north up Clumber Street, Milton Street and York Street, before stopping after about twenty minutes outside a long, large building. It had regimented rows of windows down its entire side, and a handful of sorry-looking men and women stood outside its main gate.

'Do you know what this place is?' she asked.

'No, miss.'

'It is St Mary's workhouse. I assume you have met fellow patients who have arrived from the workhouse?'

'Yes, miss.'

'And what do they say about it?'

'That the food is worse than in the asylum, miss.'

Ann allowed herself a brief smile before continuing. 'That is true, Mary. If you refuse to eat gruel or milk pottage then you will most certainly not thrive here. And tell me, what do you know of the workhouse test? Do you know anything of it?'

Mary shook her head.

'I see. Then let me tell you a little about the workhouse, Mary. You will not have your own room; you will be in a dormitory with a dozen other women, and rats running across the floor. You will have ill-fitting rags instead of freshly laundered clothes. The air will be foul and there will be no outside walks around well-kept grounds. You are as like to catch a fever as you are in the most congested of hospital wards. And you might enter that building with your virtue, but you will undoubtedly not emerge with it.

'I know all of this because I have been inside many times, paying visits with Friends, when I was one of them. And I also know that those without work are sent here in order that they qualify for poor relief: that is the workhouse test. You must live in the workhouse to receive the relief.

'Why am I telling you this? Because if you have no home to go to, and are unable to find employment, then this is where you will assuredly end up; this or somewhere very much like it. Perhaps you would go to the Southwell workhouse, being from that side of town. The point I am making is that, you will not be in the asylum forever, and unless you make yourself employable, unless you truly want to make your own way, then here you will be; and what use will you be to your brother inside here? Now, come with me.'

She set off up Mansfield Road at a brisk pace, and did not stop until they had reached the top of the hill. Ahead of them was the racecourse and cricket ground; and if they turned back on themselves, as they now did, the whole of Nottingham was spread out below them, with a thin layer of smog across the whole scene, and barely an inch of space to break up the dense framework of factories, shops and houses.

'I do not believe that you are mad, Mary,' said the matron. 'And I am quite sure that you do not believe it either. But it is much more difficult to prove sanity than it is to allege madness. No doubt we are all a little touched by insanity in our own ways; but once you are deemed to be of unsound mind, your behaviour must be beyond reproach if you are ever to return to your former life. Do you know where we are now, Mary?'

'I don't think so.'

'This is Gallows Hill. You would not know so, to look at it now, but it was less than a year ago that the last public execution took place here. Of course, if you wish to witness that sort of thing, you can still do so at the Shire Hall. But William Wells was the last person to be hanged here, nine months ago.

'He was a respectable man, Mary. He had married well and owned a farm of two hundred acres, as well as his own racehorse. But he became a slave to gambling, lost his farm and his horse, was reduced to travelling from fair to fair trying to make a living. He had debts at the Red Lion and the Wheatsheaf – and no doubt at other establishments as well – and assaulted a man in Basford Road in order to steal his watch, two sovereigns and some silver. He was caught in the act, and was found to have just ten shillings of his own.

'This is what people are driven to in reduced circumstances, Mary. And I can assure that you would need to steal significantly less than a watch and two sovereigns to find your way to the gallows. Do you understand what I am saying?'

'Yes, miss – that if I steal, then the worst that could happen to me is that I be hanged. And then I will be no help to Will at all.'

'No, Mary. This is not the worst that could happen to you. We have one more site to visit.'

She picked up her skirt and began walking back down the hill. Halfway down Mansfield Road, they forked left down York Street and then Glass House Street, until they arrived at a large, imposing building. Parts of it looked like a castle, with a high wall, turrets and narrow slits for windows, but the rest of it reminded Mary of the workhouse they had just visited.

'We are at the House of Correction,' said Mrs Morris, 'and it is undoubtedly true that there are many who would rather be hanged than be incarcerated here. There is a patient in the house, whose name it would not be appropriate for me to share, who was unfortunate enough to be sent here when she was unable to work due to a temporary illness; and it still makes her suffer to speak of what she experienced here. Do you hear that noise, Mary?'

Mary listened intently and could just make out a creaking sound, mixed with the distinct babble of water.

'That is the treadmill by the West Wall,' continued Ann. 'It is thirty feet long and it is operated all day. There are three other treadmills inside, bringing up water from the well in the rock below. Over there is the pump where some of the water emerges. I know that you are strong, Mary – I have seen how you work on the laundry, and how you recover after the chair. But tell me, how do you think you would fare upon the treadmill for eight or ten hours at a time, unable to stop walking even for a second, and whipped if you attempted to do so? There is no respite in this place; only pain and suffering, day after day.'

Mary knew a little about both the workhouse and the House of Correction from other patients in the asylum; she knew that lunatics were not welcome in either place, because they disrupted the other inmates, and there was a steady flow of paupers away from both institutions and into the asylum. She had heard tales of people with putrid bedsores from being tied to the bed frame, of whipping welts that would not heal and of food infected with bugs. She had even strongly suspected in one case that the asylum patient she was speaking to was exaggerating her symptoms purely so as not to be sent back to the workhouse.

Seeing these places in their intimidating reality – when previously they had just been concepts from stories – did bring home to her with more clarity what it might be like to be placed in them. It was upsetting, certainly; but mixed in with Mary's upset was a mild sense of anger that the matron had felt obliged to bring her out here.

'Why are you showing me all this?' she asked.

'To make you understand how this will end for you if you do not change.'

'I understand well enough. Thank you for bringing me out today, but I have seen sufficient. I know that I must never steal, or cheat, or be idle, and that if I do any of those things, I will see this place again.'

Ann took hold of Mary by the shoulders and wheeled her round to face her. 'You do *not* understand!' she said firmly. 'If you did, you would not be so – so naive! Such naivety might appear becoming in a seventeen-year-old, but you are now twenty-four Mary, and it is certainly less so in you.

'There are two ways of being discharged from the asylum, and that is as someone who is recovered, or as someone who is incurable but harmless. You might think it does not matter which of these applies to you, so long as you are out – but it does, Mary, it *does*! If you are deemed incurable, your parish will know of it, your family will know of it, any employer will know of it – not that anyone will employ you, because who would offer a job to a lunatic, even a harmless one? Do you think the mistress of a country estate will want you in her house, with her husband and her children? Do you even think your family will want you back in such circumstances?

'Perhaps you think that it is Mr Morris and I who will decide the basis on which you are discharged? Well, it is certainly not us alone – there are other factors at play here, Mary, and we are doing our best to help you, but you have to help us.

'You must seek to be discharged as recovered; not as incurable. I know that the very fact of saying you are recovered indicates that you were suffering with something from which you needed to recover, and that you do not believe you were ever suffering at all. No matter, Mary! How you arrived at this point is of no consequence now; all that matters is how you behave from this point onwards. You *have* to start thinking about yourself. It is the only way that you will avoid this place, or the workhouse, or the gallows – and the only way that you will help your brother.'

She let go of her hold on Mary. She did not think that she had ever grabbed anyone by the shoulders before, let alone spoken to them in such a forceful manner. But she did not know what else to try, or by what means to make Mary realise just how precarious her very existence was.

'I am sorry,' she said. 'I believe I was – overcome, for a minute. I can help you, and I can counsel you, but it is not for me to shout at you in the street.'

She made as if to return to the asylum, but Mary took hold of her hand and pulled her back. She clasped it tightly for a moment, and then released the pressure a little, lest Mrs Morris thought she was trying to restrain her in some way.

'I do understand,' she said slowly.

Chapter 19

Ann was distracted. She sat at the kitchen table, idly fiddling with a new contraption that Mr Dale had given her – a cylindrical box containing a glass bottle of sulphuric acid, surrounded by two dozen thin pieces of wood, all individually wrapped in paper. She unwrapped the paper from one of the strips of wood, removed the bottle stop, tentatively put the end of the wood into the acid and then removed it. Nothing happened. She tried again, leaving the wood in the acid for longer and withdrawing more quickly, and this time a sharp burst of flame erupted from the tip of the wood. It caused Ann such surprise that she immediately dropped it in her lap, where it quickly burned a small hole in her dress before she was able to extinguish it.

The matron sighed and moved the box to one side. Mr Dale was frequently sourcing the latest fire-lighting devices for his apothecary shop, as he knew how useful they might be in the asylum; it took a considerable amount of time for the candles and lamps in the asylum to be lit from a tinderbox. But it seemed this latest example could be added to the list of other devices that had not worked as Mr Dale had hoped.

Earlier that morning, Ann had received a visit. A woman in her mid-forties had turned up and asked to meet with Mary Reddish. Under normal circumstances, and with any other patient, the matron would have showed her into the airing yard to await Mary's arrival. But there was something about the visitor's manner – her urgency to see Mary perhaps, or her absolute conviction that she would be allowed to do so – that made the matron hesitate.

'Are you a relative?' she asked.

'I am most certainly not.'

'Then could I inquire after the nature of your relationship with Miss Reddish?'

'I am her former employer,' said Mrs Barwick, 'and I have visited her twice previously at these premises. I strongly suggest that you allow me to do so again.'

These were words to raise Ann's suspicions, and her hackles, even further. 'I have not made your acquaintance on either of those previous occasions,' she said calmly. 'I would be grateful if you would indicate to me now the purpose of this latest visit.'

'That is between myself and Mary,' came the answer. 'I don't believe it to be a legitimate concern of yours.'

If Mrs Barwick had been the person paying for Mary's fees in the asylum, Mrs Morris might have had little choice but to allow her access. But she knew that Mary was a pauper patient, paid for by the parish, and that this visitor had no say whatsoever over Mary's treatment.

'I'm afraid I will have to ask you to leave,' she said. 'Miss Reddish is currently unable to receive visitors.'

'Unable to receive visitors? What does—'

'I am afraid I am unable to provide further details. Perhaps she will be sufficiently recovered in a week or two. In the meantime I bid you a good morning.' She walked away, and indicated to one of the nearby attendants that the lady was not to be allowed to enter the asylum any further.

Now, two hours later, she still did not know the purpose of the visit, but she had an instinctive feeling that she had made the right decision. She still needed time to think, however; to work out why Mary's former employer might be visiting her, and how the visits could potentially be affecting her recovery.

Ann put her coat on and walked out of the asylum and down the drive. She walked up through the gardens that formed a buffer between the asylum and the houses on the edge of Nottingham, and at the end of the gardens she emerged on to the heights of Mill Hill Lane and its trio of windmills. She often came up here when she needed time to herself, even if just for twenty minutes or so; she could look down on the asylum and then to the town beyond, and the sense of perspective that the view offered her would often be mirrored in her own thoughts.

Today, however, she felt like walking further, so she continued past Green's Mill and Saint Stephen's Church – pausing, as she always did, for a few quiet moments at the grave of Joseph Taylor, the victim of the second asylum murder over that terrible Christmas a dozen years previously – and into the village of Sneinton itself.

As she walked, she thought about Mary, and decided that she had certainly appeared more positive since the visit to the workhouse and House of Correction; she had continued her exercise without being reminded, and she seemed to have been eating well. Her face was ruddier in complexion, and she had undoubtedly not lost any additional weight, even if she had not yet gained any either.

But the visit from Mrs Barwick was disconcerting, more for the fact that it had happened at all than because of any particular detail within it. Mrs Morris had gone back to check the visitor logs and had seen that Mrs Barwick was quite correct when she said she had visited twice previously; which made it unusual that Mary had not mentioned her at all.

Ann had now reached Sneinton Hermitage, where houses of different shapes and sizes were cut into a wall of rock. Stairs led up from the caves to gardens and further houses on top of the rock-wall roof; there was even a coffee house in one of the caves that was well used by residents, and which in the summer offered a welcome respite from the heat outside. It was quite the oddest scene that Ann had seen in Nottingham, and she liked to stroll this far and gaze upon it for a few minutes, before heading back up towards the windmills and the top of the hill.

On her return to the asylum, Ann saw that Mary was taking a walk with Hannah in the grounds, and she told the assistant that she was free to go, as she wished to speak with Mary herself. Once the pair were alone, she asked Mary how she was in general terms, and then broached the subject of Mrs Barwick.

'You had a visitor this morning,' she said. 'And I'm afraid to say I did not allow her entry. That may have been the wrong decision, but I wanted to inform you about it.'

Mary asked who the visitor was, and the matron told her.

'Is there anything you need to speak with me about?' she asked.

Mary hesitated. Mr and Mrs Morris had undoubtedly shown her great kindness, above and beyond what their positions called for, but she had felt unable to tell them about Mrs Barwick's visits, for fear that it would impact on Will in some way.

Now, however, the situation had surely changed. She knew that Mrs Barwick had lied to her: Will was in the same job as when he had left home eight months previously, and Mrs Barwick had not found him a new position. She felt no lingering sense of duty to her former employer and so she proceeded to tell the matron what had been taking place – how Mrs Barwick had approached her to find out about Catherine, how she had said that Mary's actions would benefit Will, and how she had ultimately been proven not to be a woman of her word.

'And what do *you* believe?' asked Ann, when Mary had finished speaking. 'Do you think Miss Mills had a baby and then killed it?'

'No, miss. I don't think she had another baby at all.'

'Then why did you engage with your former mistress at all? It appears that she has led you on something of a wild goose chase.'

'I don't know. Because of what she said about the baby clothes in Catherine's bag, and feeding another woman's baby. I thought that it made sense; and at that time I did not know Catherine at all to make me think any better of her.'

Ann now understood why Mary had been quite so upset outside I & R Morley, when she learned that Will had not been taken on by the firm: it was the confirmation that Mrs Barwick had neither the power nor the inclination to find Will a new position with a different company. If she had allowed herself physical contact with the patients, then Ann would have taken Mary's arm in hers at that point, and given it a reassuring squeeze. That she did not was not due to any lack of compassion on her part, but because she felt it helped the patients to maintain this type of dividing line. But when she spoke, her tone and manner were as empathetic as she could make them.

'All that you have been told,' she said, 'and all that you have related to me, has come only from the mouth of your former mistress. Should any of her words be believed? I do not know. Perhaps there is indeed a poor baby who has been killed, otherwise she would not be so anxious to find the culprit – any culprit, perhaps. And it may be the case that Miss Mills had baby clothes in her bag and was feeding another child. But it is not for us to attribute any greater significance to them than they may reasonably warrant. My own experience of Miss Mills – and as this is her sixth admittance into the house, I feel I have some knowledge of her disposition – is that she is not capable of such an act. I assume you feel the same way?'

'Yes, miss.'

'Very well.' Ann began to guide Mary back in the direction of the asylum building. 'But there is something I believe you must do, Mary. You must tell Miss Mills of what has taken place.'

Mary nodded, but nevertheless seemed disconcerted by the idea.

'You don't believe that you should do so?' asked the matron.

'It's not that. I know that I should do so; I have not treated her well. But I am sure she will think badly of me; she has every right to do so.'

'People may sometimes surprise us, Mary. All that you can do is what is right, and hope that Miss Mills has it in her heart to forgive you. But I think it may be of benefit to you to tell her of what has been happening.'

They had reached the main entrance, and as they went into the hallway Ann called for an attendant to accompany Mary back up the stairs to the ward.

'Oh, before you go, Mary,' she added, 'have you had any contact with Miss Mills in the past few days?'

'A little.'

'How does she appear to you?'

'She is calmer than she has been, certainly.'

'But she has not said anything to indicate the source of her distress?'

Mary shook her head.

'Has she ever indicated to you that she experiences difficulties with issues of a feminine nature?' the matron persisted. 'With her monthlies, perhaps? I am sorry if my question embarrasses you. But I grew up in a household with three sisters, and I'm afraid embarrassment was a luxury we could ill afford.'

'No, miss. I would say so if she had.' Mary turned to go away, and then said: 'I did think something myself, that I could have told you when we last spoke about Catherine, only I wasn't sure it was important.'

'Tell me nevertheless, and I can be the judge of that.'

'It was just that I remembered a woman in my village who reminded me of Catherine – sorry, of Miss Mills.'

'In what way did she remind you of Miss Mills?'

'Everything – what she said, how she said it, the way she lashed out.' She gave the matron all the details she knew about her former neighbour, and Mrs Morris thanked her.

When she was back inside the asylum, the matron went to look over Catherine Mills's notes again. She had been admitted in 1818, shortly after the birth of her child. If she was struggling with looking after her new baby, it was easy to see how that could have affected her mind. But her subsequent admissions had been in 1821, 1823, 1824, 1826 and 1827 – years when there was no suggestion that she had given birth again. The particular triggers for those admissions remained something of a mystery, just as they had been at the time. Ann's conversation with Mary had given her the beginning of an idea, however.

Mary went back to the laundry to continue ironing and folding the bedclothes. The thought of having to approach Catherine Mills was weighing heavy on her, but she knew that she needed to do so at the first available opportunity. In a strange way, it seemed that only by accomplishing this task would she see a clear way out of the asylum. Mr and Mrs Morris, Hannah Greendale and even Mr Ellis had recently been providing assistance towards that goal, of course. And following her trip into Nottingham with the matron, she had been seized by a new determination to improve herself to such a degree that it would be impossible *not* to discharge her. It had become absolutely clear that the only way to help Will was by being on the other side of the asylum walls; no one on the outside was going to help him more than she would, not even her mother and father, and once she was out she could visit him at his place of work, see him on his day off and encourage him that there was always the possibility of an end to his current employment, and other opportunities to be explored. While there was still little that she could yet do in a practical sense, the very fact that he knew she was watching out for him would – as she well knew from her own recent experiences – be of significant comfort.

How her relationship with Catherine was tied up with all of this, she wasn't quite sure. But somehow she felt that only when she had tried to make things right with her fellow patient – even if every apology she offered was thrown back in her face – would she feel sufficiently cleansed to enable her to go out into the world and try to forge a different life outside the asylum.

On the final day of February, Dr Pennington made the formal decision that Mary Reddish would no longer be treated in the chair, writing in her notes that she was 'nearly convalescent' and adding that 'the chair is discontinued'.

At their weekly meeting the day before, he had told Thomas that the patient appeared to be making good progress, that she continued to improve in mind and bodily health and that good effects were ascribed to the chair. Thomas held his tongue. The assessment of the patient was largely his own, which had subsequently passed down to the physician; it was inevitably the case that Dr Pennington himself, who was based outside the asylum's four walls, had had relatively little direct experience with Mary in comparison to the day in, day out contact established and sustained by the director.

It was now true that Dr Pennington ascribed the improvement in Mary to the effects of the chair, when Thomas knew that this was clearly not what had taken place. But the overall evaluation was correct, and the director was happy to agree that use of the chair be ceased with immediate effect.

Chapter 20

March 1828

Mary had now been in the asylum for more than eight months. During that time, she had thought of her parents dozens of times every day; she wondered how often, now, they thought of her.

She imagined that in the early weeks there would have been discussions, or even arguments, about coming to visit her. Sometimes when she tried to visualise these, she thought that it would have been her mother pleading to come and see her, and her father arguing that she had brought disgrace upon the family and should be ignored. But deep down she knew that it was more likely to be the other way round. Her mother was the one who was the protector of the family reputation, and the one who would stubbornly defend her position no matter how long had passed. If she truly believed that Mary had stained that reputation, then she would remain out of contact. Mary had also hoped that her sister Elizabeth at least – if not her older brothers – might take it upon herself to visit the asylum independently. But it would be impossible to do that without her mother finding out, somehow, and in any case Elizabeth would always take her lead from her mother's actions.

In some ways, the looming conversation with Catherine at least offered some sort of distraction; it took her thoughts away from Will, and her parents, and Halloughton, and

Southwell, and all the other people and events that dominated her waking thoughts.

She found her chance three weeks after her walk in the grounds with Ann, and this time it was in Catherine's own bedchamber where the opportunity arose. Mary was walking past with the laundry; the door was ajar; she spied Catherine sitting on the bed, and hurried in.

The second-class chamber was furnished in a similarly simple fashion to Mary's own room: a chest of drawers, washstand, bedstead and chair constituted the only furniture. She had hoped that Catherine would be in one of her more tranquil spells, but this was extinguished as soon as the older woman opened her mouth.

'Fuck me, if it isn't the Virgin Mary,' she said, looking up. 'What's the matter? You look as if you pissed on a nettle.' She patted the bed next to her. 'Sit your arse down there.'

Mary gave a half-smile and sat down awkwardly on the chair opposite. She was taken aback that Catherine seemed so lively; the last time she had seen her, she had appeared almost mute, suffering as she was from the ongoing effects of the rotatory chair.

'You seem very well,' said Mary tentatively.

'I *am*, Mary!' Catherine said loudly, causing her fellow patient to flinch. 'I am twelve days free of that bastard chair. Pennington knows I hate it and he plays on it, the little shit. Speaking of which, if I need to dash out, don't mind me; he's put me on half an ounce of castor oil to get my bowels going.'

'You are finished with the chair, then?'

'Who knows? For now. I don't mind telling you, Mary, it makes me so queer that I don't know what I'm doing half the time.'

Mary was immediately relieved at the prospect of Catherine facing a potential reprieve from the chair. But Catherine's apparent return to something very much akin to her normal self meant that Mary had no reason not to approach the subject she had gone to the room to address. She knew what it was that she had to say, but sitting opposite Catherine, seeing her in her rediscovered boisterousness, made it more difficult than she had imagined to broach the topic at hand.

'Could I ask you a personal question?' she said.

'Only if it's dirty.'

Mary ignored the remark. 'I just wanted to know – when you were found in Loughborough, before you came here, why did you have baby clothes in your bag? What were they for? And why were you trying to feed another woman's child?' She felt cowardly for tackling the issue in this slightly circuitous way, but she could think of no other way of doing it.

'Did I tell you about those things?' asked Catherine confusedly, and Mary slowly shook her head. 'Then how do you know that?' Catherine asked. 'Was it Mrs Morris told you?'

'Oh, no!' said Mary, horrified at the thought that the matron might be held responsible for any breach of confidence. 'It wasn't Mrs Morris at all.'

And she proceeded to tell Catherine everything that she understood the other woman needed to know: about the actions of Mr and Mrs Barwick and the circumstances in which she had arrived at the asylum; about Mrs Barwick's visit to the asylum and the story of the baby found dead in Loughborough; and about how she had agreed to try to find out whether Catherine had been involved in the crime.

'And I'm so sorry that I ever agreed to it!' she cried, moving over to sit on the bed. 'I only did so because I thought it could help my brother. And I don't think there was ever a single minute where I thought you had actually killed a poor baby. I don't expect or deserve your forgiveness, but I had to tell you.'

'You don't need to ask to be forgiven,' Catherine replied, suddenly a model of calm. 'I'm too old to be taking offence every time someone does something that doesn't sit well with me. I don't like talking about myself, mind. But because you've been decent to me, Mary, whatever the reason behind it, I'll tell you what I know – which isn't much. Trying to feed another baby? I don't know anything about that. I don't remember it, and I can't explain it. But the baby clothes? They are my John's. I like to carry them with me. I know it's daft, and he's halfway to being a strapping young lad now, but it comforts me, having them with me. I've been a shit mother, Mary, I know I have. But still, I like to remember when he was tiny.'

Mary nodded, and sat quietly next to Catherine. She stayed for a few more minutes, and then left without feeling the need to say another word.

Thomas closed the books in front of him, and pushed them away across the table. He had been reading for the best part of three hours, and was no closer to understanding puerperal insanity – an affliction beginning in mothers in the weeks after childbirth – than when he started. As far as he could see, there were two main types of the illness. The lesser form was melancholia, which was generally described as a period of lethargy and depression; the more hazardous form was mania, characterised as it was by disruptive and violent behaviour. But nowhere could he find a case history that combined both forms in a single patient, such as in Catherine Mills; and there was certainly no evidence that the symptoms could last fully a decade after the birth of a child, as hers appeared to have done.

He decided to pay a visit to Dr John Storer, who had welcomed him to his Thurland Hall home all those years ago, and who was still a well-respected figure at the asylum.

Dr Storer, who was now almost eighty, had been something of a peripheral figure in Thomas's life since that day, an absence that he sometimes regretted given his battles with

Dr Pennington, but he had recently assisted the director by helping him to borrow all manner of books on illnesses after childbirth from the recently established Nottingham Subscription Library, and Thomas was due to pay him a courtesy visit.

He made his way into town and to Thurland Hall, where he was greeted warmly and asked to stay for some tea. He happily acquiesced, and once inside was surprised to see that the hall appeared to be in a state of some disarray.

'Please accept my apologies for the mess,' said Dr Storer. 'We are in the process of moving, and there is rather a large amount of boxing up to be done.'

'No apologies are necessary,' replied Mr Morris, 'but I confess I was not aware of your departure. Are you to leave Nottingham?'

'No, no,' said the doctor. 'We are only going to Lenton Firs, just on the Derby road on the other side of town. I shall be sad to leave here, but the location is rather too rambunctious for a man of my advancing years. It should be considerably quieter over in Lenton.'

Mr Morris paused to take in this information. Although he had seen too little of Dr Storer over the preceding years, his host was someone whose viewpoint he respected. Once he had moved outside the town centre, however, he was unlikely to see him at all. He decided there and then to seize the moment that had presented himself.

'Forgive me for asking,' he said, 'but could I possibly trouble you by asking your views on a particular patient? It is a most perplexing case.'

'Of course, please do. It will be a welcome diversion.'

An hour later, Thomas left the hall.

Over the next few days, the director had read through all of the library books assiduously, only to discover that they offered merely a limited expansion of his existing knowledge.

Now, as Ann entered his study and saw the pile of books in front of him, he was prepared to acknowledge that he was at something of a loss.

'I am attempting to explain the symptoms of Catherine Mills,' he told his wife, 'but I will confess that I have been left confounded. I have assessed all of her symptoms – her melancholy, her flightiness, her obscenity – and I have concluded that these are all evidence of puerperal insanity.'

'Of course they are,' replied his wife. 'She is bawdy, she swears constantly, she is obsessed with matters of a sexual and bodily nature, and she is prone to outbursts of violence. Miss Reddish made the same connection when speaking with me about Miss Mills not a few days ago. But the reason you are presumably confounded is because she cannot be suffering from puerperal insanity when she has not recently given birth?'

'Well, quite,' said a flustered Thomas, who was vaguely disconcerted that his wife and a patient appeared to have independently arrived at the same conclusion as him. 'I was also going to say that her symptoms are a combination of both mania and melancholy, which I cannot see ascribed to any other patients previously.'

The matron came over and pulled up a chair so that she was sitting next to her husband at his desk. Slowly and deliberately, she closed the volumes that were open in front of him. 'Not everything is to be found in books and case studies,' she said. 'Had it never crossed your mind that Miss Mills's symptoms – her ricocheting between mania and melancholia – occur according to a cycle? According to a monthly cycle?'

'Naturally, it has,' replied Thomas. 'But I fail to see how this helps with her diagnosis. If she was pregnant, then perhaps one could see that a fear of her puerperal symptoms returning following childbirth could affect her mind. But she is not pregnant, she continues to menstruate, and yet she still suffers these symptoms?'

'It is precisely because she continues to menstruate, that she *does* suffer these symptoms,' said Ann patiently.

'Please do go on.'

'Miss Mills is thirty-seven,' the matron continued. 'Ten years ago she was admitted for the first time – three weeks after giving birth to her only child.' She pulled out Catherine's patient notes and presented them to Thomas. 'Since then she has been admitted on five further occasions. She has been described – by Dr Pennington, but presumably in agreement with yourself – as wild, and abusive, and very violent, but also as tranquil, and coherent, and quiet.

'I believe that Catherine Mills wished dearly to have another child, and to be a mother to that child in a way that she was unable to with her first. But for whatever reason, her body will not allow her to do so, and it is the regular monthly reminder of that which contributes to both her melancholia and her mania.

'Of course, her symptoms are similar to those of puerperal insanity, because they are based in the very same root. She is suffering in her body and in her mind every month, and she simply needs the cause explained to her so that she can understand it, and go to live her normal life.

'Yet what has our solution been? To restrain her to her bed. To put her in the chair. To give her anything that will make her vomit – six grains of zinc sulphate here, a large dose of powdered squill there, and then the South American vomiting root to finish her off.'

Thomas was silent while all of this was being said, but after pausing for a moment at the end of his wife's words, he said: 'Surely defective fertility should be considered as worthy of treatment as any other condition? There is clear evidence that effecting successful cures for mental afflictions may be compromised if such physical inadequacies are not addressed.'

Ann shook her head in exasperation. 'Defective?' she repeated. 'What foolishness! You appear to believe that a woman's well-being – indeed, her whole character and behaviour – is governed entirely by the successful functioning of her reproductive system, and that any so-called inadequacies can be held responsible for an almost limitless number of nervous disorders.'

'But you said—'

'I do not deny that some of Miss Mills's behaviour may be attributed directly to her reproductive functioning,' said Ann, anticipating her husband's challenge. 'Her original mania was as a result of childbirth, and I believe that her ongoing difficulties may be occurring in a monthly cycle—'

'Which indicates that her behaviour is indeed related to her reproductive function?' interrupted Thomas.

'But it is such a very small part of who she is,' said Ann, finishing her sentence. 'I have said that it contributes to her symptoms, not that it is entirely responsible for them. In concentrating so definitively upon that small part, and whether she is functioning correctly or not, you miss everything else that is of importance to her case. Her child has been raised largely by her mother and sister; do you consider that she would be so desperate for another child if she was engaged in looking after her own? The father of her child refused to take responsibility and proceeded to shun her; where would she be now if she had a stable, loving husband to return to? Her own father died when she was young. Her condition is about her family, her circumstances, and her life – and yet you have reduced it to whether her reproductive system is working or not.'

'And you believe that our treatment of her has unequivocally made those symptoms worse?' asked Thomas.

'I do; and not just Miss Mills.' She produced some more patient notes she had been carrying. 'Sarah Howard, brought in last July following a stillbirth; we have bled and blistered her, and she has attempted to strangle herself. Ann Wood, admitted in September having been in a depressed state of mind ever since her last confinement; we have blistered her. I could continue, but I shall not.'

Her husband bowed his head, chastened. 'I do not doubt the veracity of anything that you have said,' he acknowledged. 'But my thoughts at this very moment are not with Catherine Mills, or Sarah Howard, or Ann Wood. I only feel that I should have attended to *you* more after you had given birth.'

The matron shook her head. 'Not all women are the same, Thomas. I experienced nothing but happiness – and a little tiredness, I will allow – following my own lyings-in. But I firmly believe that the fact I did so was down to good fortune, not to any inherent strength of character on my part. In the same way, the fact that Miss Mills and the others are not the same cannot be accredited to any flaw in their own characters. You should be thinking of *them*, and not of me.'

'What, then, should I do? What treatment can be offered for a difficult life?'

'Perhaps there is not always a treatment,' Ann said, looking directly at him. 'There is only understanding and acceptance, and hoping that one is not too late to make a difference.'

'But will that cure her?'

'She has been here five times already, and has not yet been cured. You and Dr Pennington may mark her as "recovered" in your little book every time she leaves, but she is no more recovered than she would be had she broken every bone in her body. Let us hope that the next time she is discharged, it will be the last.'

Chapter 21

April 1828

'I consider that I owe you an apology, Catherine,' said Thomas, allowing her to walk just in front of him as they went down the steps of the asylum and into the grounds. 'You have been subjected to the rotatory chair these past few months, and I fear that the logic for using it was not sound.'

'What logic was that, then?'

'I'm afraid I am not at liberty to say. But I hope that you will accept my apology for any treatment you may have undergone unnecessarily.'

They followed the route of the driveway, and then walked a little up the hill. 'You've always been good to me, mostly,' replied Catherine, 'and Mrs Morris, too. But if you're wanting me to say I understand you putting me in that chair when you didn't need to, you'll be waiting a fuck of a long time for anything to come out of me, excuse my language.'

'Of course,' said Thomas, 'that is your prerogative,' and the pair continued walking.

The director thought that might be the end of the matter; he knew that his wife had already spoken to Catherine at length about her provisional diagnosis, and Ann had reported back that the patient appeared calmer, and accepting of what she had had to say. But as he was attempting to steer Catherine back towards the main entrance, she stopped him and said: 'I don't *like* it here, you know.'

'Pardon me?'

'I don't *like* it here. In case you were thinking that, you know, it was easier for me to be here than back at home.'

'Not at all.'

'Not that it's easy at home,' Catherine added quickly. 'Memories, see? A big old house it is, and it used to be a grand old place – we used to play in the orchard and the barn, and swim in the pond. There's an attic running the whole length of the house, and I used to go up there and lie down and watch the sun go across the sky. But it's all gone to pot, now. It feels like there's hardly any of us left. Martha and Thomas, they died before I was born. Then my father died, then our John, and suddenly there was just the three of us left.'

'You had your own child, though?'

'True – by a father who had to be taken to court to admit that he'd had his way with me. You'd think that pissing and shitting myself in that chair was shameful enough, but going to that court was more shaming than anything that's happened to me here.'

They reached the steps back up to the asylum, and Thomas took a moment to survey the scene around him; not the building itself, but the grounds, which were filled with an abundance of mature plants and trees, the bulbs already dominating the flower beds and the wisteria and azalea just coming into bloom. It was the sixteenth spring that he and Ann had seen arrive at the asylum, and each one seemed to be more spectacular than the last. He said good morning to the gardener, and was about to go inside when Mary and Hannah emerged through the large front door.

'Ah!' he said. 'A happy coincidence! Hannah, please could you accompany Miss Mills back to the ward? I wish to have a word with Miss Reddish.'

Hannah took Catherine inside, and Thomas led Mary away from the building to a bench near the fruit trees that he had planted early on during his directorship, before the asylum had the luxury of a gardener to undertake such work.

They sat down, and he said: 'Mrs Morris informed me that you had spoken to Miss Mills. That required a degree of courage, Mary.'

'It was the least I could do,' she replied. 'I am afraid I used her badly, and I am not proud of it.'

'How were matters left between the two of you?'

'She was most generous. I hope that all will be well.'

'I am glad to hear it,' said Mr Thomas. 'We are all prone to make mistakes, Mary; it is the manner in which we address them that shows our true character. And your mistake was made for the most worthy of reasons. Have you received any further news of your brother?'

She shook her head.

'Then the very best that you can do for him is to recover well enough to be able to help him on the outside,' he continued.

Mary looked around her, at the few patients who were deemed well enough and responsible enough to be out in the grounds, and thought of all of those remaining inside, who might not see any more of the outside world than the airing yard during their months or years of incarceration.

'You say to me that I must recover,' she said, 'but what must I recover from? Mrs Morris has said to me that I am not mad and never have been. So how can I recover from what I never had?'

Thomas paused before replying. 'What you have had, and what you are believed to have had, are two very different entities, unfortunately. There are now in existence, notes that stipulate what your behaviour has been, and what treatment you have received to change that behaviour. You cannot wish these away or pretend that they do not exist; all you can do is show that you have changed.'

'I have not, though.'

'But profess that you have, nevertheless. There may even be elements of your character that *have* changed. Your quickness of temper, for example – I think it would be injudicious for us to say that you did not suffer a little from this in the past. Yet perhaps it is something that you would consider to be less intrusive now? If so, then such a change can only be of benefit to you in your efforts to be released. It is of no benefit to you if you are the same person with the same flaws who entered here; you must be flawless, and entirely harmless.'

'Mrs Morris said the same to me before.'

'And she is right.' He stood up and turned towards the asylum entrance, to signal that their conversation was nearing its end. 'I am only a doctor, Mary, not an alienist; I don't pretend to understand all the workings of the mind. But what I do understand is that there are people who must be reassured. Our subscribers must be reassured that their money is being well spent. Our governors must be reassured that the treatment is appropriate. And the people of Nottingham, whose taxes support us, must be reassured that dangerous lunatics are not going to be released on to the streets of their town.'

Mary also got up from the bench, and they walked back together. It was true that her temper had played a part in her being admitted to the asylum, but Mary had a lingering sense of bitterness that Dr Pennington's view of her, as it was recorded in his casebook, was now the accepted view of who she was, and what she had been. Did his notes tell of how Mr Barwick had entered her bed, and locked her in her room, and betrayed her to her mother? Did they detail how she had been shouted down in court when she tried to relate what had happened? She could have been cleverer, she knew, and dealt with it all differently; but was it for her to have been cleverer, or for Mr Barwick never to have treated her badly in the first instance?

'The notes that you mention,' she said, 'what do they say?'

'How do you mean, Mary?'

'What do they say about me? What sort of person do they say I am?'

'I'm afraid I don't recall them in detail, Mary. The house is built for eighty patients and my memory is not so prodigious that I can bring to mind the details of all of them.'

'Which bits do you remember, then?'

'You really wish to know?'

'Yes.'

'In that case … I believe it may say that your behaviour has been violent, and impetuous. And that your moral conduct has not been correct. But it also records your improvement and your increased tranquillity.'

Mary shook her head in despair. '*My* moral conduct has not been correct?' she repeated. 'Would that I could write; I would tell a very different story, and a much truer one.'

Mr Morris remained silent, knowing that what she said was in all probability right. And it was the case, of course, that there were precious few other patients whose history he knew with anything like the detail that he knew Mary's. He would not have been able to recite even a few lines from the vast majority of their notes.

But he knew that, over the past months, Mary had become a particular project for both him and his wife. She had entered the asylum at a time when he was despairing of ever making a real difference to any of his patients, such was the grip of Dr Pennington and the governing committee over the procedures to be followed. But, together, he and Ann had demonstrated that if they were given the chance to manage patients in their own way, they *could* make a difference. Mary was an obvious candidate because she was young, appeared to be relatively lucid, and did not have any serious underlying mental incapacity to inhibit her progress. Now that they felt they had made progress with her, they could start to try similar methods with more challenging patients who presented with more problematic behaviours.

Mary, meanwhile, although she was upset at what the director had told her, was also relieved that he had not mentioned some particular details that she had feared would be in her notes. She had never told Mr or Mrs Morris the full story of what had transpired between her and Mr Barwick, partly out of embarrassment at what he had attempted to do to her, and partly out of shame at what she had offered – in her desperation – to do for him. Her intention was to never speak to anyone of it again; she had done so once, in the courtroom, and had not been believed. Neither of the couple had asked her to provide any detail other than she had rejected a gentleman's advances, and she was grateful that they had not done so.

'*De puerperarum febre*,' said Dr Pennington. The room remained silent, and so he repeated the words again, this time looking directly at Thomas. '*De puerperarum febre*. "Of puerperal fever", in case you are not familiar with the Latin language. That was the title of my thesis, more than thirty years ago. Please do not presume to lecture me on the bodily effects of childbirth.'

Thomas looked around at the rest of the house committee for support. He had decided it was best to talk about Catherine's case when others aside from Dr Pennington were present, for when he revealed what he knew would be a controversial diagnosis for her. James Dale was at the committee meeting, as well as two of the other visiting governors.

Thomas had outlined the background to the case – Catherine's previous admissions, the puerperal mania resulting from her first confinements and the recurring problems that had since been coming to light on a monthly basis. He pointed out the physical symptoms – mastodynia, dysmenorrhoea – and also the psychological ones: irritability, abusiveness, vulgarity and so forth. He explained how the chemicals in a woman's body were thought to change before and during her menses, and how this was likely to be directly affecting Catherine's pattern of behaviour. He was careful not to attribute any improvement in her to the whirling chair, but instead said that the simple fact of her knowing that there was a specific cause for her behaviour had led to an improvement.

'With respect,' he said to Dr Pennington, 'that is entirely my point. We must look beyond the physical effects of childbirth, such as puerperal fever, to those that affect the mind.'

'I am also familiar with puerperal insanity.'

'And yet this case is also not particularly about puerperal insanity – not in any meaningful, long-term way. It is about Miss Mills's perception of herself. To be afflicted in such a way as she has been is not manageable if one does not know the cause. But to know that the reason for the behaviour is interpretable, that it will last but a few days, and that it is entirely natural, these are of significant value. I have been assessing the general health of Miss Mills over recent days, and all the relevant markers – her pulse, temperature, excretions – indicate that she is much improved.'

'And yet she has had no particular treatment to aid this improvement,' said Dr Pennington. 'The chair has been deferred these past few weeks. What use is a diagnosis – if a diagnosis this actually is – that does not lead us towards an individual course of treatment? Will families pay fifteen shillings a week for – nothing?'

'They will undoubtedly pay fifteen shillings a week to learn that their loved one is suffering from a specific malady, and not from chronic and permanent mania,' replied Thomas.

'But how long will they continue paying for? They will be in the asylum for a week at most.'

'The diagnosis will not be immediate,' said the director. 'But if they are discharged soon afterwards, then is there not merit in that? Is that not what we are all here for? At the very least, it will boost our recovery rates.'

Dr Pennington appeared to be about to speak, but Mr Dale cleared his throat and the doctor held himself back. 'I do not confess to know a great deal about these matters,' said the apothecary, 'and it does appear to be a most unfortunate condition. It seems to me that offering her the opportunity to recover in a calm, safe environment, with no intrusive treatments, not only affords her the best chance of returning to full health, but also acts as a protection to members of the family who might otherwise become the target of her violent outbursts.'

'Well, perhaps I—' began Dr Pennington.

'Very good,' said Mr Dale. 'And thank you, Mr Morris, this has been most enlightening.'

Chapter 22

May 1828

It was a few more weeks before the director felt in a position to speak to Dr Pennington about Mary. Long-term patients needed both the director's and physician's agreement to be discharged from the asylum as cured and harmless, and he wanted Mary to be in as healthy a state as possible when he spoke to the doctor, so that the likelihood of him trying to block her discharge was minimised. It was by no means certain that this would be the case, once Dr Pennington realised the extent to which he had been deceived, but Thomas wanted to give Mary as favourable a chance as possible of leaving.

At the regular Wednesday meeting between the pair, they went through the details of the three new admissions who had arrived since the previous week, and then moved on to those who were convalescent and could potentially be considered for discharge. Because the asylum was full to capacity, there was always pressure to move patients on, especially paupers such as Mary who brought in less money than those of the first and second classes. Hers was the last case to be considered.

'I believe,' said Thomas to his companion, 'that her mind is firm, and she is in a fit state to be discharged.'

'Are you quite sure? Her behaviour does appear to have improved, but perhaps it would be better to keep her in the house for six more weeks now, than to readmit her for six months later.'

'I am sure.'

'And her violent outbursts, how can you be certain that she will not return to them as soon as she is released?'

Thomas paused to compose himself. 'She is not in the asylum because she is violent,' he said. 'She is violent because she is in the asylum.'

'And yet her violence began before she was admitted?'

'Because she was in the process of being deprived of everything,' replied the director. 'Her employment, her reputation, her liberty.'

'A set of circumstances which, while unfortunate, the majority of us would tackle without resorting to brutality,' said Dr Pennington. 'Nevertheless, I see you are determined that she should be discharged. I will not obstruct you; my own dealings with the girl indicate that she has much benefited from the treatment and care she has received.'

He signed the discharge form, and Thomas did the same. The director made as if to leave the room, but then stopped himself, and turned around. 'It is settled, then,' he said. 'And there is no going back now that the papers have been signed. But there is one matter with which I should acquaint you. Miss Reddish is not fit to be discharged as a consequence of the treatment she has received; quite the opposite, in fact.'

Dr Pennington looked bemused. 'You are not making any sense, sir.'

'Am I not? I had intended my meaning to be quite clear. Miss Reddish is in a state to leave the asylum not because she has received the treatments you prescribed, but precisely because she has *not* received them.'

'Have you taken leave of your senses?'

'Not at all. I believe I have only just begun to detect them.' Thomas walked over to the desk where the patient casebook was still open on Mary's page from their earlier discussion. '"Antimony tartar, three grains, three times a day",' he read out loud from the ledger. 'A more accurate description over recent weeks would be one grain, once a week. "Continues to use the chair". She has indeed continued to do so, but since the end of October these sessions have been significantly reduced, to perhaps one minute at a time.'

'This is outrageous, you can't—'

'In addition to the near cessation of these treatments,' Thomas continued, 'she has been taking one hour's exercise every day, walking a distance that I estimate to be no less than three miles on each occasion. She has been given a diet that is rich in fruit and vegetables. She has been kept in gainful employment whenever possible. And she has been moved to a quiet room where she has slept soundly and not been disturbed by the other patients. I am minded to think that, of all the weapons we have at our disposal, sleep is the most powerful of all.'

'Disgraceful!' shouted Dr Pennington. 'One minute in the chair? That is barely sufficient to get up to speed.'

'Precisely,' replied Thomas calmly. 'She has benefited from barely using the chair at all.'

'How has she benefited? What could possibly replace the invigorating effects of the chair?'

'Invigorating?' said the director. 'Is it invigorating to be unable to stand? To vomit for hour after hour? To lose consciousness entirely?'

He reached into his pocket, and pulled out a printed copy of an address that Dr Storer had made in 1811 to the governors and subscribers of the yet-to-be-opened asylum. Five hundred copies of the speech had subsequently been produced and circulated in order to advance the interests of the asylum, and one of those copies had been provided to Thomas at his interview. Its contents had been one of the most significant factors in persuading him to take up the role of director, and he flourished it now in front of the physician.

'"In whatever state we contemplate the miserable victim of insanity",' he read, '"whether in a paroxysm of fury, or of mirth; whether in his loud lamentations or mute misery, every circumstance of his sad case, makes an irresistible appeal to our sensibility, and calls upon us as men and as Christians, to exert ourselves in procuring for him that relief, which it is our province and our duty to impart."'

'I am aware of the address,' said Dr Pennington angrily. 'I was present when it was made. And I have not gone against it; all my prescriptions for Miss Reddish have had the express aim of procuring relief for her symptoms.'

Thomas flicked through more of the pages, and read them to Dr Pennington. 'An establishment designed for the *aid and comfort* of the afflicted individuals,' he said, struggling to keep his voice under control. 'An authority that is *well regulated and temperate*. Do you consider that all you have done for Miss Reddish has been well regulated, temperate, and designed for her aid and comfort?'

'I consider that severe maladies require severe solutions,' came the reply.

The director shook his head. 'Your solutions are no better than those in the worst madhouse,' he said. 'The asylum that I believed I was joining was intended to promote proper moral and physical behaviour; but how can that be achieved when our own actions fall so far short of what is correct? I was also told there would be minimal use of restraints—'

'As indeed there is!' interrupted Dr Pennington. 'Or are there chains and manacles attached to patients that I cannot see?'

'But the restraints in use are quite as bad as those you have mentioned,' continued the director. 'Rendering a person insensible through use of the chair is a restraint. Overusing an emetic to the point that a patient cannot walk is a restraint. There may be no manacles involved but the patient is as immobile as if they were chained to the wall. And there are indeed actual chains in the basement rooms, in case you had conveniently forgotten.'

'You have not acquired the experience to know what you are talking about,' said the physician, 'but no matter. You have directly gone against my express instructions with regards to the treatment of Miss Reddish, and for that I intend to have you dismissed. I would assume that the attendant Mr Ellis was also a party to this deception, as he operated the chair in question; he should also therefore be relieved of his position.'

'The hiring and firing of staff is entirely my responsibility,' said Thomas. 'And I have not gone against your instructions, except in the detail of them. Miss Reddish continued to receive the chair, albeit for a shorter period than you would have liked. She was also given antimony tartar, although less regularly than you had stipulated. These are simply examples of discretion being used, not of serious transgressions.'

'You may split hairs for as long as you like; but I am wholly content to let the governors decide. You have no influence there, and they will see your duplicity for what it is.'

'On the contrary,' said Thomas, 'I believe they will take a favourable view. I have already sought the counsel of a man much respected by the both of us, who has an intimate knowledge of the asylum and its workings, who has intimated to me that he believes my course of action was correct.'

'Who do you mean?'

'Dr Storer. I was visiting him recently and I sought his advice on some matters. I am sure he would not object to you confirming the accuracy of my communication of his views.'

Thomas could see that Dr Pennington was somewhat taken aback by this revelation, but he also noted that he quickly regained his composure.

'You are correct,' he said, 'I do hold Dr Storer in the highest regard. But he has no position of responsibility at the house, and has not had for some time.'

'You are resolved to go to the governors, then?'

'I am.'

Thomas nodded. 'Please excuse me for one moment.' He went out of the room and was absent for two or three minutes, before he returned with James Dale at his side. Dr Pennington looked in surprise at the apothecary, but maintained what self-command he had left as the two gentlemen greeted one another.

'Am I to presume that you have been brought here to support Mr Morris in the position he has adopted?' asked the physician coolly.

'I do not support any one individual against another,' Mr Dale replied, a little nervously. Although he was a key member of the house committee, and had been ever since its inception, opposing Dr Pennington was not something that fell to him naturally. The two men were broadly equal within the asylum, but decidedly unequal outside of it, and such dissension did not come instinctively.

'Then what is your view?'

'In this particular instance, it is my view that no rules or regulations have been broken,' Mr Dale said. 'The casebook accurately records the treatment that was prescribed, but as time progresses there may occasionally be variance in this, for any number of reasons. The other committee members may have a different view, but my own is that it is not a disciplinary matter.'

Thomas breathed a sigh of relief. This was the issue that he had raised with Mr Dale previously at the Flying Horse Inn. At the end of that meeting, Thomas had arranged the one thing that his friend had requested: namely, an introduction to Miss Reddish herself so that he could ascertain in his own mind whether or not her condition was such that she presented no danger to either the asylum or the wider public.

Mr Dale was only an apothecary, but he had spent fifteen years helping to decide on the rights and wrongs of discharging individual patients from the asylum, and he felt he did have a sense of which patients would present no difficulty on the outside. He had met with Mary, and spoken to her at length, and his assessment was in harmony with that of Thomas, in that her discharge would present no danger to others.

'I see,' said Dr Pennington. He looked at the director, and added: 'It may be that the committee has the same stance as Mr Dale; or they may well take an opposing view. I do not intend to drag the name of the asylum through the mud in order to find out. I am sure that our subscribers would fail to be impressed by the knowledge that the director of the establishment they so generously support is behaving quite so erratically. In taking – or not taking – this particular course of action, I believe it is clear that I am placing the needs of the asylum above my own. Perhaps, sir, there will come a day when you will feel compelled to do the same.'

He gathered up the casebook and the rest of his patient notes, and left the room.

'Thank you,' said Mr Thomas to Mr Dale, when the door had been closed. 'I am very grateful to you for your assistance.'

His friend looked slightly uncomfortable, and appeared to hesitate a number of times before he finally spoke. 'It gives me no pleasure to do so,' he said, 'and it is only the particular circumstances of the case, and the evident sanity of Miss Reddish, that justifies my opposing Dr Pennington in this way. He is a very good man, you know. I realise that you and he have not always seen eye to eye, but he is held in a great deal of esteem by those who know him well; not only for his own practice but for all his beneficial work carried out at the Vaccine Institution and the hospital. He is also an old man, and treating him in such a way does not sit well with me.'

'I understand,' said Mr Thomas, 'and if I have placed you in a position of any difficulty then I apologise. My intentions have always been to act in the benefit of the patients.'

'I believe that is beyond question; had it not been, I would not have been waiting in the meeting room today for any help I could provide. But I would not want to embark on such an engagement again; the cohesiveness of the house is not served well by it.'

At the same time that Mr Thomas was speaking with Dr Pennington and Mr Dale, his wife was the passenger in a gig that was travelling out towards Halloughton. The driver had already passed through Carlton and was about to enter the village of Burton Joyce, nearly halfway through the journey. The gig was an extravagance, Ann knew, but when she arrived at the home of Mr and Mrs Barwick she wanted every advantage in place that would successfully enable her to say exactly what she wanted to say, and in the way that she intended.

The road was muddy following an hour's rain that morning, and Ann held a blanket tightly across her lap to protect her skirt as the gig jounced through puddles and ruts in the road. As she did so, she could not but help think of Mary making the journey in the opposite direction almost a year previously. She would have known her destination by then, surely, but would she really have had any concept of what life in the asylum entailed? Would she even have known much about it from her life lived largely in the countryside, with only a few teenage years spent in the centre of Nottingham?

Ann hoped that, whatever Mary's expectations had been, her ordeal over the past eleven months had been mitigated by the care she had received from herself and the director, and indeed the rest of the staff. She hoped this for all her patients, of course, but for Mary it was particularly the case. It was hard for Ann to put her finger on the exact reason that this was so, but if she was forced to look hard for an answer, she would have said it was because Mary appeared to her the most vulnerable patient she had ever come across.

The asylum was filled with women who had been fighting all their lives, and who had been toughened by their experiences; and also with women who had been marked by some form of insanity ever since they were young girls. For different reasons, the majority of these women – in both groups – had a certain resilience to their situation, the matron felt. The first group treated the asylum as yet another obstruction placed in their way; the second group were largely oblivious to there being any obstruction at all. Mary, however, gave every indication of having been set down in the asylum in full control of her faculties, but without any real idea of why she was there. She gave the impression of being self-possessed, but in truth was as bewildered as any woman who had ever walked through the asylum's doors.

For Ann, this awakened her sympathy, her professional concern and perhaps a small amount of maternal instinct. She had occasionally wondered, though, what exactly it had awakened in her husband, who had paid Mary's case just as much attention as she had herself. Mary Reddish was a pretty young woman, and when that attractiveness was added to her vulnerability, it made for a dangerous combination. Ann had never challenged her husband about it, and nor would she ever do so. He would be as aware as anyone of the potency of the combination, and he would recognise the pitfalls that lay ahead. She trusted him to avoid them; but it did not necessarily mean that she did not think about them.

The gig pulled off the main road, and within a minute they were in Halloughton. Ann told the driver to wait, and then got down from the seat and knocked on the door of Manor Farm House. It was opened by Mrs Barwick, who took several seconds to recognise the face in front of her – such was the unlikelihood of seeing it at her front door – before eventually registering that it belonged to the matron of the asylum who had refused her permission to see Mary on her previous visit there.

'Mrs …' she said, realising that if she ever knew the matron's name, she had now forgotten it.

'Mrs Morris, from the General Lunatic Asylum.'

'Yes, I recall. Do come in; I am happy to extend to you the courtesy that was denied to me when we were acquainted previously.'

'There is no need, I do not intend to impose myself on you.'

'As you wish.'

'I simply wanted to let you know that Mary is making

excellent progress, and is likely to be discharged from the asylum in the very near future.'

Mrs Barwick looked at her suspiciously. 'You have travelled all this way to tell me this? Which is to say, I am pleased for Mary. But presumably you could have communicated this by letter?'

'You are quite right,' said Mrs Morris. 'I also wanted to speak to you about a matter that has come to my attention regarding another patient, but which also involves Mary.'

'Indeed?'

'Quite so. It is clear to me that, on your first visit to the asylum, you provided Mary with wholly false information relating to Catherine Mills. There is no need for me to go into any detail; you will be aware of what you said.'

Mrs Barwick did not reply.

'In addition to providing this unfounded information, you proceeded to make false promises to Mary about the assistance you could provide to her brother, were she to help you in the way you intended.'

Still Mrs Barwick did not speak, but she had retreated a step further into the doorway.

'I have no formal evidence regarding what it was that compelled you to make these false allegations against Miss Mills,' continued the matron, 'nor what it was that made you approach Miss Reddish. But I can only assume that either you, your husband, or the magistrate on whose behalf you were presumably acting, believed that the asylum – my husband's asylum – provided the opportunity to attribute this appalling crime to exactly the type of woman who could not defend herself against it.'

'You have no right—' began Mrs Barwick, but the matron interrupted her.

'My only concern is the welfare of my patients, which is why I do not intend to take this any further,' she said. 'I have also not informed my husband of my suspicions, but you should be in no doubt that he would consider the matter less leniently than I have done.'

'Have you quite finished?'

'I have not. I believe that those who have strayed from the path of honesty – as you have most certainly done – should be given the chance to return to it. But if there is any suggestion that there are parties outside the asylum attempting to divert justice from its proper course, or that there is anyone *within* the asylum enabling those parties to accomplish this, then I will not hesitate to investigate, and to inform the appropriate authorities of my findings.'

She took a large folded sheet of paper from her jacket, and presented it to Mrs Barwick.

'This is the most recent annual report for the asylum. In it, you will find the names of all the visiting governors, voluntary subscribers, and benefactors. I have no doubt that you will be familiar with many of the names, even if you are not in a position to have met many of them. These are the men who will be informed if I discover that anything untoward has been taking place at the asylum, or if I suspect that any such behaviour is taking place from here on in. I trust that I have made myself clear to you.'

Chapter 23

June 1828

On Monday 2 June 1828, Mary was discharged from the asylum. Catherine left on the Friday of the same week.

Before they both departed, Mary was able to speak to Catherine for a final time, in order to address the last area of concern she had regarding her acquaintance – she wished she could say 'friendship', but feared that was now impossible – with the other woman.

In the day room of Catherine's ward, with the sun cascading through the window and forming a rectangle of light on the wall opposite the sofa on which they sat, Mary told her how the director and matron had colluded with Hannah Greendale and Mr Ellis to ensure that Mary's treatment was not exactly as prescribed, and how she had benefited from improved diet, sleep and exercise. She revealed that her later sessions in the chair had barely taken place at all, but how Dr Pennington had not been aware of this; and how it was possible that he had seen the improvement in her, attributed them to the chair, and as a result taken the decision to prescribe the chair to Catherine.

'Knowing the effects of the chair, and the dread I felt of it,' Mary said, 'it distresses me more than you can imagine to know that any actions on my own part could have led to you being placed in that foul contraption for even one second.'

'Did you come up with that plan to keep you out of the chair, then?'

'No, but I agreed to it.'

Catherine shrugged. 'Who wouldn't? I'd put my own mother in that chair rather than go in it myself. And I'm sorry to say, Mary, but I'd definitely put you in there rather than me.'

Mary smiled to herself, and let the matter rest there. Catherine, meanwhile, spent a minute or two taking in what Mary had said. She had known from her previous conversation with Mr Morris that something untoward had taken place regarding the chair, but had imagined that perhaps there had been an error in her treatment plan, or that it was a different patient who was intended for the chair. She had never considered that she had only been placed in the chair because its use with another patient – Mary, indeed – had been manipulated in such a way that false benefits had been credited to the treatment. But nothing particularly surprised her about the asylum any more; she had learnt simply to accept what came her way as best as possible, rather than try to explain what had already happened or predict what was yet to come.

'Then there's something that maybe I should have told you,' she said to Mary. 'I reckon I'll be out of here before too long.'

'That's wonderful!'

'Well, it's something. I'll be going back to live with my mother and sister. And my John, of course.'

'I'm sure everything will work out,' replied Mary.

'Let's hope so. I figured out that I didn't really quite understand how bad I really was, until I found out that you and Mrs Morris thought I could have killed a baby.'

'Oh, no, I never—'

'There's no need to sugar-coat it; I would've thought the same myself if I could've seen me from the outside. A right piece of work, and that's the truth. Throwing that cue at you in the day room … what was I thinking? Well, I know that now, and just need to make sure I'm not so bad that my mother and sister can't live with me any more, and I can help to bring up John.'

'They will be thrilled to have you back,' said Mary. 'And John will be, too. I'm sure it will be a very happy household.'

Throughout this conversation, Catherine had been holding on to Mary's hand, which was placed on her arm. She kept it there now, as she looked down at her feet and said quietly: 'You could be part of it, if you liked.'

Mary turned to fact Catherine, but the other woman's gaze remained firmly on the floor. 'What do you mean?' she asked.

'Nothing untoward,' replied Catherine quickly. 'It would be nice just to have a house of women, and for one of those women to be you, is all. Someone who knows me from in here. Who can keep half an eye on me, maybe. You'd be paid a wage, as much as we could manage.'

Mary took her free hand and put it on top of Catherine's, so that three of their hands were now clasped together. The thought of leaving the asylum for the relative security of Catherine's home in Leicestershire was in many ways an appealing one, contrasting as it did with the uncertainty that awaited her if she went back to her own family in Woodborough. The simple knowledge that Catherine's family had been visiting the asylum, while hers had not, was surely evidence of the different welcomes that could be anticipated in each home.

And in certain respects she felt that a life without men in it would be welcome to her. All of her troubles had come, in some way, from the inadequacies of the men that had been in her life: Ernest's jealousy, Mr Barwick's sense of entitlement, Dr Pennington's imperious confidence that he knew what was best for her. It was very tempting to go and live with Catherine in a house filled with women. But she did not want Catherine to have any expectations that she could not meet.

'It gladdens me greatly,' she said, 'that you would make me such an offer. And I would very much hope that we will meet again when we are out of here. But I don't think that to come and live with you would be – would be the right thing to do. I need to go back and see if I still have a family who wants me.'

'I understand,' said Catherine, 'of course I do. You're a bright young thing, and I'm an old fussock. I just didn't want to not ask, if that makes sense. And I'd like to thank you for being a friend in here, which you have been. You have been, Mary. Even if you've fucked me over at least three times.'

She embraced Mary, and soon afterwards Mary left the day room.

When she was discharged, Mary was given back the clothes that she had removed when she entered the asylum, and was astonished at quite how strange it was to be putting on those garments that had once been so familiar to her. She dressed slowly, drawing out each moment that she was reacquainted with every item, and seeing each action as a careful, deliberate resumption of her former life.

But there was little time to linger, as she was due to be discharged from the asylum at ten. She felt unable to force any breakfast down, so after she had dressed she sat in her room for a few minutes, then made her way quietly down to the ground floor. She didn't wish to say goodbye to others on the ward; she had kept herself to herself as much as she could, largely through fear rather than hubris, and there was no one who she felt would miss her enough to warrant an individual farewell. In addition, her own experience was that seeing people leave the asylum only served to reinforce the desperation of one's own position, rather than offer any additional hope of an imminent release.

The director and matron were on the ground floor to meet her, and they completed the final paperwork while she stood awkwardly in the background, not quite knowing what to do with herself. Then they took her outside, where the overseer had come to pick her up in the cart. She felt an immediate stab of rejection that there was no one from her family to greet her; she had expected nothing different – how could she after a year of no contact? – but that did not mean she had not hoped for it.

She thanked the Morrises, and shook them both warmly by the hand. She said goodbye to Hannah, who had come out of the laundry to say farewell, and gave her an embrace. Then she climbed up into the back of the cart, and the overseer hauled himself up onto the front seat.

Ann and Thomas stood and watched. 'We did well by her, I think,' said the director, and his wife gave her assent by her silence, though in truth she felt a little that she had left matters incomplete, and she would still have wished to have found out more about the actions of Mrs Barwick.

Why, she wondered, had Mrs Barwick pointed the finger of accusation at Catherine specifically – how, indeed, would she have known her history? Was there someone in the asylum who had supplied information about various patients to the magistrate who had been so keen to see the baby murder solved? Or had that same magistrate sent Catherine to the asylum in the first place, making him fully aware of the reasons for her admittance?

And what of Mr and Mrs Barwick's role in placing Mary in the asylum; had they been acting entirely in accordance with their own views, or had there been an unseen hand guiding their actions and ensuring that Mary was committed to the same place as Catherine? Mary had only been admitted a week after Catherine, so it was surely the case that there was no time to put such a plan in place, and yet Ann was sceptical of such a fortunate circumstance simply falling into Mrs Barwick's lap. Ann could not rid herself of the feeling that, somehow, Mr and Mrs Barwick had engineered Mary's admission for their own particular needs. But with Mary's departure, Ann's chance of answering these questions had now gone, and she fully expected never to see Mary or Mrs Barwick back at the asylum.

For his part, Thomas was thinking of broader considerations. Mary had been the couple's very own project, and he fully believed that they had proven that a regime of sleep, work, exercise and appropriate medication could work far more effectively than the array of treatments and medicines that were habitually thrown at the mentally afflicted. Not that he believed she had ever been truly afflicted; but, still, she had shown signs of mental anguish, and they had successfully tackled those. Soon, it would be time to depart to a place which they could run entirely as they wished, without outside interference or pressure. They had shown that they were capable of running such an establishment, and one where they would be able to try their methods on those who were deeply, persistently disturbed.

Thomas had arrived at the asylum having lost some of his faith in the efficacy of medicines, and believing that a moral foundation was needed for patients to recover. He still believed that was the case, but he now felt that some medicines did have their part to play, as long as they were the right ones. Purges, emetics, blistering, the whirling chair – none of these had their place in a modern asylum, he thought. But tonics, herbal medicines, soothing poultices, restorative spices – all of these had their part to play. They needed medicines and treatments where the cure was not worse than the condition.

Whether there were medicines that could cure the mind was, of course, a different matter; but Thomas had become more convinced as time went on that mental illness was a physical or neurological problem, not simply a moral or spiritual malady. If that was the case, then there should also be a physical or neurological solution; but one that was improved at all times by the correct moral and spiritual behaviour. The different areas should work in tandem with each other, not against each other.

He thought back to the evening, sixteen and a half years

previously, when he had walked home to the asylum after meeting Dr Pennington, Dr Storer, James Dale and all of their friends and colleagues after meeting them for dinner in town. That night, he had felt a rush of safety and security wash over him as he entered the building. In time, that feeling had dissipated, as everyday worries and the pressure of running the asylum had accumulated. But it had lasted for many years before it gradually ebbed away; and now he wanted it back again. It was regretful that he would need to find it somewhere else; but he knew that he would.

Mary felt the cart start with a jolt, and they set off down the drive. She looked back as the imposing frontage of the asylum slowly receded from view. Its every window, every door – all of which had meant nothing to her when she arrived – now had its own story, signalling a familiar view from the gallery, a place of work, or even the stairwell that led to the hated basement.

They turned out past the entrance lodge, and down the short road at the side of the asylum. Mary could see the director and matron were standing hand in hand on the front steps, watching the slow progress of the cart. Then they were lost to her field of vision; the overseer pulled on to the main road, and they headed back towards Woodborough.

Epilogue

Dr John Storer died in 1837, aged ninety, and he was buried in the chancel of St Mary and All Saints church in Hawksworth, Nottinghamshire. His name is commemorated in the John Storer Clinic at the Queen's Medical Centre in Nottingham.

Dr Charles Pennington died in 1829, aged seventy-one. He had maintained an extensive private practice in Nottingham for more than forty years, as well as being the asylum's physician for seventeen years. His remains were interred at Bulwell in Nottingham, where his epitaph said that he was 'active in his profession, useful to his townsmen, kind to the poor, affectionate to his family, devout and thankful towards his maker'.

Catherine Mills was admitted to the asylum on nine more occasions following her discharge in 1828; she died at the asylum on 15 February 1846, aged fifty-six, from bronchitis. She was admitted to the asylum fifteen times during her lifetime, spending a total of fourteen years there from the age of twenty-eight onwards. The executor and witnesses of her will were all asylum officials. She was buried in Ravenstone, Leicestershire, with her mother, who predeceased her by just three years.

Thomas Morris and Ann Morris resigned their positions on 6 October 1831, and went to run a private asylum in Derby, called Green Hill House. They were joined there by Mr Morris's nephew Thomas Fisher, the former director of Lincoln Lunatic Asylum. After three years, they moved on to manage the small Barford Asylum near Leamington Spa, and in 1842 they retired and went to live with their lawyer son Thomas and his family in Warwick. Thomas died in Warwick in 1854, aged eighty-three. Ann then went to live with their daughter Ann in Essex, and died in 1861, aged eighty-five.

The fate of Mary Reddish is not known.

The General Lunatic Asylum near Nottingham continued to expand throughout the remainder of the nineteenth century, housing more than 400 patients at its peak. In 1856, it changed its name to the United Lunatic Asylum, and in 1875 it became known as the County Lunatic Asylum, as a new Nottingham Lunatic Asylum was being built in Mapperley for patients from the city. That new facility opened in 1880, and the Sneinton site became for county patients only.

The Sneinton asylum finally closed in 1902, after ninety years, when the new Radcliffe Asylum for the county of Nottinghamshire opened, in a location well away from the city centre. Most of the existing building was demolished, and the site was eventually turned into a public park; although for a number of years, a small part of the building continued to be used as the headquarters for a company of the Boys' Brigade.

Today, that part of the building has also gone; and a single gatepost, in Dakeyne Street, is all that remains of the first asylum.

Author's note

For a number of years I lived in Sneinton, about half a mile from the site of the old General Lunatic Asylum; but it is a site that, unless you were aware of the small plaque there, you would be unlikely to realise had previously been home to such a significant institution.

In 2020, some asylum records that had been under restricted access became available to the public, and I began looking in detail at both the asylum and some of the patients who had been there. The result is this book, which is partly based on real events, but where many elements of the narrative are necessarily the result of my own imagination rather than historical records; for example, the only biographical details given about Mary Reddish in the asylum records are that she was twenty-three, single, and a house servant from Halloughton. And the story of the asylum itself is one that I felt needed telling, because of the leading role it played in how the care of mentally ill people began to change in the early nineteenth century.

Until 1808, the provision of asylums was met through an uneasy combination of profiteering and philanthropy. There were small private madhouses that were run purely as businesses; and there were larger charitable institutions that survived on personal donations and subscriptions. The concerns that existed about both of these types of asylums fell into two broad categories: how to ensure that patients within them were genuinely insane – and had not, for example, simply been placed there by an unscrupulous relative for personal gain – and how to ensure that those who *were* genuinely insane were cared for in as humane a manner as possible.

By the mid-18th century there was significant evidence that both of these needed urgently addressing, and in 1774 the Act for Regulating Private Madhouses sought to do just that. It required madhouses to be licensed every year, to have inspections carried out, to limit the number of patients who could be admitted and for a medical certificate to be produced before a patient would be accepted. Owners who admitted a person without a certificate could be fined £100; those operating without a licence could be fined £500.

There were problems with this legislation, however. Pauper patients – those whose families could not afford to pay for their confinement, and whose fees were being paid for by their parish – were largely excluded, and the requirement for a medical certificate did not apply to them. The licensing and inspection regime was flimsy, with little indication that proper checks were being placed on madhouse owners. And, as the title of the act indicated, it applied only to private madhouses, and not to the charitable institutions.

These larger charitable asylums varied widely in the quality of care provided. Some, like Bethlem Royal Hospital ('Bedlam') in London, featured appalling conditions, with patients chained and kept in squalor, often entirely naked with just a single blanket for warmth. It was only in 1770 that the practice of allowing members of the public to pay a penny for admission, in order to gawp at or abuse the patients, was stopped, but there was no subsequent improvement in conditions for patients. In 1814, MP and Quaker Edward Wakefield visited and described how he saw many patients who were 'totally inanimate and unconscious of existence', but others who were perfectly lucid, and educated, and held normal conversations with him. Other establishments, like the nearby St Luke's Hospital for Lunatics, eschewed the use of restraints and attempted a kinder treatment regime. But in any case, the asylums were few and far between; there were others in places such as Norwich, Manchester, Exeter and Leicester, but there was not the geographical scope to take in the necessary patients.

The reality was that most insane paupers were either in workhouses, or still living in their own communities, usually with their families. There was limited state or county oversight of the system. Local magistrates would be involved in sending dangerous lunatics to 'some secure place' – usually a house of correction – but it was the parish that determined the destination for many more, including those sent to private madhouses.

When, in 1807, the Select Committee on the State of Criminal and Pauper Lunatics attempted to ascertain exactly where lunatics were being accommodated, their findings confirmed what was already suspected. Of the 2,398 lunatics and insane persons reported, 1,765 were in poorhouses, workhouses or houses of industry; 247 in madhouses; 113 in houses of correction; 37 in gaol; and only 22 were in asylums. The remainder were in other separate categories, such as staying with friends.

The overall figures were incomplete, as some counties did not respond; but as an indication of where the proportion of pauper lunatics were held, they were instructive, and were a vindication for Charles Williams-Wynn, the MP who had pushed for the committee to be established. When the select committee produced its subsequent report, the findings further supported the MP, stating of pauper lunatics that: 'In their present situation there is no probability of their cure, and they remain a burden on the public as long as they live.' The committee proposed that new asylums should be built, that power should be given to the magistrates of any county to charge the expense of an asylum to the county rates; and that all pauper lunatics within the district where the asylum was built should be taken there, and maintained there at the expense of their respective parishes.

These new asylums would not replace the existing charitable

institutions, or the forty-five or so licensed private madhouses already in place around the country. But they would be a new way of providing care, and of making counties and parishes – and all the ratepayers living within them – responsible not only for the ongoing expenses of the insane members of their community, but for paying to build the asylums in the first place. As with the existing charitable asylums, the new facilities would be public; unlike them, they would also be publicly funded. The state, or at least the provincial part of it, was finally becoming fully involved in how this particular part of its population would be looked after.

The relevant legislation was drawn up, and debated in the Commons in April 1808. Two months later, An Act for the Better Care and Maintenance of Lunatics, being Paupers or Criminals in England, became part of the law. (It actually included Wales as well, but not Scotland and Ireland, where there was not the same system of parochial relief for the poor.) It began by stating that 'the practice of confining such lunatics and other insane persons as are chargeable to their respective parishes in gaols, houses of correction, poor houses and houses of industry, is highly dangerous and inconvenient'. It was more commonly known as the County Asylums Act; or, in tribute to its driving force, Wynn's Act.

Counties did not have to adopt the premises of the act; it only gave them the power to do so. But for those who did want to start building their own asylums, there was nothing to stop them forging ahead; and Nottingham was in a prime position to take advantage of the new legislation.

There was already a subscription fund up and running in the town to raise money for a facility that would treat the mentally ill, and it had been in place for many years. When the Nottingham General Hospital opened in 1782, the regulations made clear that it would only treat the physically ill – 'none who are disordered in their senses are to be admitted'. It was firmly felt that a separate facility was needed to treat the insane.

In order to achieve this, the hospital founders began to

gather support and money. As with the hospital itself, the asylum would be funded through public subscriptions, donations and legacies. Fundraising began in 1789, and by 1803 it had reached £5,000 – around the same price that had been needed for the construction of the hospital. A potential site for the asylum was found between Mount Street and Park Row, close to the hospital, although it was later decided it would be both too small and too public.

This was a setback, but nevertheless the will to provide such a facility was there, as was a reasonable amount of the funds needed. Once the 1808 Act was in place, and the possibility of a new source of funding through the rates had been confirmed, there was no reason not to press ahead.

In July 1808, a new site for the asylum was bought, costing £1,911. It was a four-acre plot in the parish of Sneinton, just outside the Nottingham boundary. The plans were drawn up by the Nottingham surveyor Edward Staveley and the architect Richard Ingleman, who had previously designed houses of correction in Southwell and Devises.

The foundation stone for the new asylum was laid on 31 May 1810, and the drive for subscriptions continued. In a town where the infirmary, the Vaccine Institution and now the asylum were all being supported either wholly or partly by voluntary contributions, there was constant activity needed in order to find new donors, legators and subscribers.

The asylum was set up, and would be run as a joint venture between the town of Nottingham, the county of Nottinghamshire and the subscribers. More specifically, it was an agreement between the Justices of the Peace for the County of the Town of Nottingham, Justices of the Peace for the County of Nottingham and the committee of subscribers. These justices of the peace played a key role in every step of the process. They formed a significant part of the board of visiting governors, which provided overall management of the asylum and was made up of twelve county magistrates, three city magistrates, and seventeen subscribers (including two MPs and a rear admiral). At their Quarter Sessions, the JPs set the level of rates that the parishes would have to pay for the building and upkeep of the asylum.

Between the three parties, the various costs were split into twelve parts, with the voluntary subscribers paying seven parts in twelve, the county four parts in twelve, and the town paying one part in twelve (the expenditure of the last two being based on their relative populations). In reality this meant that by October 1810, for example, a total of £15,788 had been raised, and this was split £1,316 from the town, £5,263 from the county and £9,209 from the subscribers.

This might have appeared a disproportionate amount for the subscribers to be raising. But this part of the money did not only come from individuals making small annual subscriptions. There were plenty of these – 133 in 1811, mostly paying £2 a year. But there were also eighty-two people making single donations (generally around the £20 mark, but some of £100 and more), nine benefactors by legacy (including the largest single donation of £1,880), and collections made after sermons at eighty-one different churches. The donations came in from Babworth in the north to Bunny in the south; from Beeston in the west to Bingham in the east.

There were some key decisions that had to be made, and one was about the admission of criminal lunatics. The title of the act – being for lunatics who were 'Paupers or Criminals' – indicated the wider thinking on this, but in Nottingham the presumption was somewhat against it, with the articles of union stating that: 'No person, who shall have been charged with murder, treason or felony, and acquitted on a plea of insanity, shall be seemed admissible, unless with the consent and approbation of three-fourths of the visiting governors, present at the time of considering the question.'

The original act offered little guidance on the size of the accommodation, or indeed on the buildings themselves, beyond saying that they should have separate wards for male and female patients, and also for convalescents and incurables, with separate day rooms and airing grounds for the male and female convalescents, and be in an 'airy and healthy situation, with a good supply of water', and with 'dry and airy cells for the lunatics of every description'. With regards to the total number of rooms needed, that was for the counties to decide.

In 1809, the overseers of the poor had been asked to assess the number of insane people in their parish, and they recorded that in the county of Nottinghamshire there were twenty-nine inoffensive lunatics, twelve dangerous lunatics and four dangerous idiots, plus eleven others in the town, making a total of fifty-six. It was decided to build the asylum with a capacity of up to eighty, and in the early years this was plenty; but eventually it would prove to be inadequate, and the asylum had to be substantially extended.

The final cost of the asylum – to be officially called the 'General Lunatic Asylum, near Nottingham', but also known as Sneinton Asylum or Nottingham Asylum – was £20,869, consisting of £16,651 for the main buildings and walls, £1,911 for the land, £1,788 for fittings and furnishings, and £519 for a lodge at the entrance.

It came in at more than five times the cost of the hospital built thirty years previously. Partly this was because it was larger (the hospital opened with just forty-four beds), and it was also because the asylum management had to buy their own land, whereas the hospital had an acre of land donated by both the Duke of Newcastle and the Nottingham Corporation. But there were also problems with the actual construction of the asylum and laying the foundations, due to unevenness of the rock below, which pushed the final cost above what had been anticipated.

The original hope had been that the asylum would open in the summer of 1811, but that was a date that proved to be over-optimistic, both in terms of the necessary funds being raised and the construction work progressing quickly. The opening ceremony took place on 10 October 1811, and it opened to patients on 12 February 1812.

Acknowledgements

I am indebted to Jeremy Waters' book *Morris: The History of a Family from Witney & Hampton-in-Arden* (private publication, 2018) for providing me with details about the lives of Ann and Thomas Morris before their arrival at the asylum.

I am also extremely grateful to Michelle Hunter of Green Dragon Genealogy for her work in interpreting and transcribing medical records from the asylum.

I would like to thank the team at Legend Press, especially my editor Cari Rosen, for their unstinting enthusiasm for this book, and for their skill and dedication in bringing it to the page.

I am also very appreciative of those who kindly agreed to read the story in its early stages.

Finally, thank you to my wife, Lynn, and children, Amy and Luke, for putting up with me while I was writing this book; and, of course, for everything else.

The General Lunatic Asylum, Nottingham, circa 1816

Credit: Nottingham City Council

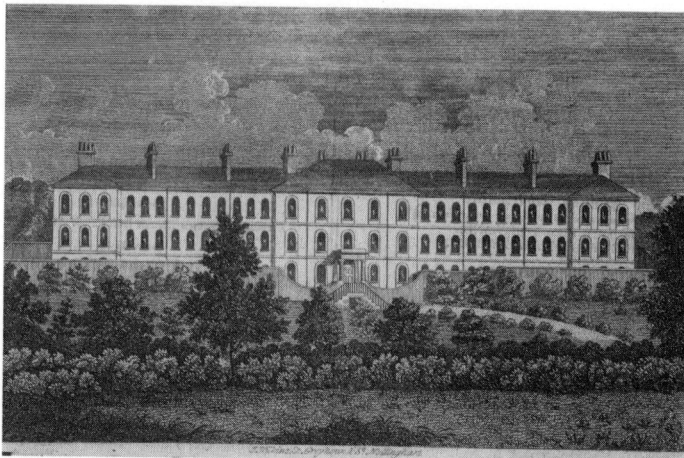

Thomas Morris silhouette from c. 1824

From public family trees on Ancestry.com. With thanks to descendants of the Morris family who made these available.

Advert for director and matron, May 1811

General Lunatic Asylum, near *Nottingham*.

WANTED, a Director to execute the duties of Apothecary, Secretary, and principal Superintendant; and also a Matron, to regulate the Female Department in this institution.

The qualifications of the candidates being equal, a person educated as an apothecary will be preferred; and if the wife of the director can undertake the duties devolving upon the matron, it will prove an additional recommendation.

Further particulars, and printed inquiries, may be obtained by applying to Doctor STORER, the vice-president; or to Doctor PENNINGTON, the physician to the institution, at Nottingham; or to Mr. Pennington, No. 14, Chapel-street, Lamb's Conduit-street, London, between the hours of eight and nine in the morning.

Nottingham, 27th May, 1811.

Map of east Nottingham, 1831, based on surveys made by Staveley & Wood in 1827-29 (the asylum is in the top right corner)

Patient notes of Mary Reddish, from Medical Superintendent's Case Book, 1827

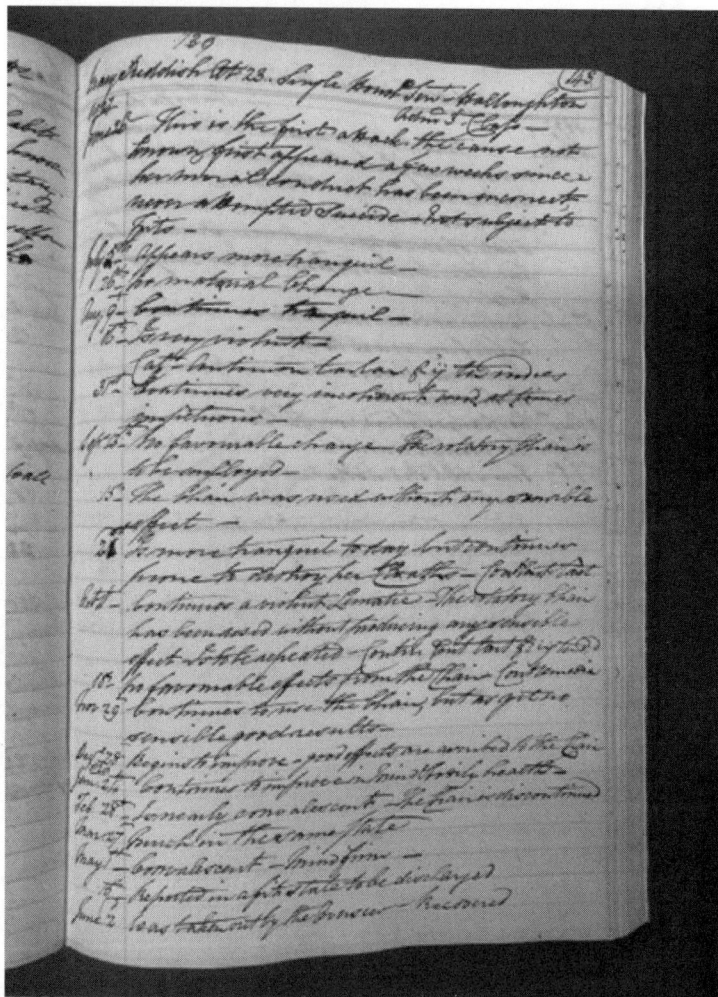

The only remaining part of the asylum, a gate post, in Dakeyne Street, Nottingham

Plaque upon the remaining gate post

This pillar marks the last standing remains of the County General Lunatic Asylum opened in October 1811.

It housed over 400 inmates in its peak in 1900 and officially closed in 1902.

It was the first County Asylum to open in the country.

Selected sources

PRIMARY SOURCES

Nottinghamshire Archives

C/QAL/10 R - Nottingham Mental Hospital, Carlton Road, Nottingham. Working plans, etc. R Ingleman (1810)

DD/2425/3 - Photocopy of letter from Charles Pennington to Mr H L Pinkerton of Staffs

DD/177/1 – First (1811) and sixth (1816) reports of the state of the General Lunatic Asylum near Nottingham

M/11562 - Letter signed from T Morris to 'Sir' (1827)

SO/HO/1/1 - Minutes of proceedings of meetings relating to purchase of land and establishment of the General Lunatic Asylum, 1803-1810

SO/HO/1/2/1-2 - Minutes of proceedings of the Visiting Governors 1810-1845

SO/HO/1/3/1-2 - General Lunatic Asylum House Committee, minutes of proceedings of meetings 1811-1836

SO/HO/1/9/1 - Medical Superintendent's Case Book 1824-1829, General Lunatic Asylum

SO/HO/1-20 - Misc. semi-official records

SO/HO/1/31 - General Lunatic Asylum ledger, 1812-1824

SO/HO/1/60/5/1-2 - Indexes of patients, 1812-1919

Nottingham Local Studies Library

Fourth (1814) and eighth (1818) reports of the state of the General Lunatic Asylum near Nottingham

University of Nottingham

Ingleman, Richard. *A specification, containing the particulars of the work to be executed, the materials to be supplied, and the utensils to be provided, in constructing a general lunatic asylum near Nottingham* (1810)

Second (1812) and twenty-second (1832) reports of the state of the General Lunatic Asylum near Nottingham

The Wolfson Centre for Archival Research, Birmingham

SF/2/1/6/2/1/1 - Warwickshire South Women's Monthly Meeting minute book 1790 – 1797

SF/2/1/6/1/1/5 - Warwickshire South Monthly Men's Meeting minute book 1790 – 1809

Wellcome Collection

RET 1/5/1/16 Letter from Thomas Morris to George Jepson (1811)

RET 1/5/1/17 Letter from Thomas Morris to George Jepson (1812)

RET 1/5/1/19/7/5 Letter from Thomas Morris to George Jepson (1814)

RET 1/5/1/19/7/7 Letter from Thomas Morris to George Jepson (1814)

RET 1/5/1/20/2/6 Letter from Thomas Morris to William Tuke (1815)

RET 1/5/1/24/5/16 Letter from Thomas Morris to George Jepson (1820)

RET 1/5/1/26/13/5 Letter from Thomas Morris to George Jepson (1822)

Leicestershire Record Office

DE2392/150/9 - Catherine Mills of Knighthorpe, examination for bastardy (1820)

Parliamentary records

Report of the Select Committee on the State of Criminal and Pauper Lunatics (1807).

County Asylums Act, or An Act for the better Care and Maintenance of Lunatics, being Paupers and Criminals in England (1808)

County Asylums Amendment Act (1811)

Report, together with the Minutes of evidence, and an appendix of papers, from the Committee appointed to consider of provision being made for the better regulation of madhouses in England (1815)

Report of the Minutes of evidence taken before the Select Committee on the State of the Children Employed in the Manufactories of the United Kingdom (April-June 1816)

Other

Archive records relating Dr John Storer and Dr Charles Pennington. Supplied by Bromley House Library, Nottingham.

SECONDARY SOURCES

Allen, Terry. *Knight Thorpe Hall* (2000). Supplied by Loughborough Local Studies Library.

Bartlett, Peter. *The Poor Law of Lunacy: The Administration of Pauper Lunatics in Mid-Nineteenth Century England* (1993). Doctoral thesis, University College London.

Bartlett, Peter. *Legal Madness in the Nineteenth Century* (2001), *Social History of Medicine*, Volume 14, Issue 1

Beckett, John. *Luddites*. Accessed on Nottinghamshire Heritage Gateway website.

Bosworth, Ennis C. *Public healthcare in Nottingham 1750 to 1911* (1998). Thesis submitted to the University of Nottingham for Doctor of Philosophy degree.

Briscoe, John Potter. *Bypaths of Nottinghamshire History* (1905). Accessed on Nottinghamshire History website.

Burrows, George Man. *An Inquiry into Certain Errors Relative to Insanity* (1820), pub. Thomas and George Underwood.

Charlesworth, Edward Parker. *Remarks on the Treatment of the Insane* (1828)

Clarke, James. *Medical Report for Nottingham* (1812). The Edinburgh Medical and Surgical Journal.

Cockburn, Anne. *An Edition of the Daybook of John Reddish, 1780-1805*. University of Nottingham thesis, 1979.

Crane, Jennifer. *1774 Madhouses Act*. University of Warwick website.

Duckworth, Jane. *Nottingham General Lunatic Asylum: the evolution of an institution and definitions of madness in women* (1998). University of Nottingham Part II Dissertation.

Elliott, Juliet. *Halloughton Unravelled* (2003).

Fothergill, Samuel. *The Medical and Physical Journal for July to December 1813* (1814), pub. Richard Phillips.

Fry, Terry. *The General Lunatic Asylum, Nottingham, 1812-1902* (1994). Dissertation for Advanced Certificate in Local History, University of Nottingham.

Fry, Terry. *Nottingham Vaccine Institute*. Articles from the Thoroton Society Newsletter.

Gorman, Martin. *Physician Extraordinary: Dr John Storer, Lord of the Manor of Hawksworth, Nottinghamshire and founding President of Bromley House Library* (2021).

Gregg, Pauline. *King Charles I* (1984).

Haller, John. *The use and abuse of tartar emetic in the 19th-century materia medica* (1975). Bulletin of the History of Medicine, Vol 49.

Halliday, Sir Andrew. *A general view of the present state of lunatics and lunatic asylums in Great Britain and Ireland, and in some other kingdoms* (1828).

Mellors, Robert. *Men of Nottingham and Nottinghamshire* (1924).

Nichols, John. *The Progresses, Processions, and Magnificent Festivities, of King James the First* (1828)

Parr, Hester and Philo, Chris. *'A forbidding fortress of locks, bars and padded cells': the locational history of mental health care in Nottingham* (1996). Bristol: Historical Geography Research Group.

Parry-Jones, WL. *English Private Madhouses in the Eighteenth and Nineteenth Centuries* (1973). Journal of the Royal Society of Medicine, Volume 66, Issue 7.

Phillimore, William. *Some Account of the family of Middlemore of Warwickshire and Worcestershire* (1901). Accessed on Internet Archive.

Roberts, Mathew. *Rural Luddism and the makeshift economy of the Nottinghamshire Framework Knitters* (2017). Sheffield Hallam University Research Archive.

Rutherford, Sarah. *The landscapes of public lunatic asylums in England, 1808-194 (in three volumes)* (2003). Thesis, De Montfort University.

Scull, Andrew T. *Mad-doctors and Magistrates: English psychiatry's struggle for professional autonomy in the nineteenth century (1976).* European Journal of Sociology, Vol. 17, No. 2.

Shelford, Leonard. *A Practical Treatise of the Law concerning Lunatics, Idiots, and Persons of Unsound Mind* (1833)

Smith, Leonard. *Cure, Comfort and Safe Custody: Public Lunatic Asylums in Early Nineteenth-Century England* (1999)

Smith, Leonard. *A gentleman's mad-doctor in Georgian England: Edward Long Fox and Brislington House* (2008). History of Psychiatry, 2008, 19 (2).

Smith, Leonard. *Perspectives on death in the early county lunatic asylums, 1810–50* (2012). History of Psychiatry 23(1) 117–128.

Spence, Ursilla, and Bishop, Mike. *An Archaeological Resource Assessment of Modern Nottinghamshire (1750 onwards).* Nottinghamshire County Council.

Sutton, John F. *The Date Book of Remarkable and Memorable Events Connected with Nottingham 1750-1850* (1852).

Tuke, Samuel. *Description of the Retreat* (1813).

Waters, Jeremy. *Morris: The history of a family from Witney and Hampton-in-Arden* (2018).

York, Sarah Hayley. *Suicide, Lunacy and the Asylum in nineteenth-century England* (2009). Doctoral thesis, University of Birmingham.